Someone Like You

You

by

Syd Parker

To my love, who keeps me grounded.

ACKNOWLEDGMENTS

When I started writing this book last year, there were only six states plus Washington, D.C. that allowed same-sex marriages. I'm happy to say at the time of publishing, there are now nine states that allow same-sex marriage, including Maine. Three of these states, Maine, Maryland and Washington, legalized same-sex marriage by means of public vote, a sign that the general opinion of the public in those states is the same as ours, that we deserve the same rights as everyone else. I opted not to change the states in this story, but I wanted to acknowledge that fact and say a heartfelt thank you to the people of those three states for standing up and letting your voice and your vote in our favor be heard.

To Sarah, for your continued patience and support for my "hobby"; thank you for letting me share my out there ideas and for pointing me in the right direction, whether I agree or not. Here's to lucky #7.

Loewen, you always have been and always will be one of my biggest "fans". From the first jumbled mess of a manuscript I sent to you to the darkness of the last one, you have given me tweaks that made them all better. Thank you for tell me to scrap "the umpteenth time".

Terry, you are the orchestrator of all things big. Without you, I wouldn't have found my footprint or lived my dream.

To Aspen, thank you for allowing me to take your incredible talent and create a love story that I hope does you proud. I am in awe!

And finally, to my mother, who never let us settle for doing anything half-baked, for pushing us to live a life that could be respected, for raising all seven of us to be responsible, hard working adults. Most of all, thank you for loving us enough to discipline us; I wouldn't have made you proud otherwise.

Chapter 1

"I can't do this. I'm sorry, A." Alexis Tataris scrubbed her palms over her face, her eyes aching from the tears she had cried. It was the end of a long, emotional conversation. Well, not a conversation really, more like Lex telling Aspen all the reasons she couldn't stay. Not how she wanted to stay and work through things, not asking how they could make it better. No, it was Lex stating all the reasons she had failed and now couldn't look at herself in the mirror without hating herself.

"You're a coward, Lex." Aspen Lane's voice wasn't harsh or angry, but broken, the low, resigned tone of someone who knows they are defeated. Her stormy blue eyes searched Lex's darker ones, looking for some glimmer of hope. What she saw was guilt and recrimination. Their marriage of five years was crumbling before her eyes, and she had no way to save it. "Your reasons for leaving are fucked up. You think this doesn't hurt me just as much as it hurts you. I lost a baby too. However, I'm not walking away."

A fresh tear pooled in the corner of Lex's sad brown eyes. She wanted to stay, just wanted to wrap her arms around Aspen and forget all the pain of the last eighteen months. They had tried in vitro three times and were thrilled when the fourth attempt finally worked. Five months into the pregnancy, Aspen miscarried. The loss hit them both in a way that neither was prepared for. They made the choice to stop trying and adopt, knowing that fate was telling them that they were needed in someone else's life. Lex thought she could move on, but every time she looked in the mirror; she saw a woman that she had begun to hate. She saw herself as a failure, and failing Aspen wasn't something she was strong enough to handle. So, instead, she chose the only other option she felt she could live with. She decided to leave.

Aspen leaned forward and lifted Lex's chin, so they were eye to eye. "You're wrong. You think this is better for me, but you're wrong. I'm nothing without you. You're ruining the only perfect thing we've ever had."

Lex's bottom lip trembled, and she swiped at the errant tear. She couldn't face Aspen. How could she fix things if she couldn't even look her in the eye? She shook her head, unable to utter a word. She felt the walls closing in and the air leaving her body. Unable to take anymore, she found her legs and walked out the door, the sound of her heart fracturing into two ringing in her ears.

Aspen felt her knees buckle from the weight of her pain, and she hit the floor; her body wracked with sobs, the emptiness inside too much to bear.

It took two months for the tears to subside, another two months to care to eat, and by the time she found her way to her aunt and uncle's farm in Vermont looking for solace, she was fifteen pounds lighter and a ghost of the woman she had been.

She stood on the back porch, her eyes taking in the countryside around her. She smelled the first hints of summer wafting in the air, the smell of green grass tickled at her nose. She scanned the surrounding area; smiling for the first time when she remembered the summers she had spent with her Aunt Ginny and Uncle Neal. This had been where she found herself, found her calling. She hugged the satchel under her arm, and the corners of her mouth turned up in a wistful smile. She recalled the first few drawings she had done here.

Her aunt had been kind enough to say they were good. Aspen chuckled at the thought of those early pictures, so amateurish, but harkened to a time when life was less complicated and certainly less painful. *Do not cry, Aspen. Seriously, it's been four months, stop with the fucking river of tears.* She cinched her shoulders back, drawing on the strength of this place to look past yesterday and forge a new tomorrow.

As if sensing her presence, Aspen turned and found her aunt studying her closely. She tried to smile and knew she had only succeeded in what probably looked more like a grimace. "Aunt Ginny."

Her aunt opened her mouth to reply and then thought better of it. What that child needed was a hug and fast. She pulled her niece into her arms and hugged her fiercely, not the first and definitely not the last of the hugs she would give. When she felt Aspen still in her arms, she pushed her away and held her at arm's length. "Baby girl, I missed you."

A smile crept over Aspen's features, and she felt the pain of the last few months start to leave her body. She loved her mother, no doubt about that, but her bond with her aunt had been something very special. Aunt Ginny was the first to know she was a lesbian. She was the first one she told about Lex, and the first one that Aspen had talked to when she lost the baby. She felt at home here, and she hoped that meant she could start to heal. "Hi, Aunt Ginny. Thanks for letting me stay."

"Nonsense." Ginny Thomas waived a hand, dismissing Aspen's comment. At sixty-one, she had seen a lot and her blue eyes twinkled with a thousand lost tales. Her brown hair, the same shade as Aspen's, sat in a haphazard pile atop her head. Her glasses sat perched on her head, long forgotten after this morning's perusal of the paper. She still carried her trim figure with ease and looked every bit the farm girl in her wrinkled white tee—shirt and worn out blue jeans. Her smile was effortless, and it had been said of Ginny Thomas in her younger days that anyone that met her fell in love with her. "Come inside. I'm just getting your uncle's lunch together. He's riding the fence with Lacey making repairs. He should be back soon, and you know your uncle."

"He will be ready to eat." Aspen laughed as they said the words in unison. Her uncle Neal was as gentle and sweet a man as she had ever known. He was as thin as a rail and looked as though he never ate, although she knew the truth. She had been blessed with the same culinary skills as her aunt and Aspen knew that her uncle ate very well. Perhaps it was his constant chatter that kept the weight off, or maybe working on the farm every day. Her aunt and uncle owned a farm in Vermont. It sat on a hundred acres of what Aspen believed was the most beautiful countryside in the northeast. She felt like she knew every inch of the property like the back of her hand, having tagged along with her uncle every summer.

"Grab your stuff and get in here." Ginny interrupted her ruminations and as she walked in behind her, Aspen inhaled the air around her one more time. Yes, this is where she needed to be to move on.

Hours later, long after Neal had retired, Aspen sat curled in a rocking chair on the back porch, listening to the first bugs of summer. Crickets chirped an eternal tune and blended effortlessly with the gentle ruffle of the trees in the late evening breeze. She heard her aunt join her and took the offered cup of tea with a smile. She could smell the hints of lavender, and she felt more at ease with this small reminder of her childhood. She and her aunt spent many a night sipping tea and talking about her life.

After a few moments, her aunt broke the silence. "Have you talked to your mom lately?"

Aspen smiled. She knew this was her chance to get everything out if she wanted. She wasn't sure yet, but the thought was comforting in a way. "Last week. She said to tell you hello."

"Hmph." Ginny nudged her chair again, and the creak filled the air. "Damn woman still hasn't called me back."

Aspen laughed out loud. "Can you blame her? You called her cooking crap."

"Ornery old woman." Ginny snorted. "Her food does taste like crap." Their relationship had been this way as long as Aspen remembered; the older sister picking on the younger one. Her mother had given it back equally, but there were times like this where they went weeks without speaking, reviving the old sibling rivalry. "Called her three times this week, and she still hasn't called me back."

"Oh, you know Mom. She has to stew a while before she forgives anyone." Aspen chuckled to herself. Her aunt was right. Her mother's cooking was crap. She wasn't sure how the cooking gene missed her mom, considering both she and her aunt had it. However, it had and apparently being reminded that she couldn't cook had raised her ire. It would probably last a couple more days, and then she would call and the whole older sister/younger sister rivalry would start again. "Did you say you were sorry?"

Ginny snorted again. "Ha, why should I? She ought to be apologizing for almost killing me with that."

Aspen shook her head. This was the one area where Ginny had never grown up and couldn't be charged with giving any kind of sound advice. Fortunately, in everything else, she was wise beyond her years. "Really, Aunt Ginny?"

Ginny's low laughter reverberated through the dark and warmed her soul. "Did you tell her about Lex?"

A small feeling of guilt washed over Aspen. She hadn't told her mother yet about Lex leaving. She just couldn't bring herself to talk about with her. Telling her mother held an ominous air of finality, and she hadn't quite gotten to the point of shutting the door completely and locking it. Holding onto a small sliver of hope helped her survive these last few months alone. Besides, her mother's reaction would probably be somewhat volatile and tying her mother up so she wouldn't murder Lex wasn't something Aspen had the strength to do right now. "No, I just can't tell her."

"Want me to talk to her about it?" Ginny offered quietly. "I already pissed her off, might as well keep going."

Aspen shook her head and chuckled softly. "No, but thank you. I need to put on my big girl panties and just do it."

"Well, I imagine she will want to take her Smith and Wesson and have a little *conversation* with Lex." Ginny knew her sister well. Her temper got her into trouble once or twice in their younger days. "Thank god, she's half blind and a terrible shot to boot."

"Aunt Ginny." Aspen put her hand on her chest in mock horror. "How dare you talk about my mother that way?"

"Ha, I'm talking about my sister that way. I knew her way before she was your mother, and she's got a short fuse." She absent-mindedly rubbed the small scar on her forehead. A well—placed toy train had left a permanent reminder that her younger sister was wired a little tightly in her earlier days.

"She's settled down now. I just don't want her to have to deal with my being hurt."

"Oh, she won't deal with it. She'll bottle it all up inside like she does everything else." Ginny was right. Aspen's mother never wore her heart on her sleeve. She locked it all up inside and stewed on it. It was what led her to stop talking to people instead of dealing with the issue. She tried to say it was because discussing *feelings* made you weak. They both knew better; she just didn't know how to talk about it, so she got mad instead. "You need to tell her, though. Otherwise, she will be mad at you for not telling her."

"I know. I know." Aspen sighed loudly. "You know talking to her is impossible sometimes. I am not ready for hours of Momma Susan's I told you so's. I don't need to be reminded that she thought marrying Lex was a bad idea and that trying to have a baby was an even worse idea."

"Oh shoot, that was her opinion and lord knows what they say about opinions." Ginny snickered loudly. "I think hers were a little jaded anyway. She never did think anyone was good enough for you. She isn't like your father. I think maybe she was just scared for you, knowing what the world is like today. I think she loved Lex just as much as we did and her reaction will be from hurt. However, she would be the last one to tell you that you were doing something right."

"You never tried to discourage me from marrying Lex." Aspen sipped her tea quietly, a gentle late evening breeze licking at her skin and calming her somehow.

"I saw your eyes when you talked about her. You reminded me of myself all those years ago when I fell in love with your uncle. That man hung the moon. I knew the second I saw you after you met Lex that your heart belonged to her forever."

"Too bad she didn't feel the same way." Aspen's voice trembled. She had lost her baby and her soul mate and some days she ached from the emptiness inside. She was trying; god knows with all she had in her, to move on. However, the wounds were still so fresh and so painful that there were days she thought she might die from it.

Ginny leaned over and clasped Aspen's hand, squeezing gently. "Honey, she's just lost. Everything that was right with her world has suddenly turned upside down. If I know Lex, she feels like she has failed you, and she's not the type of woman who can live with failure."

"I know." Aspen squeezed her aunt's hand, reveling in the strength she offered. She needed it to face the next step in the grieving process. "But damn her for leaving me and not facing this together."

"Maybe she couldn't stay. Perhaps she thought that you were looking at her the same way that she saw herself and rather than stay and continue to let you down, she chose to leave. I can understand how she feels."

13

"You sound like you are defending her. You are supposed to be irate and stand up for me." Aspen chuckled sarcastically. She knew what her aunt was doing and while she appreciated the effort, part of her wished that Aunt Ginny would hurl a string of expletives at Lex. At least, it might make her feel better.

"Goodness no." Ginny gasped. "I'm just saying I can understand how Lex must be feeling. It's hard to look at the person you love knowing you let them down."

Aspen cocked her head. She heard something in her aunt's tone that gave her pause. "It sounds like there is more to this than just understanding."

Ginny sighed loudly. "I was a lot like Lex. I see a little of her in me. It's hard to explain without sharing something with you that only two other people besides me and Neal know." She gave Aspen's hand one last squeeze then gripped the arm of her rocking chair and started to rock. She was silent several beats longer.

"What is it, Aunt Ginny? It can't be that bad." Whatever it was that Ginny was holding onto gave Aspen a start. It wasn't like her aunt to have difficulty talking about something. If anything, she could talk the ear off a brass monkey, so the silence was somewhat disconcerting.

After several more seconds, Ginny finally broke the silence. "I have kept this a secret for over thirty years, but I think you need to hear it. It may help you to move on. A few years after your uncle and I got married, we decided it was time to have children. Neal wanted a son, and your grandma, well she was just like every other mom in the world. She wanted grandchildren to spoil. We tried for several years with no luck. We had almost given up hope of ever having children when I finally got pregnant. Meanwhile, your mom was four months pregnant with you. We were so excited. We were going to have kids about the same age; all the cousins growing up together."

Aspen could hear the catch in her throat. She didn't need to hear what had happened, she knew the outcome. Ginny and Neal had never had children. She hadn't realized that it wasn't because they didn't want to. "How long?"

"Five months."

Aspen sucked in a breath. The same time that she lost her baby. She was finally starting to understand that there was so much more than she ever knew about her aunt that made them kindred spirits. "Uncle Neal left when you lost the baby?"

"No, honey." Ginny shook her head in the dark, a rueful smile on her face. "I did."

Aspen's swift intake of breath did little to mask her shock at her aunt's revelation. "You left?" She still wasn't sure she had heard correctly, not able to believe that her aunt and uncle had ever had issues.

"Yes." Ginny let out a sigh. "I couldn't take the pain in his eyes. To me, it wasn't pain for me and what I had lost. It was pain for losing his chance at a son to carry on his name. I couldn't see past my own hurt long enough to realize that Neal was devastated for me. He knew how much I wanted a baby and when we lost our son, I was broken. Every time I looked in his eyes, I felt like I had failed the man I loved. I couldn't move past my own pain and the fact that I had let him down, so I ran."

Aspen was still reeling from her aunt's words. Nothing in her aunt and uncle's fairy tale story could have suggested anything but years of happiness, and yet, here she was sharing something with her niece that made her a little more human. "Where did you go?"

"I went to your great Aunt Sarah's house. It was the one place I could go where I knew that I wouldn't get looks of pity from every direction. Aunt Sarah never married. In fact, to this day, I would swear she was a lesbian, though she wouldn't tell anyone, not in that day and age. But, I knew out of everyone, she would be the one that could understand what I was feeling."

"Why didn't you stay with Grandma?" Aspen queried.

"Oh honey." Ginny squeezed her hand. "Grandma was a lot like your mom. She would have told me to stop wearing my heart on my sleeve and just deal with it. She would have told me to keep trying, and I couldn't do that."

"Well, at least now I know that Mom comes by it honestly." Aspen chuckled softly. "I swear that woman has a jar somewhere that she stores her feelings in, just so she doesn't have to talk about it."

Ginny snorted loudly. "You are more right than you know. Grandma used to tell me to tuck those feelings away and move on. It didn't help any to leave them out and dwell on them all the time."

"So what happened? I mean how long did you stay with Aunt Sarah?"

"Oh longer than I should have." Ginny's voice caught in her throat. "I almost lost your uncle. I didn't talk to him for the longest time. I had your mom tell him where I was, but nothing more. I remember the one time he tried to get me to come back home. You think your uncle is skinny now; you should have seen him then. He was nothing but skin and bones. That almost broke me. He came to tell me that he had turned the nursery into a music room, something I had always wanted. He wanted me to know that he didn't need a baby to love me or to make us a family. He just wanted me. However, I was stubborn. I couldn't go back and let him down."

"But he told you he was okay."

"He did. I heard the words. I just didn't listen. All I saw was me taking away a man's dream. I figured he could find a woman who could give him babies and not be tied to me the rest of his life. He was young. It wasn't too late." Ginny sat back in her chair, and it creaked loudly. The sounds in the night were dying down slowly, and she yawned in response. "He left in tears and I ached even more. I stayed for two years before I finally grew up enough to realize that I was only hurting myself and breaking your uncle's heart by being an ass. When I came home, I was finally able to understand that your uncle loved me for me and when he married me, it wasn't because he thought I could give him a houseful of kids. It was because he wanted to spend his life with me."

Aspen shook her head. "He waited all that time?"

"He did." Ginny took a sip of her now cold tea. "I am the luckiest woman alive. He could have very well moved on without me, which is what I told him to do. I'm not saying you should wait. Lord knows; two years was an eternity to wait for someone to start thinking straight again. I only want to help you understand how Lex is feeling. I'm not saying it is right, I'm just saying I know where her head is."

"I know." Aspen sighed loudly. "I just wish I could make the ache go away. It helps my head to hear what you went through, but not my heart. I hurt all over. When I think of what Lex and I had, it rips my heart out."

Ginny heard the pain in her niece's voice, and her heart went out to her. From her own experience, she knew that it felt like a white-hot knife searing her soul. Time didn't take the pain away; it could only dull it. "She's probably feeling the same. The difference is you're stuck around to deal with the pain. You are a lot like Neal in that regard. He was my strength and what helped me heal, once I let him. It's going to be hard, but you just have to keep waking up and facing each day. Eventually, it gets a little easier."

"God, I hope so." Aspen admitted. "Right now I feel like it will never go away. I can function, but it's not me. It's a shell of the woman I was. When I look in the mirror, I don't recognize myself anymore."

"I know it's hard to see right now, but you will get better. I almost broke your uncle Neal, but he was stronger than that and didn't let me. Don't let this break you, honey. You've got me and Neal to lean on, as long as you want."

"I know." Aspen stared off into the night, a thousand pictures playing in her head. "Thank you for telling me what happened with you. I don't think our story will end happily like yours, but I know my heart will go on. At least, I hope it will."

"It will, honey. It may take a while, but we are strong, resilient creatures, and we aren't given anything we can't handle." Ginny leaned forward in her chair and yawned loudly, long past her bedtime. "You just have to believe that one day, you will be healed."

"I don't doubt that." Aspen smiled wryly. "I just wish it would happen more quickly."

"I can't promise that it will happen soon, only that it will happen eventually. Until then, you have us…for as long as you need."

"That means a lot, believe me." Aspen leaned back in her chair and rocked slowly. She nudged her aunt. "I'm okay. You need to get to sleep."

Ginny stood up slowly and stretched her hands over her head. "You going to bed?"

"Not yet." Aspen shook her head. "I'm gonna sit out here a bit longer. There's something about being out here that calms me down."

Ginny leaned over and kissed her cheek. "Alright, honey. I'll see you in the morning."

Aspen watched her aunt retreat into the house before she settled back in. She heard the slight creak in the chair, felt the soothing rhythm of the gentle rocking as she closed her eyes and willed her mind to think of nothing but the soft breeze on her skin. She would let herself feel again tomorrow, but for tonight, she would just be. It was the first small steps in what she knew would be an arduous journey.

Chapter 2

"You have to do what?" Cassidy Scott's voice raised to a particularly annoying level that made Lex long to put headphones in and drown her out. "You can't be serious."

"Dead." Alexis Tataris twirled her black ponytail, a sign she was stressed. "It's the only way. Rhode Island doesn't grant same—sex divorces from another state. It's easier to file where we got married, but we can't file for divorce until we can prove we've lived there for six months. At that, they won't finalize the divorce until one of us has lived there for a year. Her aunt was nice enough to let us use her place." Lex felt the heat rise in her neck. Actually, her ex had said she would stay there alone, but Lex had surprised them both and offered to move with her…if it was alright with all the parties involved.

"So why can't she just live there a year? She can file, and you can go there when you need to sign everything." Cassidy pushed back. "I don't see why you both have to live there."

"That's not fair to ask of her, especially since I'm the one asking a huge favor here. I'm asking her to pick up her life for a year just to give me a divorce." Lex's brown eyes flashed. "I'm lucky she agreed at all. She could have told me to kiss her ass. Besides, I'm just going for six months, babe. After that, I can come home. She's agreed to stay the whole year."

Lex looked away guiltily. In all honesty, Lex could have rented a place in Massachusetts and filed there, but she would have been out the money for a full year. There was a huge part of her that wanted to feel what it felt like to be near her ex-wife again. To remember, if even for a short time, what she had felt before. Lex had never fully moved on, but she would never tell Cass that. Instead, Lex sold the idea for legal reasons. It wasn't the most honest thing, but she couldn't stop herself. "Besides, it's just a business arrangement. You still get to have me."

Lex regarded Cassidy. Honestly, she wouldn't have chosen to get married again. Living in domestic sin was good enough for her. Nevertheless, what Cassidy wanted, Cassidy got, and a quick look at her pouting face confirmed that. "This is the only way."

"You mean it's the only way since I am the one that wants to get married?" Cassidy asked petulantly.

Lex rubbed the bridge of her nose wearily. This was a fight they had had one too many times before. She wasn't sure why it mattered so much, but she didn't feel the need to give in tonight. "Well yeah. I told you before that there is no point in getting married. I'm not going anywhere."

"Hmph!" Cass wrapped her arms around Lex's neck and pulled up on her tip—toes. "I don't want to marry you because I want to tie you down. I want to marry you because I love you. I had hoped you felt the same way about me."

Lex felt herself soften. She kissed the tip of Cass's nose. "You know I love you, Cass. It's just that…"

"Yes, Lex, I know." Cass yanked on her ponytail and searched her face. "However, you were young and well, that wasn't me."

Lex's mind flashed to a different time and felt her heart clench. No, she thought, you aren't her. She was her first love and if pressed, Lex would probably say her greatest love. She shook her head. That was then. This was now. She forced herself to return Cassidy's gaze. She tipped the corners of her mouth into an indulgent smile. "So you're okay with this?"

Cassidy shrugged. "I'm not sure okay is the word I would use. I just think it's stupid you have to be there with her. It's a divorce for God sake. It's a piece of paper. Grant the damn thing and move on."

The *her* in question was Aspen Lane, Lex's ex—wife. They had married when Lex was twenty—three and separated when she was twenty—eight. The reason for Lex's leaving was stupid really, at least looking back. She and Aspen had tried to have children unsuccessfully, stopping after Aspen's miscarriage. Not really sure how to handle the disappointment of losing a child, Lex fell apart. Instead of looking to the person that would have soothed her soul the most, she had run, too afraid to face her own imagined failure. "It is what it is, Cass."

Cassidy regarded the pained look in her eyes. Lex did her best to hide it, but on the rare occasion that she saw it, Cassidy experienced a pang of fear. In the back of her mind, she knew Lex had never gotten closure with Aspen. In the three years that they had been together, there were times she saw something in Lex's eyes and knew part of Lex would never be hers. "Okay."

"Okay." Lex saw Cassidy finally resign herself to what had to be done. In a way, maybe it was a blessing. Lex could get the closure she needed, and then they could be free to move on with their lives without Aspen's ghost. Three was a crowd anyway. "Besides it's not like we will be together that much. You know I'll be on the road most of the time anyway."

"Yes, I know." Cassidy shrugged. Lex's job as a sports columnist took her out of town more often than she liked. Early on, it had caused several arguments, but when Cassidy figured out that Lex wouldn't give up her job, she realized she either took Lex as she was or not at all. She took what she could get. "So tell me why you have to live in the same place."

Lex shrugged. "It's stupid for us both to get a place. Besides it is Aspen's aunt's farm, and the rent is cheap." Cheap was actually free. There was a bunkhouse that had been fully renovated and since her aunt was no longer operating the farm, it was empty. When she had run the idea by Aspen, Aspen had initially said she would make the move and take care of the divorce, but Lex wouldn't hear of her doing it alone. It was her request. She needed to be part of it. Cassidy wrinkled up her nose. "There better be two bedrooms."

Lex chuckled. "Yes, babe, there are two bedrooms. Did you think I was going to sleep in the same bed with her for the next six months?"

"You never know." Cassidy toyed with a button on Lex's shirt. "I know you never got over her."

Lex tensed and swallowed the lump in her throat. Truth be told, a part of her hadn't ever gotten over Aspen. There were so many times over the two years after they had broken up, that she almost picked up the phone and called begging for forgiveness, pleading with her to take her back. Somehow words just didn't seem like enough to bridge the distance that she had put between them.

"It's okay. I know." Cassidy smiled sadly. She put her hand over Lex's heart. "First loves. You never stay with them, but you never forget them."

Lex waited while Cassidy fidgeted against her, a string of sighs escaping her lips. Lex finally pushed her back and held her at arms' length. She forced Cassidy to meet her gaze. "Come on, spit it out."

"Well..." Cassidy's eyes searched hers. "If there is anything you need to do while you are there, I'm okay with it."

Lex furrowed her brow in confusion. "What do you mean?"

"It's just that, well, I know you didn't ever get closure."

"And…" Lex tired sometimes of having to pull everything out of Cassidy. Granted Lex had never been the best communicator, but Cassidy beat her hands down. She couldn't just say what she was thinking and make it easier on both of them. There were times Lex thought she did it on purpose just to get under her skin.

"I want you to get closure and if that means you need to sleep with her or something; you can."

Lex nearly choked. "Damn, woman! I'm going there to get a divorce, not get back together. How on earth is sleeping with her going to get me closure?"

"You know, break up sex." Cassidy said matter of fact, as if that explained everything.

"Still not following." Lex dropped her arms and pulled away. Cassidy never ceased to amaze her. She was immature at times and insisted on her way more times than not, but there were moments like this that she gave unselfishly.

Cassidy's manicured fingernail tapped on the counter nervously. Her stomach felt unsettled. It was a spur-of-the-moment suggestion, but she had always known that Lex held onto her past relationship because she had never said good-bye. It was impossible to move forward when she still had a foot in the past. "You never had your chance for closure. You never said good-bye. I think you need to do that."

"I can do that without sleeping with her." Lex's mind suddenly hurtled back ten years to the day she met Aspen Lane. A mutual friend set them up on a blind date. The second she walked in the door, Lex was lost in her steel blue eyes. She felt a jolt of electricity when they shook hands. Lex Tataris was caught – hook, line and sinker. Her skin felt hot just thinking about Aspen, and she got the familiar itch in her fingertips. The one that she got anytime she even thought about touching Aspen. She shook her head, and the image faded into gray again.

Cassidy saw the emotions in Lex's eyes and knew where her mind had gone. She felt tightness in her chest. "Maybe you can. I'm just saying that when you get there, please do what you need to do to shut that door. I want a future with all of you."

Lex saw Cassidy's lip tremble and knew what a sacrifice it was for her even to offer the suggestion. As difficult as Cassidy could be sometimes, Lex did love her. It may not have been a soul consuming love, but Lex had known early on that she would only find that once in her life, and she had screwed that one time up. "You have all of me."

"Do I?" Cassidy looked at her askance. "Show me."

Lex knew she meant to get rid of her wedding ring. That had been the one thing Lex couldn't let go of. The pictures, everything else was gone. It had been too hard to see those after the breakup. She would sit for hours and stare at Aspen's picture, those blue eyes looking into her soul, until she ached so bad that she would drink herself into oblivion to forget. She met Cassidy during that time. She wasn't looking for anyone, but having someone fill the gaping hole in her chest seemed like a good idea. "I…"

Cassidy sensed her hesitation, and it firmed her resolve a bit. Yes, she may not really want Lex to sleep with Aspen, but she did want her to get her out of her system and if that was the only way then so be it. "You don't have to say it, and I'm not forcing you to, but I hope you reach a place while you are there that you will finally be able to let go."

Lex felt a lump rise in her throat. Say good-bye. Let go. Those words had a finality that hit her in the stomach and almost knocked her over. Could she say good-bye? Was she ready to let go? All these years, she held on to the past; maybe not to Aspen, but to the thought of her. She shook her head. It was only fair what Cassidy was asking of her. She looked at the woman she had loved for three years and smiled. "By the time I come back, I'll have it all taken care of."

Cassidy felt herself relax. That was one thing about Lex that she loved. When she gave her word, she kept it. "I know you will." She narrowed her eyes and studied Lex closely. Lex was good at not saying what she felt but her eyes always betrayed her. She saw a spark of sadness in them and hoped when she got back, it would be gone.

Lex twisted her short ponytail again. Cassidy may have been calm, but she was anything but. The thought of having to spend six months in the same place as Aspen was starting to sink in. In the five years they were together, to say that she took her breath away every day would have been a gross injustice. It was more like she took her breath away every second of every day.

She wasn't a believer in the notion of soul mates per se, but Aspen made her believe in miracles. Maybe that was why it was so hard when they couldn't conceive. It shook her faith and made her question everything. Maybe they weren't right for each other. Perhaps fate was telling her, she's not the one. Stupidly, Lex listened to her fears. Instead of leaning on the one person that could have made everything right, she pulled away. She kept running until she turned and couldn't see behind her anymore. She had lost herself, and she had let the light that would have called her home burn out. That was yesterday, and she needed to focus on today.

She just needed to treat this like a business arrangement. That was how she separated her emotions from everything else. She made decisions with a level head; at least, the decisions that didn't involve Aspen. With her, every choice she had made was with her heart. It was as if she had reached in and wrapped her hands around Lex's heart and had not let go. She felt tightness in her chest. If she was going to survive the next six months, playing the business angle was going to be the only thing that worked.

Lex pushed her thoughts to the back of her mind and smiled at Cassidy. "Have I mentioned that I love you?"

Cassidy smiled. "Yes, but remind me again."

Lex closed the distance and kissed her softly. She felt the familiar tug in her loins. It felt comfortable with Cassidy.

Never out of control, never enough to make her ache, but for Lex, it somehow became enough. She had long ago resigned herself to the fact that fate wouldn't strike twice. She had her chance at wonderful, and she had blown it. But good was...well it was good enough. Right? She broke the kiss. "Besides, it's only three hours away. I can come home for long weekends when I'm not on the road."

It was late summer and baseball season was in full swing. Pre—season football was getting ready to start, and Cassidy knew Lex would be on the road more often than she was home. "I'd like that."

"Me too." Lex admitted with a smile. "What about you? What are you going to do with all your free time?"

Cassidy smiled wildly, for the first time since the conversation had started. "Work on next spring's line up." She was a clothing designer for Saks, and the spring release was a huge deal for them. "Now I can do it without you here to distract me." She teased.

"Hey!" Lex feigned offense. "I distract you."

"Very much." Cassidy admitted. "It's difficult to think when you're around, much less keep my mind on my job. With you gone, I may actually make my deadline."

Lex kissed her again. "You know I have a thought."

Cassidy cocked an eyebrow. "Yes?"

"The six months will be over about the time you go to New York for the fashion show. What do you say we make it our official engagement trip?"

"You mean it?" Cassidy eyed her suspiciously. "You said you didn't want to rush."

"I know." Lex shrugged. "But you're right, there's really no reason to wait."

Cassidy squealed. "Oh my god, I love you." She kissed her soundly then pulled away and started jumping around excitedly. "I have to go call my mother."

Lex watched her leave and chuckled slightly. She made the decision without thinking. She hoped it would give her a goal, something to focus on during the next few months. She was going to need it. She wasn't sure she could be anywhere near Aspen and not get consumed by her again.

Chapter 3

Aspen threw the covers off and sat up, trying to catch her breath. Her heart raced, and she had to check her surroundings to make sure she was in her own bed. The dream had been so real it terrified her. No stranger to night terrors, her recent conversation with Lex made them even worse.

Years of emotions came pouring out like a swollen river overflowing its bounds. She had done a good job of tucking those years in a neat little box in the back of her mind, but one call, one word, the sound of Lex's voice and the box opened and spilled its contents.

This dream had taken her back to the last time they had tried to conceive, and she had miscarried. Only in the dream, she went full term and had given birth. They brought the baby home from the hospital. Their lives were as perfect as three people could want for. She woke up to Lex taking the baby—their baby from her. She had run screaming after them, but no matter how hard she had run; she hadn't been able to catch them.

Aspen scrubbed her palms over her eyes and kicked her feet to the floor. She inhaled quickly. The floors were freezing. She reached for the socks she had kicked off during the night and pulled them onto her feet. Her mind flashed to Lex and the shiver this time had nothing to do with the cold.

"Aspen?" Her mother's voice carried up the steps, and she was immediately transported back to her childhood. "Honey, are you up?"

Aspen groaned loudly. Even though her stay here was temporary, she was already looking forward to leaving. After almost five years, she had given up her place in New York four months ago, needing to get away from the hectic pace and not wanting to worry about how she was going to pay the rent all the time. "Yeah, be down in a sec." She stood up and stretched her arms over her head and pulled her housecoat on, cinching it around her waist to stave off the cold. She started down the steps, and the familiar creak of the steps made her smile.

"Morning, sleepyhead." Susan handed her daughter a cup of steaming coffee and pointed at a loaf of bread."

Aspen took a sip and shook her head. "Just coffee."

"Honey, you need to eat." Susan's eyes assessed her daughter. "As it is, you're skin and bones."

Aspen half—expected her to force her into a chair and make her eat, just as she had twenty—five years ago. Instead, she let it slide and sat back down to work on her crossword puzzle. "Are you running into town today?"

"Yes." Susan looked up from her crossword puzzle. "You want to ride along?"

"No, but I'm going to have you pick up a few things for me."

Aspen turned the mug in her hands until her mother looked up, rested her glasses on the tip of her nose and looked at her expectantly. "I'll pick up anything. Just make a list." Her eyes flicked to the coffee mug. "Something you want to talk about?"

Aspen's eyes dropped to the table before meeting her mother's waiting gaze. "Lex called me last week."

Her mother's brow furrowed. "Lex...as in our Lex?"

Aspen nodded. "Yes." She wrung her hands together. Even talking about her was bringing emotions to the surface, ones that were better left unfelt.

"Well, what did she want?" Susan pressed lightly. She could see the unrest in her daughter's eyes, and it made her hurt for her all over again.

"She wants a divorce." The words were so matter of fact, but Susan could hear in her tone just how much it hurt. She had always held onto the hope that one day Lex might wake up and realize what she gave up and come back. Aspen's news poked a hole in that.

"Kind of late for that, isn't it?" Susan asked without censure. "You've been separated for five years. Isn't that overkill?"

Aspen shrugged. "I guess. Her girlfriend is insisting they get married, and they can't until we are divorced."

"Hmph!" Susan uttered with a disapproving look. "So, she called to tell you that and to expect the papers to sign?"

"Not exactly." Aspen smiled ruefully. "She lives in Rhode Island now. They recognize same-sex marriage from other states, but they won't let us divorce there. We can only get divorced in Vermont or in a state that recognizes gay marriage."

"So, she'll just drive on up to Massachusetts and do it there." Susan offered as though that was the solution that everyone else in the matter had missed.

"Well that's the other news." Aspen said quietly. "The state won't grant a divorce unless the party petitioning for a divorce has resided in the state for a year, or…"

Susan furrowed her brow, not liking the tone of her daughter's *or.* "Why do I think I'm not going to like the sound of that?" Like it or not, her daughter was grown up, and she couldn't protect her from getting hurt, but Lord knows; she wanted to. She had been there five years ago when her world came crashing down. She was the one that listened to her daughter cry herself to sleep every night for months. She was the one that watched her daughter go through life like a zombie, and God help her; she wanted to do whatever she needed to do to protect her.

"Because you aren't." Aspen sighed loudly trying to build up the courage to get through the next part of her news. She practically spat out the subsequent part, tripping over herself to say it before she got her wits about her and forgot the whole crazy idea. "A year is a long time for her to relocate, so I might have offered to move to Vermont for a year and file where we got married." There she had said it and felt immediate relief. "I'm going to stay at the ranch."

"What?" Susan looked at her daughter in disbelief. "Ginny didn't say anything to me about this."

"I asked her not too." Aspen admitted. "I knew you would be upset."

"Of course I'm upset, honey." Susan had set her pencil aside earlier, but she picked it up and tapped it nervously on the table. "You're dropping everything for her again and not getting anything from her."

Aspen grimaced. "That's not entirely true."

"What do you mean?" Susan eyed her daughter suspiciously.

"Lex is moving there too. She felt it was only fair to suffer with me."

"Oh that's rich. Now, she decides to step up."

Aspen reached over and stilled her mother's hand. "Please don't be upset with me. Right now what I need is your support. I know you don't agree with it, but I feel like it's something I need to do. Besides, we will only be together for six months, and it isn't like she will be there full time. She travels for work, remember?"

"How could I forget? Susan frowned. "I always thought she should have found a different job and settled down. Couldn't she have just been one of those boggers and written for the computer thingy like you do?"

31

Aspen chuckled. "You mean blogger. She does blog Mom, but she needs to be at the games to be able to do that."

"Pshaw. Details honey." Susan squeezed her hand. "Are you sure about this?"

Aspen nodded then hesitated. Was she sure? At the moment, there wasn't a definitive answer. Confusion had set in, and she hadn't settled on quite where she was with her decision. "I think I need this. We never really had the chance for closure. It was like I had my hand on something, and it got ripped away with no warning."

"That's because she ripped it away and broke your heart in the process." Her mother's tone held the censure she expected.

"Mother." Aspen shot her a look. "Not helping. I'm already questioning my decision. You aren't making it any easier."

"Maybe that's a sign."

"I don't need a sign. I finally need to say goodbye good-bye Lex and the past, so I can move on with my life. It's been five years, and I'm no closer to being over her than I was five years ago."

"Honey, are you really sure?" Susan's concerned eyes regarded her closely. "I just don't see how this can end well."

Susan sighed loudly. "Well or not, it's end I'm looking for. I didn't get that before and there is this thing in my life just hanging there, unresolved. I feel like I am frozen in time, unable to move forward. Perhaps, I can finally get some closure and get past all of that."

"Well I can't say that I agree with this, but you're an adult. It's your choice, I'll stand by whatever decision you make." Susan never understood holding on. She believed in dealing with your grief and moving on. Her husband had died three years ago, and while she did miss him, she didn't let it dominate her life. Aspen must have gotten that from her father. The two of them could horde feelings like no one else, tucking them into some untidy box that they could pull out later and disassemble once again. Susan couldn't allow herself to do that, burdening herself with feelings and emotions when a person ought to let go. "Your aunt Ginny is going to give Lex a piece of her mind, I don't doubt."

Aspen smiled. "Was that ever a question?" Although, she knew better. She remembered the conversation she and her aunt had years before and Aspen knew if anyone was going to stand up for Lex, it would be Aunt Ginny. She drained the last of her coffee. "I may run into town with you after all. Do I have time for a quick shower?"

Her mother checked her watch. "Of course. I've still got to finish my crossword puzzle."

Aspen pushed her chair in and squeezed her mom's shoulder as she walked past. No matter what happened in her life, her mother had been there. From her first broken heart in high school up to now, she was her rock. Her mom didn't cry with her, instead she lived her life with a silent stoicism that allowed her to give Aspen a solid shoulder to cry on, and the knowledge that it would get better with time. She knew at the end of this next journey, she would be waiting on the other side waiting to pick up the pieces. Aspen just hoped her heart wasn't shattered into a thousand pieces and there was something left to salvage.

She pulled her hair up and looked at her reflection in the small country mirror. The new signs of age that were starting to show up did little to improve the face looking back at her. She barely recognized herself anymore. She touched a wrinkle beside her eye and sighed loudly. At thirty—three, she was too young to look as worn out as she did. Or feel as worn out for that matter. The hurt she carried around like a badge was getting heavy.

She leaned in closer and narrowed her eyes. She felt her mind alter and a new determination slipped inside and took root in her conscious. No matter what happened with this whole Lex thing, she would walk away from this looking forward and no longer holding onto the past. Her very existence depended on it.

Chapter 4

Lex cinched her garment bag further up her shoulder and rang the doorbell again. She cocked her ear and listened. Nothing. "Shit." She pulled her blackberry out of her pocket and thumbed through texts until she found the right one. She studied the text then looked over her shoulder. It had been a long time since she had been at Aunt Ginny's farm, but she was pretty sure she recognized her surroundings.

She decided to take a chance and turned the knob on the front door, somewhat relieved that it gave easily. She wouldn't dream of leaving her door unlocked in Providence. Grabbing her suitcase, she bumped the door open with her foot and stepped inside. She was immediately ensconced in rich, warm wood. The newly renovated *bunk house,* as Aspen had called it, was closer to a mountain cabin than any bunkhouse she had ever imagined.

The only item that gave the building's origin away was the unfinished beam ceiling that towered two stories above her. She glanced to her left, and her gaze lit on a cozy kitchen. Her mind reeled back ten years, and she could see Aspen standing at the island making her cobbler and teasing that Lex didn't stand a chance once she tasted Aspen's cooking. She might as well say good-bye to her heart now.

Lex chuckled, breaking her reverie. Like everything else about them, those memories were turbulent waters below a crumbling bridge. She walked past a sizeable living room area with two stuffed, wing back chairs facing a fireplace. A floor—to—ceiling mantle held a large, flat-screen TV and several pictures. Seeing one of Aspen, with her head thrown back stopped her in her tracks.

She weaved through the chairs and picked the frame up. Aspen's head was thrown back, her eyes closed and a smile that went from ear to ear. Lex sucked in a breath. She had forgotten that anytime she saw Aspen, her heart stopped. She ran her thumb over Aspen's face and felt the familiar tug in her heart. *Do what you need to do to say good-bye and move on.*

Cassidy's words played in her ears. She shook her head and set the frame back on the mantle. She was here to end things officially and say good-bye, so she and Cassidy could move on, not reminisce about the one she let get away.

She gathered her suitcase from the spot she left it. She paused when the open living space stopped, and tee'd down two hallways. She mentally flipped a coin and turned left. She passed a small powder room and opened a door at the end of the hallway, revealing a large master bedroom. She saw several personal items on the bed stand and knew she had chosen Aspen's room.

Lex was about to close the door when Aspen's scent wafted towards her, evoking images that she had no right thinking about. She closed the door guiltily and almost ran to the other door at the opposite end of the hall. She opened the door to an nearly identical room. She flopped her garment bag on the bed, set her suitcase on the floor and surveyed her room for the next six months.

The bed was larger than she had expected, and she smiled. The first bed she and Aspen had shared was a full bed, barely bigger than a twin. They didn't complain at the time. Neither one minded spending the night entwined in each other's arms. Lex felt a current course through her body, and she mentally pulled her mind back to reality. The sooner she got her mind focused on the plan, the better.

She went through a small door to her left that opened into a spacious bathroom with a vanity, commode and a large sunken, soaking tub. "Do not even go there, Lex."

Lex washed her hands and splashed water on her face. The drive wasn't tedious at all, in fact, had the circumstances been different; she might even consider it relaxing. Today though, her mind had not thought of anything else except the reason she was making the trip in the first place.

Her eyes sought the mirror as they did most times she was in the bathroom lately. Age was creeping up on her quickly, and so far she hadn't figured out a way to outrun it. Cassidy liked to tease that Lex was her cougar. In actuality, the age difference was only eight years, but being on the other side of thirty, there were times Lex felt like she could have been a cougar.

She ran a hand over her ever—present ponytail and grimaced at her own face. She thought that maybe being on the road as much as she was, coupled with her harried schedule, wasn't treating her as well as she thought. She enjoyed the freedom, the change of scenery, loved sports and everything about them, but she knew something was missing. She had given hope to the feeling that perhaps marrying Cassidy would give her the settled in feeling she had been missing for so long.

Lex took one last look in the mirror. She fished around in her bag for her Red Sox ball cap. She pulled her ponytail through the hole in the back and pulled the brim low over her forehead. She cupped her hands around the brim and pushed it back into shape. Curiosity got the better of her, and she set out to find her new roommate.

She wandered out the front door and down a narrow well—worn path to an aged barn. The doors were propped open, and she peeked inside. Rows of once filled stalls sat quietly, a vestige to a bygone era. The scent of hay penetrated her senses, and her nose crinkled with a threatening sneeze. She pinched her nose and swallowed it back down. She reminded herself to take an allergy pill daily while she was here.

She cocked her head and heard a soft, muted voice coming from the back of the barn. She saw long brown hair peeking out from under a worn cowboy hat. Lex's eyes raked over Aspen's body in a familiarly protective way. They stopped at her deliciously round bottom. Lex subconsciously licked her lips.

Aspen's hips swayed with every brush of her hand. She was brushing the honey—colored mane of one of the three horses left in the nearly empty barn. She was humming an unrecognizable tune, and Lex snickered.

Aspen hadn't heard her come in, and the sound scared her. She wheeled around and immediately shot Lex a reproaching look. "You scared the shit out of me."

Lex's gaze met her steely blue ones, and she exhaled loudly, completely caught off guard by Aspen's breathtaking beauty. If anything, she had gotten more beautiful with age. Lex had hoped that she would show up old and fat and so far from adorable that any leftover emotions she had would fly out the window. One glance and Lex knew she might as well try to stop the sun from shining. "I'm sorry. I didn't mean to scare you."

Aspen's face softened, and she smiled shyly. "Hi, Lex." Her heart raced in her chest. They had talked on the phone several times prior to arriving, but nothing could have prepared her for the rush of excitement at seeing her again.

Lex trembled. She had always loved when Aspen said her name. It rolled off her tongue like smooth honey, golden and just as sweet and filled her with love. "Hello, A."

Aspen blinked at Lex's nickname for her. There were some things a person didn't forget. She felt heat creep into her cheeks, and she pushed it down again. "Did you just get here?"

"A bit ago." Lex returned her smile. She hooked her thumb over her shoulder and gestured towards the house. "I hope you don't mind. I went ahead and got settled in my room. I wanted the one facing east so I moved your stuff into the other bedroom."

Aspen looked at her in disbelief. "You're joking, right?"

"Nah, it was pretty easy. You didn't come with much. I just piled it on the bed."

Aspen was about to scold her when she saw the old mischievous twinkle in Lex's eyes. She couldn't forget that. All she had to do was look at Lex, and she knew she was up to no good. "Well, I can honestly say I didn't miss your twisted sense of humor."

"Some things never change, A." Lex took a step closer and propped her elbows on the stall door. "So who is the gorgeous blonde?"

Aspen's face broke into a smile. "This is Lacey." She ran her palm over the horse's back, feeling the muscles ripple beneath her hand. She lifted the other hand and pointed with her brush to the other occupied stalls. "That's Tarra and that's Reba. They are the only ones that Aunt Ginny held onto when she retired."

"She's beautiful."

"I agree." Aspen nodded towards the wall. There were still several saddles and tackle lining one side. "You can ride if you want. Aunt Ginny's is giving us free rein of the place in exchange for horse duty while we are here."

"This is really nice of her. I truly appreciate it." Lex's brow furrowed. "You know I don't mind paying for the room."

"No need." Aspen smiled mischievously, "It's worth more to her not to have to clean the stalls for a while."

Lex threw her head back and laughed, giving Aspen a chance to steal an unnoticed glance. Her Greek coloring and high arching cheekbones had always been two of Aspen's favorite things about her. The years were generous to Lex as well. Everything about her was sculpted perfectly, her casual attire doing little to hide her toned figure. From her olive coloring to her beautiful body, she was a Mediterranean Goddess as far as Aspen was concerned. Well, as far as she was concerned when they were still together. Now, Lex was like one of her favorite paintings. She could look, but she couldn't touch.

Lex's eyes returned to Aspen, and she smiled. "Thank you again. I hope this isn't too awkward for you. I know we…well, I didn't leave things on the best of terms."

Aspen smiled sadly. "Honestly, that's ancient history, Lex. I'm sure things will be just fine. This is a favor to a friend. We don't need to make it into more than what it is." Even as she said the words, she heard her heart call her a liar. She almost rubbed the tip of her nose, expecting it to have grown several inches.

A look of something that almost resembled disappointment flashed in Lex's eyes before she blinked it away. "Good. I'm glad. It would have been a long six months otherwise."

Aspen pulled the brush off of her hand and looped it over a hook before opening the door and joining Lex outside Lacey's stall. "You're lucky today. I've already cleaned the stalls and fed the ladies. I wasn't sure what time you would get here so I didn't plan dinner. If you're hungry, I can make us something."

Lex put her hand on Aspen's arm and jumped at the tingle. "You don't have to cook for me, A. I can fend for myself."

"Nonsense." Aspen shook her head. She dusted her hands off on her jeans. "Come on. I'm cooking for myself anyway. It's just as easy to cook for two. Pizza okay?"

"Homemade?" Lex's mouth watered. She missed the taste of Aspen's cooking among other things.

Aspen opened her mouth in feigned shock. "Do you even have to ask?"

"Silly me." Lex fell in step beside Aspen and studied her profile quietly.

40

Aspen turned to find Lex's eyes on her. "What?"

"Nothing." Lex tugged on her ponytail. "Just a bit surreal to be standing next to you right now, much less living in the same house as you for the next six months."

"Surreal is one way to say it." Aspen chuckled softly. She led them up the front steps, stopped and took her boots off before continuing inside.

Lex hesitated for a moment before slipping her own shoes off and following her inside. She watched Aspen wash her hands, turn the oven on and start pulling food out of the fridge. She sat down at the island and hooked her toes over the stool. She loved watching Aspen in the kitchen. She had a way with food. Pairing items together that Lex wouldn't dream of mixing and somehow making it into the best thing she had ever tasted.

"Can you reach the flour?"

Lex blinked and found Aspen regarding her with an amused expression. "Huh?"

"The flour." Aspen pointed at the top shelf. "Can you reach it?"

Lex slid off her stool and came around stopping next to Aspen. The nearness made her jump. She met Aspen's eyes, and her heart stilled. *Damn it, Cassidy. I'm not going there to sleep with her.* Lex stiffened, and her eyes shuttered closed. *Six months. All she had to do was make it six months. One road trip to the next. Piece of cake, right. Right?*

"Thank you." Aspen set the flour canister on the island and grabbed a packet of quick rise yeast out of the freezer. "So what have you been up to? Besides planning a wedding?"

Lex blushed. "Just beat around the bush, why don't you?" Aspen's laugh was as sexy as Lex remembered. Oddly, rather than a pull of desire, she felt a settling warmth effuse her body. She remembered at once that she missed not only Aspen her lover but Aspen her friend. Perhaps, when they walked away from this, the latter could be salvaged. They were older and more mature now and maybe the old hurts had slowly been replaced by beautiful memories tucked away that she could bring back out on a rainy day. "Jeez, Lex, I know you just got here, and we haven't spoken in five years, but fill me in on your plans with your girlfriend."

"Touche." Aspen smiled ruefully. She eyed the flour and dumped it into a mixing bowl, along with some sugar and salt. She lifted her eyes from the bowl. "Let me try that again. "Tell me about your life since…" Her voice drifted off, unable to bring herself to say the words.

Lex saw her discomfort and rescued her. "Nothing too exciting. We, I mean I moved to Providence a few years back."

"It's okay to talk about her, Lex." Aspen turned away before Lex could see her eyes glisten. She used heating the water as an excuse and when she turned back to the island, her composure had returned. "It's kind of hard to look past the obvious reason we are here. She's a part of your life, soon to be a pretty big part of it. You have every right to talk about her."

"It just feels funny." Lex pulled on her ponytail with both hands, cinching it tightly against her head. "Talking with my ex—wife about my soon to be wife. It's all just so bizarre."

Aspen nodded in agreement. "So, tell me about your job then. We can start off on neutral ground. Are you still working for your dad?" Lex's family owned a flower shop in Boston. Aspen used to tease her that her dad was trying to start the Greek mafia, and the florist shop was a front. Lex was his accountant for years.

Lex watched while she added the water to the bowl and turned it on to knead the dough. She waited till the mixer stopped so she didn't need to talk above the noise. "No, I quit that a few years back when I started traveling."

"You got out of the mafia?" Aspen teased. "You know you can check out; you just can't ever leave."

"Nice, A." Lex said sarcastically. "You know Pops isn't in the mafia. He cries when one of his flowers dies. Killing people? Fuh—geda—bout—it!"

Aspen laughed out loud. Lex had always been one for accents, and there were times she would speak with an accent and get her laughing so hard she almost peed her pants. She wiped her eyes and handed Lex a pear. "Here, cut this."

Lex grabbed the pear and found a knife after pulling out a couple of drawers. She searched several more for a cutting board. "You know where she keeps the cutting boards?"

Aspen nodded towards the sink. "Second drawer from the bottom."

Lex grabbed one and settled back on her stool. "How do you want me to cut this?"

"Peeled. Slices about yay big." Aspen held her thumb and forefinger about a quarter of an inch apart. "So how did you get away from Pops?"

"Lucky break." Lex peeled the skin around the pear and dropped it in the trashcan at the end of the counter. "I was doing the sports blog as a hobby. Gave me a chance to unwind after spending hours crunching numbers. I blogged quite a bit on the Red Sox, among other things. It was for fun, mostly. Just a way to share opinions with other sports fans. One day I get a call from ESPN, and they want to know if I'll write a traveling sports column for them. And the rest as they say is history."

Aspen frowned slightly. "Bet wifey doesn't like you being gone all the time."

Lex smiled wryly. "Oddly enough, that's one of the things that makes us work. We still get to have our lives and when I get home, she appreciates me more."

"Oh? The old distance makes the heart grow fonder thing, huh?" Aspen reached into the fridge and pulled out a package of gruyere cheese and prosciutto. She handed the prosciutto to Lex. "I can only speak for myself. I wouldn't like it if you were on the road that much."

"Oh, you wouldn't?" Lex cocked an eyebrow.

Aspen felt herself color. "I don't mean you. I mean if I, well with another person, not you, of course." She looked up to find Lex regarding her with an amused expression. "Oh, shut up. You always could get me tongue tied."

Lex's hands stilled. "Even now, Aspen?" She only called her Aspen when they were serious. Otherwise, it was always A. Her eyes studied Aspen's and saw something in them she hadn't seen in a long time. And that something sent shivers down her spine. She dropped her eyes, unable to hold Aspen's steady gaze. "What about you, A? Still doing the art thing?"

The art thing, as Lex referred to it, wasn't so much Aspen's career, but her passion. What she created paid the bills, but it was more an outlet for her creativity and something to lose herself in when she couldn't deal with something stressful. She had done some of her best work the first few years after Lex left. "Yes, Lex. I'm still doing the art thing. I have actually had a couple of shows in the city. My most popular was a series I called *Angst*.

Aspen didn't have to attribute those pieces to her, but Lex could tell from the hurt that flashed in her eyes when she spoke about the collection that it came about as a direct response to her leaving. "I'm sorry for hurting you."

"It's okay." Aspen said flatly. It was the closest she'd gotten to an apology. It wasn't enough. She needed to know why. She wasn't going to spend six months with Lex and not find out why she left. The past five years of her life had been miserable, and she needed to know why so she could move on. "Why?"

Lex tilted her head in confusion. "Why, what?"

Aspen's hands stilled, the dough all but forgotten. "Why did you leave? Wasn't I worth working through everything?"

Lex sat in stunned silence. Over the years, she had spent many sleepless nights wondering the answer to that question and more. "I wish I had a good answer for you."

"How about any answer? Let's start with that." Aspen's jaw clenched, some of the anger she had kept buried starting to surface. "I'll settle for anything right now. And not some similar version of seeing you walk out the door with no warning at all."

Lex could hear the ire in her voice and her heart hurt for the pain she had caused her. She shrugged, unable to come up with anything that made her cowardice. "I was weak. I didn't know how to handle the pain of us trying to conceive and not getting pregnant and then to lose the baby. I couldn't face the hurt in your eyes, let alone feel like some of it was failure on my part."

"So you ran away instead and left me to face it all alone?" Aspen desperately wanted to move forward, to let this part of her life go, but here, in a small room, standing face to face with the woman who had let her down, her defenses broke down. Now, all she wanted was to let her pain out, to lash out at the woman who had hurt her. She wanted Lex to feel some responsibility for the mess she left behind. "You're a chicken shit, Lex. I hope you know that. We were married and you took everything away from us. Everything. Did you ever think that maybe knowing I couldn't give us a baby made me feel like a huge disappointment? That I couldn't give you what you wanted. But, I would have stayed. I would have talked to you. I never would have left. We needed each other to get through that, and you walked away. You took the one thing in our lives that was right, and you shit on it."

Lex winced at the tear that was escaping from Aspen's eye. Without thinking, she reached over the island and brushed it away with her knuckle. The second she touched Aspen's skin, Lex froze. The reason they were here no longer mattered. The only thought that filled her mind was protecting this woman from pain. It wasn't until Aspen pulled away, that she realized she was not hers to protect. Lex gave up that right years ago. "I'm so sorry, A. For all of it, for being a complete and total asshole, for walking out. You have every right to hate me."

"I don't hate you." Aspen said quietly. "I hate what you did to us." The pain of Lex's leaving cut as freshly today as it had five years ago. She felt the wound re—opening and wondered if she would have the strength to let herself face this all over again. The silence was deafening, and she felt the need to fill it with some unnecessary noise. She sprinkled flour on the island and set the ball of dough in the middle of the island. Her pain, so long buried, was right at the surface, and she felt as though she might explode. Without thinking, she slammed her fist into the dough, sending a puff of flour into the air and effectively covering Lex in white powder. The move and the subsequent look of shock on Lex's face made Aspen laugh out loud; her earlier tears brushed aside. It was a small gesture, but it took her mind off her pain and made her feel better. She waited for Lex to say something, but for once in her life, she thought better of it, and kept her mouth shut. A bemused smirk was the only sign that anything was amiss. Aspen snickered once more, before turning her attention back to the dough, kneading it several times before working it into a circle. She flattened it out with her fingers and then laid it over her knuckles and enlarged it until it was almost a foot in diameter.

Lex watched in amazement. "Not doing the toss it in the air thing, huh?"

"Not here." Aspen crinkled her nose. A gesture she hated but Lex had always found adorable. "Aunt Ginny would have a cow if I messed up her brand-new kitchen." She laid the crust back down and pulled the edges out gently. She looked up to find Lex gaze fastened on her face. "What? Do I have something on my nose?"

"Actually, yes." Lex's face broke into a smile. She reached over the island and brushed Aspen's cheek with her thumb. It was a simple gesture, nothing sexual intended, even implied, and yet Lex felt heat effuse her body. She jerked her hand away with an embarrassed smile. "Just a little flour."

"You turd!" Lex had taken her hand and smeared flour down her cheek. It was another small gesture that reminded her so much of their years together. Lex had always been the troublemaker of the two, the one who was constantly teasing and playing practical jokes. It was obvious; she hadn't grown up any. Aspen tried to remain stern, but she smiled despite herself. She could only imagine what they both looked like covered in flour. With a laugh, she turned and grabbed a cheese grater out of the cabinet and handed it to Lex. "Once you finish grating that, I'll get this thing together. I'm starving." She said her piece, for now. They would probably talk about it again over the next few months, but for now; she was ready to move forward.

Lex sensed the change, and she took the peace pipe Aspen offered her. She started grating and within minutes, she handed Aspen a pile of gruyere with a grin. "By all means…create."

Aspen rolled her eyes and smiled. "Shut it." She had to look away so Lex wouldn't see the grin that stayed plastered on her face. Despite the heated exchange, this felt so much like a hundred other nights they had spent together; her cooking and Lex watching, or playing sous chef. It felt good. Too good, and she tried not to allow herself to get lost in emotions of yesteryear.

Aspen pulled a wooden pizza peel off a rack and sprinkled cornmeal over the surface. She gently lifted the dough and stretched it back out into a circle over the cornmeal. She spread a thin layer of sweet garlic over the crust then topped it with pears and prosciutto. She finished it by sprinkling a healthy amount of shredded gruyere over the top and brushed the edges with olive oil. She slid it onto the pre—heated pizza stone and shut the door. "You want a drink?"

"Yeah, what do you have?"

Aspen pulled the fridge open and started listing beverages. "Beer, pop, a Reisling."

"Let's do the Reisling." Lex suggested, thinking it sounded like the perfect pairing with Aspen's pizza.

"Good choice." Aspen pulled the wrapper off and scrounged around for a corkscrew. "Do you mind?" She handed Lex the bottle and corkscrew and started searching for wine glasses.

Lex poured the Reisling into the glasses Aspen set on the island. She handed a full one back to Aspen and sampled her own. "Mmm, good."

Aspen sipped her own as she cleaned up the few dishes they had dirtied and wiped down the island. She put the flour away, grabbed her glass and leaned back against the counter. "So what else is new?"

Lex shrugged. "Not much."

"Lex, we haven't spoken in five years. Certainly more has happened to you during that time than getting a new job."

Lex shot her a self—effacing smile. "Sorry. I forget sometimes it's been that long."

Aspen paled slightly. "I haven't."

Lex swallowed a lump. However hard it had been for her; it must have been infinitely harder on Aspen. She was the one that Lex abandoned. "Listen, A. I never meant to hurt you."

Aspen waived a dismissive hand and opened her mouth to reply, but the shrill buzz of the oven timer stopped her. "Saved by the bell."

"But I'm in a lot of trouble later." Lex winked mischievously and dodged the dishtowel that Aspen chucked in her direction.

Aspen set the pizza stone down on a hot pad holder and sliced it. She slid three pieces on a plate and handed it to Lex then served herself two slices before settling onto the stool next to Lex.

"Oh, my god. This is so delicious. I forgot how good you were." It was Lex's turn to blush. "I mean how good your cooking is."

"You always did love it." Aspen shot her an appreciative smile. "Don't get too used to it. After all, six months will be over before you know it."

That's what I'm worried about. Lex wasn't sure where that thought came from. Well yes, she actually did. She had forgotten how good it felt to be with Aspen. It was a feeling she knew she should fight, but as the wine and the nearness to Aspen settled in; she felt the tingle of warm familiarity steal into her subconscious, and in true Tataris fashion, she decided she would deal with it in the morning.

Chapter 5

Lex blinked against the soft rays of sunlight that stole into her room. She rolled over and stared at the ceiling. She wasn't awake enough, and it took her several minutes to get her bearings before she threw the covers off with a loud groan. She stretched her arms over her head and yawned loudly.

Her eyes flicked to the door, and she wondered if Aspen was up yet. One deep inhalation later and she knew the answer to her question. The smell of hot coffee wafted under her door, and before she knew it, it had wrapped her up in its grasp and deposited her in the kitchen. "Morning, sunshine."

Aspen handed her a cup and poured rich, dark liquid all the way to the top. The steam swirled tantalizingly towards Lex, and she hurried a bit more than she should have to take a drink. "Woo, shit. That's hot." Wisely, she blew on it before she attempted to drink it a second time. "So, what's up for today?"

"Lex." Aspen cocked her head sideways. "Just because we are in the same house doesn't mean you have to spend time with me. I know you have stuff to do, and I've got plenty to keep me busy."

Lex's face dropped before it broke out in a grin. "Yeah, sure I know, A."

Aspen held her gaze a moment longer, before breaking the connection and escaping to the fridge. "You want breakfast?"

"You don't have to make anything. I can eat a protein bar or something."

"Really?" Aspen spun around and looked at her askance. "I thought we settled this already."

Lex colored slightly. "We did. I feel bad that I'm taking advantage of you."

"You're going to have to stop thinking that. It's just as easy to cook for two. Besides, you know I love to cook." Her eyes zeroed in on Lex. "Now let's try that again. Do you want some breakfast?"

A relieved smile broke out on Lex's face. "Yes, thank you. I'm starving."

"Pancakes okay?"

Lex nodded. Aspen could have offered to make her a dirt pie, and she might have eaten it. Lex was normally very patient, but the one thing she didn't usually wait for was food. When she was hungry, she wanted to eat.

Aspen busied herself setting the griddle to heat and mixing batter. "I've got blueberries."

"Whatever is fine. If you're having them, I will too. But otherwise, don't worry about it." Lex felt a little tug. Five years, and Aspen still remembered she loved blueberry pancakes. Cassidy couldn't even remember that her favorite color was blue. Funny, how different the women she loved were.

"Blueberries it is." Aspen poured the batter onto the griddle and scattered blueberries over each drop of batter. "Can you grab the maple syrup and the butter out of the fridge?"

Lex slid off the stool and padded over to the fridge in search of the requested items. She located the butter, grabbed it and searched for the syrup.

"Behind the milk." Aspen said from the other side of the door as if she sensed what Lex was thinking.

Lex pushed the milk aside and grabbed the syrup. She shut the door and turned to Aspen with a smile. "Just like old times. You can read my mind."

"Like I said, some things never change." Aspen slid her spatula under the first of the pancakes and flipped them over to finish on the other side, leaving Lex to ponder her words. It was the second time in less than twenty—four hours that she had said that same phrase and Lex had to wonder if she was trying to tell her something.

Lex found the plates and silverware and gave them both a napkin, while Aspen finished up the pancakes. She set a stack at least twice as high as hers on Lex's plate, mindful of the bottomless pit she was feeding. Lex thanked her and doused her own stack liberally with syrup, dropping a pat of butter on for good measure. She was just about to sit down when Aspen stopped her.

"Grab your stuff and follow me."

Lex scooped up her plate and coffee and jogged to catch up with Aspen, who was just walking into her bedroom. "Oh nice, breakfast in bed."

Aspen looked at Lex over her shoulder and rolled her eyes. "You wish."

Actually, I do. Lex thought briefly, before conjuring up a picture of Cassidy's face. *Remember why you're here.* "Where are you taking me?"

Aspen set her food down and pulled the curtains open on what Lex had mistakenly assumed was just a window. She revealed a large set of French doors. "Voila. The perfect spot for breakfast."

And the perfect spot it was, Lex thought. The French doors opened up to a large deck that spanned the length of the house. In the far corner, was a sunken Jacuzzi that Lex wished she had known about last night. The views from the small table were breathtaking. Rolling hills covered with trees that were just beginning to hint at autumn's return. "This is gorgeous."

"It is." Aspen set her plate on a small table between two Adirondack chairs. "Aunt Ginny didn't mess around. It's hard to believe this is the old bunkhouse."

"No doubt." Lex settled into the chair beside her and shoved an impatient bite into her mouth. "Mmm, heavenly. I don't know how you do it. I can't seem to get a pancake anywhere close to this. Definitely, a bummer when I'm craving breakfast foods."

"It's just pancakes, Lex." Aspen chuckled lightly.

"Nothing is just anything with you." Lex met her eyes and smiled genuinely. "Everything you touch is special."

Aspen felt her chest tighten. *Don't even start thinking like that, Aspen. Remember why you are here. Closure.* She smiled at the compliment, but it stopped before it reached her eyes. She needed to keep her distance, at least with her emotions. "Glad I can accommodate."

Lex sensed the wall go up and mentally chided herself for pushing. The one thing that she knew hadn't changed with Aspen was she was slow to open up. It took her a while to trust and even longer to let someone in. The second time around was going to be even harder. The trust she had given Lex had been crumpled up in a ball and thrown back at her. She knew it was a miracle she was even in the same state with her, much less sharing breakfast on the second day of their tempestuous journey. "So, what made Ginny stop breeding horses?"

Aspen shrugged. "I think she just got tired. When Uncle Neal passed, it got to be too much."

"I'm really sorry about your uncle." Lex covered Aspen's hand with hers. "I should have called or something."

Aspen tensed beneath her touch, and she let out a long sigh. "You didn't owe me anything, Lex. We were over a long time ago. I didn't expect you to show up just because my uncle died."

"I just meant that I should have called or something." Lex pulled her hand away. "How did he pass?"

"Heart attack. It was fast, though. The doctors said he probably didn't suffer at all." Aspen blinked back a tear. She wasn't sure she was prepared for the onslaught of emotions this little trip down memory lane was going to bring up.

"That's crazy. He was always so healthy." Lex shook her head in disbelief. "I figured he would live until he was a hundred."

Aspen laughed. "That's what Aunt Ginny used to say. Her phrase was more like only the good die young, so your uncle ought to make it until he's at least a hundred years old."

"Do you remember the time he took us snow skiing?"

Aspen's laughter immediately got louder. "Oh my gosh, the time we went to Lake Placid. The one and only time he took us skiing. I've never been so mortified in my life."

"That was the funniest thing ever."

"For you, maybe. Meanwhile, I didn't come out of the lodge the rest of the trip."

"I've never seen someone actually slide under the fence and into the creek before."

Aspen rolled her eyes. "What can I say? I'm obviously gifted."

"All I know is I've never looked at a mogul the same way again." Lex looked down and realized she was eating her last bite. "Oh man, I talked through my whole stack."

"I can make you a couple more. I've got a little batter left." Aspen started to stand up, but Lex motioned her back down.

"I'm fine. If you don't stop me, I'll eat so much I won't be able to move." Lex laid her head back and stared up at the clear blue sky above them. "Just relax and finish your coffee before it gets too cold."

It was Aspen's turn to smile. Lex had remembered she hated lukewarm coffee. In fact, she was teased because she drank a cup faster than anyone else she knew. She couldn't help it. Coffee was meant to be hot enough to singe your tongue. Anything else seemed like sacrilege.

"So, what's on the docket for the day?" Lex had closed her eyes, but she opened one enough to peek at Aspen as she waited for her answer.

"Horse duty for one." Aspen mentally ticked off her to—do list. Aunt Ginny was making sure she worked the rent out of her. "I have to run Guinness into town and get him groomed. I need to pick up some supplies. Nothing too taxing."

"Guiness?"

"Aunt Ginny's dog. He's black and tan and Guiness just sort of fit."

"Cute." Lex stretched her legs out in front of her, and her bare feet peeked out from under the frayed hem of her faded jeans. She circled her foot in the air, trying to work the kink out of her ankle. "I can help with the horses."

"Ankle still bothering you?" Aspen leaned over and pulled up her pants, so she could see it. The scars were barely visible now, but she could still make them out. Lex broke her ankle in several places on a misjudged step on third base. Her body had gone one way, and her ankle had said good-bye, packed up and headed in the opposite direction.

Lex nodded. "Little bit now and then. Figure it will be something I just have to deal with. Most days it's okay and I can run through it. Today, I'm thinking I'll relax."

"That means no horse duty for you." Aspen replied firmly.

"No good." Lex's tone was kind but firm. "I'm living here too. Besides a couple of Advil will knock the edge off."

Aspen sighed loudly and pushed herself off the chair. "Just as stubborn as you always were." She gathered her dishes and nodded towards the far end of the deck. "Your room opens up to the deck as well…in case you wanted to use the hot tub."

Lex scrambled up and followed her inside. "So, what exactly is horse duty?"

Aspen rinsed their dishes and stacked them in the empty dishwasher. "You're about to find out." She flicked her eyes over Lex's attire and smirked. "You might want to change into something more conducive to shoveling shit." She walked out with a smile, leaving Lex staring after her with wide eyes.

Minutes later, Aspen handed Lex a pitchfork. "This is what I like to call mucking 101. You are sure about this?"

"I think so." Lex took the pitchfork and smiled. "What do I do first?"

"Give me a sec to let the girls out, and I'll give you your first lesson."

Lex watched her closely as she led the horses out to a small pasture where they could roam for the day. She used the few distracted moments to study Aspen. Her hair was pulled up and twisted at the back of her head. The sleeves of her thermal shirt were pushed up revealing tanned, muscular forearms. She had faded Levis tucked into a pair of old rain boots, and for the first time since Lex had gotten there, a carefree smile lit up her whole face. It erased years of worry and heartache. Lex felt warmth effuse her body, and she knew it wasn't the heat of the morning sun.

"You ready?" Aspen's voice broke through her reverie. She followed her into the barn. "Throw a couple of buckets in the wheelbarrow and bring it back here."

When she joined her at the empty stalls, Aspen was already grabbing water buckets and taking them outside to empty. She brought them back in, grabbed a handful of the straw bedding and scrubbed the inside of the bucket. She nodded towards the pitchfork in Lex's hand. "You're going to scrub the stalls." She laughed at the blank expression on Lex's face. "Find the manure, scoop it up and shake the dry straw through the tines then dump the manure in the bucket. Reba and Tarra are easy. They use the same spots at the back of the stalls. Lacey, on the other hand, she likes to leave little surprises for you. Just watch your step."

56

Lex cocked an eyebrow, and shot Aspen a *what have I gotten myself into* look. She padded into the stall and started to *muck.*

Aspen followed behind her and emptied the buckets into the wheelbarrow before taking it to a small compost pile. She shook clean, dry bedding into each stall and filled the buckets with fresh water. They were finished before she knew it. Her normal morning routine had taken half the time, and she shot Lex a grateful smile. "Thanks."

"Sure." Lex propped the pitchfork up against the wall and scrubbed her palms on her jeans. "Okay, I do have to say this whole mucking thing doesn't completely suck."

"I'm glad you said that. We do it twice a day." Aspen spun on her heel, and for the second time in minutes, left Lex with an open—mouthed expression. The shock turned into a smile. It had been less than twenty—four hours, but they had slid past awkwardness that Lex feared would temper their time together. She was pleasantly surprised, if not hopeful that when they came out of the other side of this venture, a semblance of a friendship might be had and that made her happier than she had been in years.

Chapter 6

Cassidy studied her fiancee's face closely. Lex was bent over her computer proofing her latest article. It had been two weeks since she had spent any time with her, and Cassidy was seconds away from a full-on pout. The attention she was craving was currently misdirected towards a laptop. "Hmm."

Lex looked up from her laptop and caught Cassidy's questioning gaze. She smiled ruefully. "I know. I'm sorry, babe. I just have to finish this up and send it to my editor, and then we can spend some time together."

Cassidy wasn't sure if it was the tone in Lex's voice, or the lackluster response to Cassidy's welcome that irritated her more. She met Lex at the door wearing nothing but a pair of lacy panties and one of Lex's button-down shirts. Normally, this would send Lex's blood pressure soaring, and it wouldn't be long before Lex pinned her up against a wall and gave her a proper hello. Cassidy sighed again. Something was different about Lex, and while she couldn't pin down the exact reason, she was fairly certain it had to do with her ex.

They didn't talk about Lex's time in Vermont. By pre—arrangement, Lex didn't share, and Cassidy didn't ask. She preferred not to hear the details. But now, curiosity had her wondering about the subtle change in Lex. She had known a part of Lex would always belong to Aspen. She just hoped the part that she still had wasn't overtaking the part that Cassidy had. The worry had started to creep through her, and she needed reassurance, which counted for her uneasiness and reading too much into Lex's cool reception.

Lex could feel the insecurity in the gaze that Cassidy was focusing on her. She felt a twinge of guilt but pushed it aside. She kept telling herself it was work and nothing else that kept her from sweeping Cassidy into her arms and making love with her. Her trip to Seattle was something she had needed. Time to get some clarity and wrap her head around the chaos her brain was feeling.

She stole a glance at Cassidy, and her heart went out to her. Two months ago, this had been the woman she was going to marry, albeit somewhat reluctantly. She did love her, Lex didn't question that. What made her question everything was Aspen's face flashing in her mind all the time. It was as if the past five years had been erased, and they were right back where they left off, building a life together. She knew it was only her sentimentality talking, but there were times when Lex let herself believe that the feeling was her reality and not a distant dream.

Lex slid her eyes back to her laptop, but she felt Cassidy's gaze again, and she hoped that her face hadn't reflected her train of thinking. She closed her laptop and pushed Aspen to the back of her mind or at least made an attempt to. There was a beautiful, half—naked woman in front of her, one who loved her with all her heart and would do anything to make her happy.

Lex pulled Cassidy towards her and felt her nestle in between her legs. She slid her hand under Cassidy's shirt and splayed her palm against her stomach, feeling Cassidy's muscles tense reflexively. She slid her other hand around Cassidy's neck and pulled her lips towards hers. The first touch was warm and soft, the fires of desire yet to burn deep in her stomach. She heard Cassidy moan, and her hips pressed into Lex's core.

Cassidy pulled her lips away and grabbed Lex's hands, pulling her off her stool. Her eyes were dark with desire. "Now. I want you inside me now."

Lex let her guide her to the bedroom, praying that her mind would shut down, and her body would take over. She watched Cassidy slide the shirt off her shoulders, and her heart jumped at the sight of her perfect breasts. She closed the distance between them and cupped Cassidy's breast in her palm. She felt Cassidy's hands slide around her neck and their lips met again, this time Lex pushed everything out of her mind except the two of them.

Cassidy's body pressed into Lex, and she moaned as Lex deepened the kiss. "God, I missed you. My body missed you. I need your touch." She pushed Lex's hand inside her panties and pressed her fingers into her slick wetness.

Lex felt her stomach jump. Her vision went hazy, and she felt her body take control. Her clit hardened and she pushed deep inside Cassidy, feeling wetness flood her fingers. She felt Cassidy push against her, matching Lex's even strokes.

"Please baby, make me come." Cassidy slid her tongue into Lex's mouth and stroked it deftly. Years of love— making had made them attuned to each other's bodies and the touches that would send them over the edge. She bit Lex's lip.

Lex felt the pressure on her mouth and knew Cassidy was close. She wrapped her arm around Cassidy's middle and pushed deeper inside her, finding a spot within her and stroking deftly. Her thumb massaged Cassidy's clit and she felt it harden to a taut bud, pulsing with increasing speed. She deepened the kiss and within seconds, Cassidy's body trembled against her, and she swallowed her moans of pleasure.

When Cassidy came down, she laid her head on Lex's shoulder and kissed her neck, her hand snaking inside Lex's waistband. She felt Lex still. She pulled back and searched Lex's face. "Come on, baby. Let me take care of you."

Lex smiled and kissed her lightly on the mouth. "I'm okay. Later."

"You sure?" Cassidy pushed. "I know you're close." She slid her fingers into Lex's body and smiled. "Lay down, Lex." Cassidy tried to pull her to the bed. It wasn't like Cassidy to push her. Lex had always been the aggressor, and their relationship had always been somewhat one—sided in that aspect. However, Cassidy felt her world slipping away and did the one thing she thought would cement them together again. It was wrong she knew, to try to change now, but for so long, this arrangement had worked. Lex was a top and she gave selflessly, more interested in Cassidy's enjoyment than in her own.

Lex shook her head. She pulled Cassidy's hand away from her body and held her still. Her heartbeat hammered in her head and between her legs, but she didn't feel the need to come. The dull ache wasn't enough to open herself up and let Cassidy inside. For the first time since they had been together, she felt as though she was cheating on Aspen.

She shook her head and hoped that Cassidy didn't see how fucked up she was. "I'm fine."

Cassidy sensed the wall going up and wondered if she would be able to make Lex happy. She always struggled with the feeling that Lex had never been fully hers. That was part of the reason she pushed so hard to get married. Maybe her fear of losing Lex pushed Cassidy to hold on as tightly as she could. She loved Lex, there was no question about that, but she wondered for the first time if she was marrying her for the right reason or just a desperate attempt to hold on. To keep her world from being ripped out from underneath her if Lex ever left.

Cassidy pushed into Lex's arms and kissed her softly. "I love you."

Lex returned the kiss before pulling away again. "I love you too." She saw the uncertainty in Cassidy's eyes, and she pulled her into her arms, holding her tightly. She wasn't sure what to say. She hoped she could show her without words that she was in love with her, or at least convince herself that she was. Unconsciously, Lex compared the feel of the woman in her arms to the feel of the woman in her mind. So similar, yet so different.

They hadn't known each other long before she and Cassidy had moved in together. It wasn't that she didn't love Cassidy, but it had always been on a different level than how she loved Aspen. That had been an all-consuming love that had burned within her. It made her ache. There were times when she craved Aspen so much that she felt her heart would explode in her chest. She loved her so much it hurt.

Lex felt Cassidy stir in her arms and part of her wished it was Aspen. Hadn't it always been that way? No one could compare to Aspen, and the love that they had shared. No matter how much she loved Cassidy, it paled in comparison and Lex was suddenly forced to accept that perhaps she had been trying to fill that void. Trying to duplicate those feelings with Cassidy. *I've always tried to find someone like you.*

The realization was somewhat freeing. She had a choice now. She could accept that she couldn't replace Aspen. She could let herself love Cassidy the best way she knew how. They had a good life. Lex thought it could be great if she let go of the past. Maybe that's why Cassidy had been okay with her doing what she needed to do to let go. She knew that was the only way that Lex could truly move forward, by letting go of the past. She owed it to her to at least try.

A sense of clarity washed through Lex, and she knew that she needed to find a way to say good-bye and let go so that she could move on and give herself completely to Cassidy. She just had to figure out a way to stop craving Aspen and that in itself seemed almost impossible.

Chapter 7

Lex bounded up the steps and opened the door anxiously. It had been four days, seven hours, and…she glanced at her watch…twenty—two minutes since she had seen Aspen. But who's counting? Oh right, her. "A? Aspen? I'm home." Home. It had a nice ring to it. It wasn't really her home, only a temporary stop, but over the past two months, it had begun to feel like home. Or, more accurately, Aspen started to feel like home.

Aspen wasn't home. Lex's shoulders sunk dejectedly. She walked into the kitchen to grab a drink. "Might as well work." She grabbed a beer, twisted the top off and took a long draw before she set the bottle down. Her eyes flicked to the island. It was then she saw the note. *I'm at Aunt Ginny's painting. Be back later.*

Lex set the note down and frowned. She glanced at her watch again. Three—thirty. Aspen probably wouldn't be home for at least two hours. That gave her plenty of time to finish her column for the day. Her editor was already on her for her sudden proclivity for tardiness. A habit she'd only recently reacquired because of her latest distraction. She grabbed the bottle off the island and went to get her laptop. She opened it and stared at the screen.

Twenty minutes later, she was still staring at the flashing cursor, no closer to finishing the column then when she started. Her thumb picked at the corner of the label on her beer bottle, a sure sign she was distracted. Or maybe sexually frustrated. She shouldn't be. She'd stayed in the city last night and Cassidy welcomed her back with open arms. Even after they had made love, Lex felt an odd emptiness. She attributed it to their time apart. Once the divorce was final, and she moved back home, things would certainly return to normal. She would finally be able to move on. Wouldn't she?

"Fuck it." Lex snapped her laptop shut and set it on the coffee table. She leaned out of the chair and popped her back. *God, what I wouldn't give for a massage.* It always took her a couple of days to unwind after a trip. Lately, it seemed like old age was creeping up on her and the traveling was taking a bigger toll on her than before. Maybe it was time to start thinking about a regular job again. One that kept her home more.

Lex grabbed the remote and flipped through channels. She stared at the screen, not seeing what was on and had watched fifteen minutes of Barney before she realized what she was doing. Swearing again, she stabbed the off button and tossed the remote onto the couch. She stood up and paced the room, unable to keep still. Finally, she let herself accept the reason for her restlessness. She wanted to see Aspen.

She left the house and started down the path towards Aunt Ginny's house, unable to contain her smile. It was easier this way, just accepting that seeing Aspen was what she thought about the entire time she had been gone. It should have worried her, but she shook it off. She was in love with Cassidy. What she felt for Aspen was friendship. They had, after all, been friends before they had been lovers, and she hoped they could be again.

As she covered the distance to the house, her eyes took in the scenery. The leaves had morphed into brilliant red, oranges and yellows almost overnight. The hills around the farm looked like they were on fire. She inhaled deeply, and the scent of fall filled her nose. The only sounds she heard were the birds and a gentle breeze ruffling the trees around her.

Her years in the city had clouded her memories until she had all but forgotten the mystical allure of the country. This place was magic, and it had weaved a spell in and around her and settled within her. She knew leaving again was going to be difficult. She just hoped it wasn't as hard as it was the first time.

The closer she got to Aunt Ginny's, the stronger the pull. Maybe, it wasn't this place that tugged at her, perhaps it was the people. Or person, to be exact. It didn't matter, in the two months since she had gotten here, she had felt more alive than she had in five years. She took the steps two at a time and rapped on the door.

"Lex." Aunt Ginny propped open the screen door for her to come in.

"Hey, Aunt Ginny." Lex had always called her that, and it seemed time had not erased the tradition. They had simply fallen back into the old and comfortable relationship they had shared before. She stepped over the black and tan fur ball running circles around her feet. "Hey, Guinness." She bent over and rubbed his ears and was rewarded with a round of yips and a wet hand.

"Guinness, behave." Ginny nudged him back with her foot and led Lex into the kitchen. Aunt Ginny had been the one person in Aspen's family that didn't hate Lex for leaving. In fact, she understood it a little herself. Having never been able to have children herself, she knew all too well the hurt. There had been a time when she had left her own husband. She had finally come home when she realized that Neal loved her no matter, and they didn't need children to be complete. She may not have been happy with the way that Lex left, but she understood it. "How was the trip?"

Lex rolled her eyes. "Long." She took the glass of lemonade Ginny handed her with a gracious smile. "Thanks."

Ginny waved her hand dismissively. "I remember how much you loved my homemade lemonade." She pulled out a chair. "Sit."

Lex hesitated, and Ginny chuckled softly. "She's painting, Lex. You'll see her soon enough. For now, you can keep me company."

Lex smiled shyly and regarded Ginny thoughtfully. She looked the same now as she had before. Soft, graying hair framed an oval face. Her blue eyes twinkled. Lex had once said that Aspen didn't take after her mother, but her aunt instead. Not only had she gotten her eyes, she had inherited the same mischievous streak that Ginny possessed. Aside from the thirty-year difference in ages, they could have passed for sisters. "Okay."

"So, where was it this time?"

"Seattle. The Seahawks against the Niners. Everyone is saying San Francisco has a chance this year. They have a decent coach, and Smith has got an arm on him." As Lex spoke, she relaxed into the chair. "Might have a run at a championship this year."

Ginny laughed. "Oh, Lex, you know I don't know a thing about sports. I haven't seen even so much as five minutes of a game since Neal passed away."

"True." Lex joined her laughter. "Then how about I tell you about everything but the game."

"As long as you let me make you something to eat while you're telling me." Ginny squeezed her arm, stood up and began bustling around the kitchen. Lex shook her head. Ginny was a lot like her own mother. Always trying to feed her. Fortunately, she was feeling a bit hungry, so she silently accepted the offer. "Grilled cheese okay? I have a pot of vegetable soup just about ready to eat."

"Sure." Lex watched her lift the lid, and the aroma of veggie soup filled her nostrils. She had forgotten how much she enjoyed a home-cooked meal. She had no business in the kitchen, and Cassidy didn't do the normal wife thing. Most of their meals consisted of restaurant fare or Chinese takeout from their favorite spot around the corner from their loft. "Can I help?"

Ginny waved her offer away. "Sit. Relax."

She pulled ham and taleggio cheese out of the fridge and set them on the counter next to a loaf of what Lex surmised to be homemade bread. She turned around and gave Lex a hurry up twirl of her finger. "Tell me all about Seattle."

"It's different, faster. Very artsy and the people are really nice." Lex swirled the ice in her glass. "And the views. Well, the views are, well let's just say even you would approve." Lex paused momentarily. She was surprised that Ginny's approval mattered, and yet somehow it seemed as though she should expect that now. "The city sits right on Puget Sound. It is surrounded by mountains. Mt. Rainier, Olympic National Park, Mt. Baker. It's gorgeous really. No wonder people pay as much as they do to live there."

"It sounds lovely." Ginny slid a large pat of butter into a hot skillet, and it sizzled loudly. She laid two thick slices of bread into the skillet, layered them with the ham and taleggio and topped them off with a second slice of bread. The aroma permeated the kitchen, and Lex found herself wandering closer to the stove to watch. Ginny smiled at her over her shoulder. "So, how was the food? Do those Seattle folks know how to cook?"

Lex chuckled softly and kissed Ginny's cheek. "Not even close to yours."

Ginny smiled. "Charmer." She swatted Lex's bottom and pointed down the hall. "Go get Aspen. She hasn't eaten all day."

"Aye! Aye!" Lex saluted Ginny with a wink and scurried out of the room before Ginny could swat her again.

She knocked on the door to the studio and when Aspen didn't answer, she pushed the door open and stuck her head in. "A?"

Aspen jumped and swiped at her eyes. "Lex." Her voice trembled.

"Aspen, are you okay?" Lex stopped beside her and tried to see her face. "Are you crying?"

Aspen pushed her away and stared out the window. "I'm fine."

Lex grabbed her chin and spun her around to face her. "What's wrong?"

"Nothing." Aspen shook her head and rubbed her hand over her nose. "I said I was fine."

"You don't look fine." Lex's eyes held hers. "Talk to me."

"It's nothing, okay." Aspen's eyes pleaded with her to let it drop. "I'm just having a moment." She scrubbed her palms over her eyes. She was silent a second longer before breaking into a sad smile. "What did you want?"

"Aunt Ginny. Dinner." Lex stammered. She had never been able to look at Aspen when she cried. It was never very often and the few times she had, Lex had pushed her to it. She wondered if that was the case today. She met her gaze, and her heart broke for her again. She pulled her eyes away before she said something stupid.

Her gaze flicked to a sketchpad. It was a charcoal sketch of a woman's profile. Her eyes were closed. Dark hair framed her face. Her face was almost completely shadowed except for the graceful curve of her neck and the small spot at the base of her neck. Her hand rested on her chest in gentle repose. Lex felt Aspen's eyes on her, and she smiled. "It's beautiful."

"She is." Aspen whispered softly. They both recognized Lex's strong features. Aside from that, it was a pose she remembered well. Her head resting on Aspen's lap, eyes closed, content to just be. They stared a moment longer, sharing a walk down memory lane and feeling the painful ache of a love that had flourished and died before its true potential was reached. In that brief respite, Lex felt her own heart cry.

Aspen waited for hers to shatter. She held her breath ready to feel the devastation that she was certain would come and when it didn't, she started. Something tugged at her and turned the corners of her mouth up. It wasn't despair. It was hope, and for the first time since her heart had started to die, she felt like living.

She allowed Lex her moment to grieve, to let go of yesterday. She slipped her hand into hers and felt a tingle at the touch of her palm. She pulled her to the door, opened it, and they stepped through it into a better future.

Ginny looked up at the sound of footsteps. Her eyes flicked between the two women, and she smothered a smile. She couldn't quite put her finger on it, but something between them had changed. She saw Aspen's red—rimmed eyes and bit her tongue. In this world, tears were necessary. They were part of the healing process. If Aspen was truly going to move on and begin to heal, she needed to strip herself of the old memories that haunted her and kept the wounds fresh. She had to allow them to rend completely so they could be repaired and heal. For the first time since she had arrived, Ginny saw in her something that hinted at tomorrow. She turned her head and hid her smile.

"It smells great in here, Aunt Ginny." Aspen plopped down in an empty chair and swiped Lex's glass of lemonade. She took a healthy gulp before Lex could even stop her.

"Hey." Lex spouted.

"Hay is for horses." Aspen smirked mischievously. She motioned to the fridge, and Lex pulled the pitcher of lemonade out and refilled the glass. "We can share anyway."

Ginny listened to the banter and smiled again. The only time she had seen Aspen truly happy was when she was in the studio and when she was with Lex. Aside from those times, she always felt like something was missing. "You girls behave. There's plenty for both of you. And, Lex? Get another glass out of the cupboard. There's no sense in you girls sharing when there's plenty to go around."

Lex stuck her tongue out at Aspen and grabbed a glass off the shelf.

"Promises, promises." Aspen whispered, so that her Aunt wouldn't hear. "So, Aunt Ginny, what creation do you have for us tonight that smells so divine?"

"Ham and taleggio grilled cheese and a parsley—leek vegetable soup." She sat steaming bowls of soup in front of the women and a plate of sandwich quarters in the middle of the table. She set a bowl in front of herself and sat down with an expectant smile. "Well, dig in. Don't stand on ceremony with me."

Lex and Aspen hesitated only briefly before diving into the hot soup and devouring the grilled sandwiches. Between mouthfuls of food, they raved about Ginny's cooking and how much they missed it.

"Well eat up. There's plenty more soup and I have a blueberry cobbler for dessert."

Lex groaned loudly. "At this rate, I'm going to have to take more assignments, or I'll end up weighing three hundred pounds."

"Don't worry." Aspen grinned evilly. "I'll let you muck the stables full-time and burn the extra calories off."

Lex's eyes widened. She may have gotten used to horse duty, but used to and loving were two very different things. She waggled her finger at Aspen. "Just remember, paybacks are hell."

Ginny laughed out loud. "It's good to see you two getting along. When Aspen first mentioned this whole idea, I have to admit I was a little worried how it would turn out. I should have known you two would figure out a way to like each other again."

Aspen's hand stilled, her drink paused at her lips. She met Lex's gaze over the rim of the glass. "Yeah, Aunt Ginny, I think you're right. Besides it is nice to have someone else on manure duty."

Lex shot her a glare then started to snicker. "Just remember. Paybacks."

"I'm not worried." Aspen shook her head. "You're all talk, and besides, you will do anything I ask, if we cook for you."

"True. True." Lex admitted begrudgingly.

Ginny saw the look that passed between the two women and wondered if given the right circumstances, the passion that burned just below the surface might be allowed to bubble up. *Don't push, Ginny. If it's meant to be for those two, they will figure it out.* For now, she contented herself with their company and being thankful for the tentative beginning of their new friendship.

Chapter 8

"Come here, girl." Aspen whistled and smiled as Lacey trotted over to her. She fed her the apple and stroked the star on her nose. "What do you think, girl? Think you're up for a ride?" Lacey whinnied and pawed at the ground.

Aspen patted her neck and led her to the gate. "I know. I've been bad about taking you out." Lacey snorted loudly. Aspen snorted in response. She had always loved coming to her aunt and uncle's ranch to ride, and she usually spent most of her summer with them. When Ginny had decided to retire and had sold the majority of the horses, she had let Aspen pick her favorite three. Well, two technically, but when Aspen hadn't been able to let go of her favorite three, her aunt had given in.

She listened to the muted clopping sound as Lacey followed her into the barn. "I wish Lex were here. I really need to take your sister out, and I'd rather do it with company. You can't be the only one that gets special treatment."

Lacey responded with a short whinny and a sigh. "No, Aunt Ginny can't go either. There is some chili cookout at the church." Aspen cocked her head and regarded Lacey thoughtfully. "Yep, it's official. I have lost my mind. I'm having a conversation with a horse." She snorted derisively.

Aspen saddled Lacey up and was just about to bridle her when she heard a car approaching up the long gravel driveway. She poked her head out of the door, and a smile broke out on her face. Lex was home. She shook her head at how quickly they had slid into this being their home. She conveniently forgot that Lex had a whole life waiting for her when this was over. She mentally ticked off the months. Three gone. Which meant only three were left, and they would start the divorce proceedings.

Shaking it off, she finished putting Lacey's bridle on, pushing her thoughts of Lex to the back of her mind.

"Hey!" Lex's cheerful voice caught her by surprise. "Are you finishing up?"

Aspen shook her head and smiled. "I still have Reba after this."

"You want company?" Lex's smile was genuine. She was glad to be off the road and even more excited to be back at the ranch. She didn't kid herself into believing it was more relaxing than the city or that she had a much easier time getting her articles done. No, she wasn't foolish enough to believe it was anything but Aspen that made her want to come back.

"You don't mind?" Aspen cocked her brow. "Don't feel like you have to."

"I want to." Lex met Aspen's gaze and held her blue eyes. "I could use the break. I'm tired of being stuck inside." They were well into November, but the temperatures were unseasonably warm and the sun and the cool fall air was calling to her.

Aspen's face lit up, and she handed Lex her reins. "Give me a sec, I'm going to saddle up Reba." She walked back towards the barn and stopped short of the door. She looked over her shoulder and found Lex's eyes on hers. "Thank you."

Lex shrugged as if it were no big deal, but her heart was pounding out of her chest. She felt herself being pulled into those blue eyes. It would be so simple to let herself fall all over again. With effort, she broke the connection. She rubbed Lacey's nose and patted her neck. "Between you and me, three months better get here quick, or I'm going to be in a heap of trouble."

Lacey snorted in response, all too happy to oblige another one—sided conversation. "Let's just say, Cass is getting a little tired of me being gone." Another whinny.

Lex heard footsteps behind her, and she jumped.

"Sorry." Aspen walked up beside her and let Reba's reins dangle in her hand. "You ready?"

"Yep." Aspen mounted Reba and waited while Lex pulled herself up on Lacey. "Aunt Ginny wants us to check the back fence and make sure there aren't any holes." She pointed at a bag she had attached to her saddle containing the repair tools. "I was going to do it by myself, but since you're here, you get to be my fence whore."

Lex feigned shock.. "I knew you were just using me."

"Yes, yes I am." Aspen smiled wickedly. "I rigged this whole thing just so you would come to the ranch and ride the fence with me."

"Figures." Lex nudged Lacey's sides and caught up to Aspen. "So, what are we checking for?"

"Just checking the barbwire to see if there are any breaks in it. If there are, we fix them."

"Sounds fun." Lex said sarcastically.

"And that is why you are coming along, fence whore." Aspen teased.

"And I thought you just wanted me along for my sparkling wit and sizzling good looks." Lex cocked her head and waited for Aspen's reaction. Silence wasn't what she expected as her first reaction, but when Aspen didn't answer, Lex decided not to push.

She pulled up on Lacey's reins and fell behind Aspen by several lengths. Lex wasn't sure what was going on in her head, and maybe it was better that she didn't. If her thoughts were similar to what Lex's were, it could be dangerous to be so close to her. And if she wasn't thinking the same thing, Lex preferred not to know.

74

Aspen surprised her when she slowed enough to let her catch up. "So, how was the trip?"

"Good." Lex felt Lacey slow down. She clucked her tongue. "Come on, girl." Lex clucked her tongue again and nudged her heels softly into Lacey's flanks. She felt Lacey's muscles ripple against her legs as she cantered to catch up.

When Lex caught up, Aspen smiled apologetically. "Guess I should have told you I gave you the spacey one. Lacey here is a bit curious. She's pretty good usually, but if she gets too interested in nosing around, just give her a little nudge."

"Figures you would give me the broken horse." Lex chuckled softly. "Slow horse. Fence whore. If I didn't know any better, I would say you are trying to tell me something."

Aspen laughed out loud. "Maybe. Or maybe, you're just getting lucky today." She tried to smile suggestively. Instead, she pinned Lex with a searing gaze that sent shivers down her spine.

It was Lex's turn to smirk. That answered her question as to whether Aspen was struggling with her feelings as much as she was. She felt warmth effuse her body. She was forced to acknowledge again that the next three months were going to be nearly impossible. She wasn't exactly using her time to get over her relationship with Aspen. Instead, she did nothing but concentrate on it, second guess herself, let it haunt her late at night. Yes, they had unfinished business, mostly because of her, but she wasn't sure how she could move on when she wasn't even certain she wanted to. She finally met Aspen's eyes and smiled. "I consider myself lucky just to have your company."

Aspen blushed and looked down quickly. When she looked up again, she had schooled her face, and it no longer revealed the naked heat she felt pulsing beneath her skin. "So, it was Nashville?"

Lex picked up on the change in conversation. She didn't care to talk about her trip, but it was obvious that Aspen wasn't ready to talk yet. She may never be. "Yeah. The Titans."

"Was it a good trip?" Aspen cleared her throat. It shouldn't be this difficult to have a simple conversation. Most of the time, she was fine. She pushed old emotions to the back of her mind. However, today, there was a subtle shift in her feelings. She felt a little tug in her chest, and she struggled to push it back down.

"It was okay." Lex pulled up alongside her. "Why don't we talk about what's really on our minds?"

"I don't know what you mean." Aspen said quietly.

Lex reached over and rested her palm on Aspen's arm. "Don't you?"

Aspen stared into her brown eyes, and her breath caught in her chest. "Lex, there's nothing…" She tried to nudge Reba forward, but Lex stopped her.

"There is something, at least for me." Lex's voice was strained, and Aspen couldn't ignore the painful tremble in her tone. "I know that I came here to end things. It was supposed to be easy to do this and walk away. It's not easy anymore."

Aspen's lip trembled. She waited five years to hear those words. For Lex to find her and tell her that she was still in love with her. Five long years of recrimination, trying to figure out what she could have done to fix it. And now, now when she was finally getting the chance to say good-bye and move on, Lex decided to lay her cards on the table. If only she had said something earlier. "Lex, I don't think we should be talking about this."

"Why?" Lex's heart ached in her chest. The pain was so acute she knew without a doubt what it must feel like when someone died of a broken heart.

"It's too late, Lex. You have Cassidy. I've moved on." Aspen pulled the reins to the side and tried to steer away from Lex. "Let's just do what we came here to do, and then we can both get on with our lives."

"What if I don't want to get on with my life?" Lex nudged Lacey again and pulled up next to Aspen, this time taking Reba's reins from her. She ignored the short whinny. "Will you just stop and talk to me about this?"

Aspen shook her head. "Can I have that back?"

"Only if you promise not to run." Lex studied her face and when she was content she would stay, she handed the reins back to Aspen. "Can you honestly tell me that you feel nothing?"

Aspen lowered her gaze. She could say whatever she wanted, but she knew Lex would see everything in her eyes, and it would give up her bravado. She felt Lex's eyes on hers. "Lex, please don't ask me that."

Lex leaned over and lifted her chin, forcing her to meet her eyes. "I need to know. If you tell me you feel nothing, I'll forget this and move on. But if I know you feel even the slightest bit for me, I would give up everything for a chance to be with you."

Aspen's heart soared and just as quickly, it sank. She couldn't allow herself to believe that there was any more to Lex's admission than sentimentality. They had been together for ten years, and although they had broken up five years ago, there was still that little bit that held them together. That piece of paper that let the world know they belonged to each other. Lex was obviously just feeling separation anxiety. She wasn't sure where she got the strength, but Aspen plastered a smile on her face. "Lex, that was a long time ago. We've moved on. You're getting married. I understand you are feeling a little sentimental. But don't fool yourself into thinking it is more than that."

"I don't believe you." Lex's voice dropped an octave. She leaned closer forcing Aspen to meet her gaze. "You never could lie to me."

Aspen felt herself slipping into her eyes, and she tried to pull away. "Lex, please."

But Lex didn't pull away. She leaned in closer, her scent wafting on the breeze and making Aspen's stomach jump. "Tell me you don't still love me."

Aspen swallowed the lump in her throat. Her thoughts screamed in her ears. *Just tell her it is over.* Her heart pounded in response. The war waged inside her body, and she knew she needed to get control. She balled her hands into fists and sucked in a breath. "I'm sorry, Lex. I just don't love you that way anymore."

Lex almost bought it until she saw the tears brimming in Aspen's eyes. She opened her mouth to say something, and Aspen shook her head. Before Lex could even blink, Aspen swung Reba around and nudged her into a run. Lex watched her hair whip behind her, and she knew there was no point in trying to catch her now.

She nudged Lacey, but didn't make her run. She needed time to think. Time to wrap her head around where her heart was. Perhaps Aspen was right. Maybe she was holding onto the relationship they had and the feelings that came with it. But maybe she was right, and she really was still in love with Aspen. Either way, her heart felt like someone had ripped it out. She knew she needed to find a way to make it through the last three months without having a meltdown.

Lacey whinnied beneath her, and she shook her head. "Let's get you back home."

No sooner had she said the words then she was reminded that being here at the farm with Aspen for three months felt more like home than the years she had spent with Cassidy. It was going to be a long three months.

Chapter 9

Aspen stood back and surveyed the firewood she had stacked neatly on the porch. She would have taken some to her aunt, but she was back home visiting with Aspen's mom and wouldn't be home for at least a week. Her phone buzzed in her pocket, and she jumped at the sound. She pulled it out of her pocket and hit accept. "Hello?"

"Hey, it's me." Lex's voice announced.

"What's up, me?" Aspen teased.

"I called to tell you I was heading back today. I cut my trip short. There's a big storm heading east over Michigan, and I didn't want to get stranded in Detroit, so I cut out early."

"Oh yeah, true." She had been through the Detroit airport once, and it was not a place she wanted to return to, much less be stuck in on the chance they shut down the airport. Aspen could hear her rustling with paper in the background. "What are you doing?"

"I was going to run by the store and pick up a few things. I figured I would cook for you tonight. We can have Aunt Ginny over too."

Aspen could hear the smile in her voice. It wasn't often that Lex offered to cook, but when she did Aspen ran with it. There was only a handful of dishes that Lex could make well, and Aspen secretly hoped it was going to be filets. "Hopefully, you're okay settling with just me. Aunt Ginny is at Mom's for the week."

"I can work with that. Steak's okay?"

"Yes, perfect." Aspen's face broke into a smile. "I never could resist your meat." She heard Lex's intake of breath and knew she was blushing. "Could you pick up some butter? I want to make a pie for dessert."

Lex chuckled softly. "Of course, you know I could never resist your pie."

Aspen felt the color rise in her cheeks. "Hush, you. Just get my butter."

"Yes, ma'am. Anything else?"

"Nope, that should be it. I've got stuff for salad, if you want, and a couple of bottles of wine, so we should be good." Aspen got off the phone and slid it into her pocket. She figured she could get several more loads of firewood and shower before Lex made it back. She glanced at her wristwatch. She would be cutting it close, but she should be able to at least have the filling for the pie done too.

Forty—five minutes later, she heard Lex's car in the driveway. It had been several weeks since their conversation, and although the first few days after had been awkward, they were getting back to normal again. She didn't almost spill her guts every time she was around Lex, and Lex had stopped looking hopeless. She had started to believe that this was going to be okay.

Aspen was putting a last shake of cinnamon on the apples when Lex came in, her arms loaded with bags. "I thought you were just picking up a couple of things."

"Yeah, it ended up being a little more than a few things."

Aspen started unloading the bags. "Ice cream. Chips. Beef jerky."

Lex grinned sheepishly. "I was starving. Everything sounded good."

"Well, ice cream will go well with the pie." Aspen wadded up the bags and put them in a recycling container underneath the sink. "Apple pie okay? I could freeze this and make something else if you prefer."

"Apple is fine." Lex washed her hands. "Are you hungry? I can start dinner now."

"Actually, yes." Aspen confessed. "I am starving." A loud rumble made them both laugh.

"Sounds like we woke the dragon." Lex dodged the dishtowel that Aspen sent flying her way. "Hey! You want dinner; you had better behave."

Aspen glared in her direction. "Just get to cooking or you won't get your pie."

Lex waggled her eyes suggestively. "You never denied me your pie before."

"Things change." Aspen said with a hint of a tremor. "Well, stop standing there staring at me and start cooking."

Lex held her gaze, the air between them fraught with emotion. It would be so easy to take what she wanted, possess Aspen once again. Her heart was torn in two different directions. The life she was yet to live, and the love she was leaving behind. She tore her eyes from Aspen and willed her heart to stop thundering in her chest. She swallowed the lump in her throat. "Pan...do you have a skillet I can use?"

Aspen pulled a stainless steel skillet out of the cupboard and handed it to Lex with a confused look. "No grill for the steaks?"

"Nope. Cass..." Lex cleared her throat. "I learned a new method. Much juicier." She turned the stove on and set the skillet on the burner.

"You know it's okay to talk about her. You are engaged." Aspen washed a head of lettuce and set it on the counter to dry. "How did you meet?"

"Her store. Saks. I was up for a Polk award. It's a journalism award, and I needed something to wear to the banquet. I went to Saks to get a tux. Cass was working her way through college as a sales clerk. She fitted me for a tux...and fitted herself right into my life." Her tone dropped.

"You sound like that wasn't your choice." Aspen's senses were working in overdrive. She heard regret in Lex's tone, or so she thought. Maybe she was just putting doubt where it shouldn't be. "I'm sorry. That's really none of my business. I'm sure she is wonderful, and you both are incredibly happy."

"Yeah, well she is very persuasive. We started out dating, and the next thing I knew, things started showing up in my apartment. A toothbrush, makeup, panties. Little stuff, but I blinked, and suddenly, there she was living with me."

"But you do love her right?" Aspen cocked her head to the side and studied Lex's face. "I mean you are marrying her."

"Yeah, I guess." Lex dropped the steaks in the hot skillet and watched them sizzle for several seconds, before she turned around and leaned against the counter, her arms across her chest. "I mean, yes. I do. I guess it's all just happening a little fast, that's all. I was content to just live together, but she has this picture of a big wedding in her head. I guess I just prefer the way we did it."

The admission sent their thoughts reeling to ten years before. They had married on the porch of the ranch and had a small ceremony with just friends and family. They spent the afternoon hiking, enjoying their first few hours together. "It was good, Lex."

"We were good, A. Don't you think? Everything about us was special."

"Lex, don't." Aspen felt herself closing off emotionally, protecting herself. Every day that passed, it became more and more difficult to keep her distance. "Don't talk about what used to be. This is now and this…" She pointed between them. "…this thing between us is friendship, or at least the beginning of it. We had our chance, Lex."

"Did we?" Lex searched her face, looking for something; a sign that maybe Aspen felt the same way. "What if our second chance is now, and we are ignoring it?"

"Lex, I believe in second chances, just not with me." Aspen's tone held an air of finality about it. "We had our chance. This is an opportunity for us to move on from the past, maybe be friends again. I'd like that."

Lex saw the determination in her eyes and knew there would be no convincing her otherwise. "Sure, yeah. You're probably right. What are the odds lightning strikes twice, and we get consumed by the love of a lifetime again?"

Lex's eyes burned into Aspen with such intensity that she felt her knees might buckle beneath her. Aspen's heart stopped in her chest. All her bravado was about to fall by the wayside if she didn't break the connection between them. She opened and closed her mouth several times before deciding no words would douse the flames inside her. Instead, she turned away, busying herself with anything that would push Lex's look of desire from her mind.

Lex watched her pull away, the distance between them returning. Maybe Aspen was right. Perhaps friendship was what they would find here. God knows; she needed it. Too many hours on the road left her little time to keep any real friends, and Cass's friends were all younger and too immature for her. "Maybe you're right. Friends it is then."

Aspen looked over her shoulder and smiled; relief in her eyes. "Good. Yes, that's good."

They fell into an amiable silence, working around each other comfortably. Aspen set the salad on the island and watched Lex bend over to put the pan—seared steaks in the oven. Her eyes dropped to her shapely bottom and her muscular legs. Aspen's stomach jumped. Her traitorous mind pictured those legs wrapped around her, and she gasped out loud.

Lex spun around and cocked her brow questioningly. "You okay?"

"Yeah." Aspen felt the heat rise in her cheeks. "I...uhh...I almost dropped the pie." She held up the apple pie as if explaining everything.

"Okay." Lex saved her the embarrassment of explaining the blush, instead reaching for the pie. "What does this need to cook on?"

"Three—fifty."

"Perfect, that's what the steaks are on." Lex opened the door again and this time Aspen shamelessly studied her flawless body. She felt warmth effuse her body. She may be offering friendship only, but she would be damned if she wasn't going to be stuck out in the middle of nowhere and not enjoy the scenery. "Umm, you wouldn't happen to have another skillet, would you?"

"Of course." Aspen pulled another pan out of the cupboard and handed it to Lex. "What's this one for?"

"This is for my secret weapon." Lex set the pan on the stove and fired up the gas. She pulled a package of shitake mushrooms out of the fridge and started chopping them. "Hey, can you open that bottle of wine?"

Aspen pulled a bottle of Kendall—Jackson Reserve Merlot off the counter and opened it. She handed it to Lex, who poured it into the pan and watched it sizzle. She tossed a handful of shallots into the hot liquid and watched the mixture steam.

"You are getting pretty fancy in your old age." Aspen teased, but she was impressed. "You never cooked like this before."

"Well, let's just say I've had some time to perfect a dish or two." Lex smiled and handed the bottle back to Aspen. "I've used what I need. Pour us a glass?"

Aspen took the bottle and felt the tips of her fingers brush Lex's. Electricity shot up her arm, and she pulled the bottle away a little too quickly. She met Lex's questioning gaze and smiled ruefully. "So, when did you start drinking reds?"

Lex shrugged. "Mmm, a couple of years ago, I guess. Cass prefers them. I developed a taste for them after a while." She turned and poured balsamic vinegar into the pan and brought the mix to a boil. She turned the heat down and added beef broth, Worcestershire, some tomato paste and fresh rosemary, stirring them all together. "Besides, Merlot makes a hell of a finish to the filet."

"So, I'm learning." Aspen watched her add flour—coated shitake mushrooms to the pan. Once they were tender, Lex added a teaspoon of Dijon mustard. She turned the stove to low and pulled the steaks out of the oven. The aroma of beef mingled with pepper and Merlot filled the room. "God, that smells divine."

"Thanks." Lex felt herself blush. For some reason, it mattered more to her that Aspen loved this meal than any she had made for Cass. The thought should have scared her, but it didn't. She realized that she still had a need for acceptance and love from Aspen, maybe just on a different level. "Still like it medium?"

Aspen smiled; genuinely touched that Lex would remember such a small detail. "Yep. Still like a little moo in my meat."

Lex dished salad onto plates and added the filets, dousing them both with equal portions of her mushroom sauce. "What kind of dressing do you want? Still blue cheese with a little Italian?"

Aspen's face broke out in a smile. "You remember that?"

"You'd be surprised what I remember." Lex poured dressing over their salads. "You're hard to forget."

"That's funny. I always thought I was easy to forget, even harder to remember." Aspen shot her a self—deprecating smile. "So, you want to eat in here or in the living room?"

"Mmm…" Lex sipped her Merlot while she decided. "Let's do the living room. The Patriots are on. You don't mind, do you?"

Aspen shook her head, grabbed her plate and followed Lex into the living room. She set her glass down and flopped into one of the wingback chairs with a sigh. "Thanks for cooking. I didn't realize how exhausted I was. With Aunt Ginny and you gone, horse duty is wearing me out."

"Well, I'll be here for the next week, so I can help. I am your whore after all." Lex chuckled into her wine glass.

"I believe that was my fence whore." Aspen corrected her with her own smile. She stuffed the first bite of her filet in her mouth and moaned appreciatively. "This is amazing. Whatever you are doing in Providence, keep it up. This might be my new favorite meal."

"Even better than my world-famous meatloaf?" Lex waggled her eyebrows. Her *world-famous meatloaf,* as she referred to it, was actually a charred brick of unidentifiable meat. The one and only time she had attempted to make it, she had gone to the bedroom to call Aspen for dinner and instead met her finishing up her shower and still naked. It was only later, after they had both been sated, that Lex remembered the meatloaf, which was burnt beyond recognition.

"Yes, well that was an interesting recipe." Aspen scrunched up her nose. "I think the kitchen stunk for a week after that."

"And there was no way to air it out. Every window painted shut. God, that was the worst apartment ever." Aspen's laughter filled the air. "It seems like only yesterday. Remember how we scraped by just to get that place?"

"There was no way I was living at your house. Your mom hated me." Lex cut her own steak and tasted her first bite, savoring the spicy pepper flavor. "It was a year before she looked at me without glaring."

"Can you blame her? You corrupted her only daughter."

"The look on her face was priceless."

Aspen snorted. "Maybe for you. I got a week long lecture about giving my virginity away to some smooth-talking letch. She wouldn't let me leave the house by myself for weeks."

"Good thing I had my dorm room." Lex snickered softly. "Although, I'm not sure they meant for us to abuse it like we did. Poor Steph, I don't think she signed up for the late-night sessions we gave her."

"Umm, I don't think the entire floor signed up for those late-night sessions. I seriously cannot believe I ever screamed that loud."

"Well I was really, *really* good with my tongue." Lex's dark eyes twinkled.

Aspen blushed, the conversation and the heat of the wine getting to her. "Stop it, you." She let the conversation taper off as they ate their meal. After she cleared her last bite, she put her plate on the coffee table and leaned back in the chair with a contented sigh. "You outdid yourself with that meal."

"Thanks." Lex smiled shyly. "I'm glad you liked it." She leaned over and grabbed the remote. "You mind?"

Aspen shook her head. "Nope. Watch away. I might have to prop my feet up and take a nap."

Lex watched the first few minutes of the game. At the commercial break, she found herself stealing glances at Aspen, watching her in gentle repose. Her eyes were closed and her hands rested on her stomach, her fingers laced together. Strong, narrow fingers. Artist's hands were what Aspen called them. Lex felt Aspen's fingers glide along her skin, and she trembled. Those perfect fingers that had brought her to orgasm so many times, had haunted her dreams and tugged at her heart.

"What?" Aspen's voice surprised her.

Lex looked down guiltily, but when she raised her eyes, she saw that Aspen hadn't even opened hers. "Nothing."

"So, why are you staring at me?"

"I wasn't."

One eye opened slightly, and Aspen regarded her thoughtfully. "I've known you long enough to know when you're staring at me. I can feel you, Lex."

Lex stammered a response. "I…was…just…well, I was just thinking that you have gotten even more beautiful than you were when we were…" Her voice trailed off.

"Are you trying to sweet talk me?" Both eyes were open now and Aspen was studying her. "You want my pie, don't you? Fine." Aspen pushed herself out of the chair and grabbed their plates.

Lex watched her walk away. *"Darling, I never stopped wanting your pie."*

"What?" Aspen called from the kitchen.

"Nothing." Lex sunk down in the chair, embarrassment creeping over her face. "I was just saying don't forget the ice cream for the pie."

"Uh-huh." The disbelief in Aspen's voice was apparent, but she didn't push. Steaks. Pie. Ice cream. All of this was starting to feel too comfortable, too right. She needed to distance herself again. She felt herself being pulled in by an invisible force field. Lex had the same pull over her now that she had all those years ago. Aspen had to admit the attention thrilled her, but there was no way she was opening herself up again to the same heartbreak she had experienced before. And having her heart broken by Lex another time was not something she would survive. The first time had almost been her undoing.

She mentally built a wall deep inside. She would stay strong. She wouldn't give into temptation. She wouldn't dream of following her heart. No, this time, she would listen to her head, and her head told her to run.

Chapter 10

*"Ladies and gentlemen, this is the captain. Please
remain calm. Your oxygen masks are being released as a
precaution."*

*Aspen's hands held on to the seat with a steel-like clamp.
She had felt more than heard the engine over the right wing
stop working. The slight loss of altitude had left her mildly
alarmed and when the captain had come over the intercom to
announce an emergency landing, the alarm had elevated to a
full-blown panic.*

*She wanted to watch out the window, to see the horizon.
She wanted to see the tops of the clouds and reassure herself
this was all a bad dream, but she couldn't even turn her head,
fear paralyzing her. She hated flying; hated that her fear
made her immobile.*

*She had to fly though. Lex was getting married. She
shook her head again wondering what on earth had
possessed her to hop a flight and go half way across the
world in search of a woman who was still running from her.*

*"Please place your own oxygen mask securely over your
face before assisting your fellow passengers."*

*In her head, she felt her fingers let go of their death grip
and grab her own mask, sliding it over her head. The first few
breaths actually made her dizzy.*

*"Miss? Miss?" A persistent voice broke through the
haze, drowning out the slow rhythmic timing of her breaths*

into the plastic breathing apparatus. "Miss, please, let me help you get your mask on."

She shook her head, feeling hands around her head, sliding the mask down her face. No, she thought. I have mine on. I don't need two. She started to flail her head around, feeling her face covered and instead of assisting her breathing, the newly placed mask made her feel smothered and claustrophobic.

"Ladies and gentlemen, we have some serious news. We have lost another engine. We aren't going to be able to make it to Charles de Gaulle airport. We are losing altitude fast. Our only option is to try to do a water landing."

Land in the ocean? Aspen's thoughts were a jumble of fear and fury. Her last glimpse out the window before this had all started was nothing but the dark-blue expanse of the ocean. Where were they supposed to go? She barely registered the silence around her, broken only by the whispers of flight attendants too shocked to believe and yet still tied to their duty.

She barely registered them pointing out the emergency exits. No one ever used the emergency exits. Flying was safer. Use the seats as flotation devices? Never. And yet, here she was half listening as they explained how to remove the seat. She felt the plane drop sharply and knew this was it. The captain and flight attendants worked in tandem making announcements that she heard but didn't listen to. They were more like rumbled murmurs somewhere in the back of her mind.

She didn't dare to look out the window now. Instead, she closed her eyes and laid her head against the seat. She could tell they were losing altitude quickly, her stomach jumping into her throat with every drop. Her mind flashed to her mother. Had she remembered to tell her she loved her? Probably. Her aunt Ginny? Hopefully. Lex? No, her last words would haunt her. She had told her she didn't want her. She wouldn't stand in the way of her and Cassidy. It had only hit her in a dream that she didn't want to lose her a second time.

And here she was, on a plane, heading to Paris to bust up a wedding. Or, she was until misfortune intervened. She felt the plane drop more sharply than before and knew that this was the final descent. The captain was using what power he did have to land them as upright and safely as he could in the choppy waters of the Atlantic Ocean. If he was successful, they would disembark, a vice grip on their tiny flotation device praying that they would be rescued.

Yes, she was frightened. Afraid of death, but not for the reasons she thought. No, what hurt her most was she had missed the opportunity to tell Lex that she was in love with her, always had been and of course always would be. That missive got her ass on the plane in the first place. She would tell her, and if Lex chose Cassidy then Aspen would walk away. However, if by some miracle, Lex chose her, Aspen would spend the rest of her life loving her.

The plane pitched sharply left, and her gasp got lost behind the mask. She felt smothered again and tried to paw the offender off of her face with no success. She told herself to work with the mask and not against it. Fear would only fuel her panic, and panic would be her demise.

"Ladies and gentlemen, it has been a pleasure flying with you today." The captain's voice held a sarcasm born of desperation. At that moment, there was nothing to say. She felt the giant beast shudder around her and when it hit the water, the impact jarred her to the core. The last sound she heard was the sound of a vacuum seal being broken before a roar like none she had ever heard filled her ears and drowned out everything else.

Her next minutes were on auto—pilot as she barely registered the words around her. Her subconscious took over and a will to live surged from deep within her body. Her arms gripped the seat to her chest, and she shuffled slowly, her turn to jump inching closer with every second. She reached

*the door, tried to take a deep breath and felt her lungs
tighten. She froze. No, she needed the air. She gulped
unsuccessfully. Her hands gripped the door, preventing the
hand on her back from pushing her out.*

*Please, she thought, just let me take a good breath, and
then I will jump. She opened her mouth again, and in the
second that she loosened her grip to inhale, unseen hands
pushed her, and she felt herself falling.*

"Aspen? Aspen, honey, wake up!" Lex shook Aspen's
shoulders, trying to wake her up. "Come on, A. Please wake
up. You're having a nightmare."

Aspen felt herself starting to wake up. The tunnel of
darkness disappearing behind her. She gasped and filled her
lungs with air. "Lex?"

"Yes, baby, I'm here." Lex lay down beside her and
pulled Aspen into her arms. "Shhh. Shhh. It's going to be
okay. It was just a dream."

Aspen curled her fist around Lex's shirt. Her head rested
on Lex's chest, and she could hear Lex's erratic breathing and
quickened heartbeat. Her own was still beating out of her
chest. Minutes passed before she could talk. "I'm sorry. I
didn't mean to wake you."

Lex rubbed her arm. "It's okay. You had me worried."
She hugged Aspen closely. "So, do you have nightmares all
the time?"

"Sometimes." Aspen admitted. "They've gotten worse
lately. They just feel so real."

"Well, whatever it was must have been pretty bad. You
were screaming loud enough to wake the dead."

"God, I'm sorry, Lex. I did not mean to wake you up. It
was just so real. I almost…"

"You almost what, honey? Tell me." Lex's soothing
tone, coupled with her hand rubbing absentminded circles on
her back, calmed Aspen down instantly.

"You, you were getting married in Paris, and I was trying to get to you. The plane was going down."

Lex's heart jumped. It shouldn't have; she knew better. She had no right to feel joy that somewhere in Aspen's subconscious, she didn't want her to move on. The very fact that she would have gotten on a plane, despite her fear of flying, warmed her. "It's okay, honey. I'm here. See." She squeezed Aspen against her; reminding them both, they were very much alive.

"It was just so real." Aspen said softly. "They always are. They started…they started after you left. I guess the stress of being here is ramping them up a bit."

Lex felt a pang in her heart and once again, she felt the enormity of her decision weigh on her. She was responsible for what had just happened. "A, honey, I am so sorry."

"Don't." Aspen cut her off with a rueful laugh. "Don't apologize for what's already done. We've been down that road. I'm an adult, and I will deal with it. I'm sorry I woke you up."

Lex chuckled softly, her attempt at lightening the mood. "It's really okay. I like to wake up at three o'clock sometimes."

Aspen groaned loudly. She glanced at the clock and saw the red numbers glowing 3:09. "Yeah, I'm sure." She pulled away and propped her head on her palm. "I'm okay now. You can go back to bed."

"Nah, I'm up now." Lex shifted away from Aspen and sat up, her shadow barely visible in the dark. "I've got to finish an article anyway. My deadline's today and I haven't even started it."

She pushed herself off the bed, and Aspen immediately missed her weight. "I'll get up with you. I don't want to go back to sleep and risk another nightmare. Besides, I'm starving."

"Leave it to you to think of food at a time like this." Lex paused at the door. "Let me grab my laptop, and I'll meet you in the kitchen."

Aspen sat up and brought her knees to her chest. Her heartbeat had finally slowed enough that she didn't feel like she was having a heart attack. She scrubbed her palms over her eyes, pushing unpleasant images out of her head. She swung her feet over the side of the bed, feeling for her slippers and sliding into them. She registered the chill in the air and knew winter was wrapping its icy tendrils gently around them.

She padded out of her bedroom and found Lex bent over the fireplace. She watched as she lit the kindling and fanned the first few flames.

"Good idea."

Lex jumped. She didn't hear Aspen join her. She spun around and saw Aspen's sleepy blue eyes. She felt her heart jump into her throat. Even at three o'clock in the morning, she was gorgeous. Her mind flashed to years before, and she saw them together. Young and in love. It wasn't unlike them to wake up in the middle of the night wanting each other, only able to fall back asleep after their cravings had been sated. She willed the visions away and merely succeeded in making them more vivid. "Yeah, it's a little cold."

"I think winter is coming a little early this year." Aspen shivered and wrapped her arms around herself. "Nothing a little hot coffee can't fix."

Lex watched her start the first pot. "This reminds me of our first place."

"Oh, God." Aspen rolled her eyes. "The only thing that reminds me of that matchbox is, well, a literal matchbox. That place was so small."

Lex chuckled softly. "I was thinking more the early-morning coffee then the size. Do you remember the mornings we used to get up this early?"

Aspen shook her head. "Yeah, we were crazy."

Lex cocked her head. "True. However, I remember wanting to wake up, just so I could talk to you."

"Okay, so maybe you were the crazy one." Aspen shook her head. "I don't think we slept much at all that first year."

"We were in love. Sleep wasn't as important as spending time with you."

"Aww, you're such a romantic." Aspen teased softly. "So, how about we revisit another tradition?"

"Are you thinking what I'm thinking?" Lex grinned wickedly and smirked.

"Ahh, no." Aspen looked at her askance. "I will not go skinny dipping with you again."

Lex's laughter filled the room. "You always did read me like a book. You have to admit that was a lot of fun."

"If by fun, you mean scaling a six-foot privacy fence, sneaking into a locked pool and getting caught by the security guard fun, then okay, that was loads of fun."

"I seem to remember you enjoying yourself that night. As a matter of fact, I think it was someone screaming my name who alerted the security guard in the first place."

Aspen felt her face get hot. "Oh God, I have never been that mortified in my life. I couldn't even look at him."

"Well, getting caught aside, I'd say that was one of our better traditions." Lex's eyes met Aspen's, and the memories surged between them. They were like invisible currents of barely contained electricity. Their gazes held for several more beats before Aspen pulled her eyes away.

Aspen took a deep breath. She had to break the connection. She needed to breathe again. Being caught in Lex's eyes was like spinning in suspended animation. She felt as though she was outside her body, unable to control her visceral response to Lex. She didn't like being out of control. She didn't want to lose herself again. She barely found herself the first time, pulling together some semblance of a life. She couldn't afford to do that again. If anything, her nightmare had firmed her resolve to keep her distance. She pulled her heart back into her chest. "What I was actually thinking was cinnamon rolls."

Lex watched her pull away, her eyes closing off, the view into her soul gone. "Oh yeah, those."

"Well, don't sound so disappointed." Aspen feigned offense. "If *I remember correctly,* you used to love those."

"I seem to remember loving to watch you make them more so than the actual cinnamon roll."

Aspen felt her cheeks redden again. When they had been married, she spent a lot of time cooking in just an apron. More often than not, her cooking was interrupted by a frenzied round of lovemaking. "I can promise you *that* is not going to happen this morning."

"Damn shame." Lex smiled wickedly. She picked her laptop up and planted herself on the opposite side of the island. "Will this give you enough room?"

"Yep." Aspen studied her while she worked. Lex's face had matured over the last five years. She wouldn't have noticed it as much had her forehead not been creased in concentration. The lines around her eyes had deepened some, but did nothing to detract from her handsome looks. Her long hair was pulled into its ever—present pony tail. Her skin had lost some of its summer color, but still had its beautiful Greek coloring. Aspen had to admit that she was every bit as breathtaking as she remembered. She reminded herself that looking at her that closely was way too dangerous.

"Yes?" Lex asked without raising her eyes from her computer.

"Huh?" Aspen felt embarrassment at being caught.

"You were staring at me." Lex looked up, and her eyes rooted Aspen in place.

Aspen swore silently. Those damn brown eyes. So captivating. So...so sexy. "Nothing. Just wondering what you were writing about."

"Uh—huh." Lex responded sarcastically. Mercifully, she looked away. She started paraphrasing the article she was working on. "I'm doing a series of articles on female athletes."

"That sounds interesting." Aspen pulled ingredients out of the cupboard as she listened. "What's the angle?"

"I'm looking at female athletes, in particular, who have set records in their respective sports, who are above their male counterparts and don't get the same recognition, namely similar monetary compensation. The gap between the two has closed some, but females still suffer from disparate treatment."

"Do you think your articles will help?" Aspen dumped a package of yeast into warm water and set the mixing bowl aside.

Lex shrugged. "Who knows? It's been that way for years. Navratilova, Chris Evert, the Williams sisters. Look at the WNBA. The average salary for a rookie is less than forty-thousand a year. The median rookie salary for the NBA is over seven hundred thousand, and that's the thirtieth round pick. I don't think it will change it, but I at least want to use my position to raise awareness."

"Well, you are in as good a position as any to do some good." Aspen turned the oven on the Proof setting and started adding the other ingredients to the bowl.

"I guess I just want to do more than cover sports. Don't get me wrong, I love what I do. I wouldn't change it for the world. I would just love to see the playing field be more level sometime in my life."

"It's a little like getting same-sex marriage legalized in all the states. It's a great goal; I just think there are a lot of narrow-minded people who believe differently."

Lex watched her as she let the mixer mix the ingredients. "That's the problem. There are so many people in this country that know that equality should be a way of life, in sports, in marriage, you name it, but that is the minority, and until we change the attitude of the majority, it's a losing battle. However, that doesn't mean I can't make a stink about it."

Aspen watched her eyes flash and chuckled. "Passionate much?"

"Actually, yes. Take us, for example. Because the majority rules, we had to come back to Vermont to get a divorce. How is that fair?"

"Are you not enjoying our six months of solitary?" Aspen intended the question in a teasing manner, and she hid a twinge of hurt that Lex wasn't enjoying their time together as much as she was.

"That's not what I meant, A." Lex met her eyes and smiled ruefully. "You know our time together is amazing, and I wouldn't change it for the world. I was just making a point."

"Relax, Lex, I'm teasing." Aspen put the dough in a greased pan, put it in the warm oven and set the timer for sixty minutes. "It's going to be a while on the dough. I'm going to get a jump on the girls. If I'm not back before the buzzer goes off, will you yell at me?"

"I'll help." Lex started to shut her laptop, but Aspen stopped her. "What?"

"I've got it. You write. I know you have a deadline." Aspen waived her hand in the air signaling some unseen power.

Lex watched her retreat down the hallway and fought a feeling of loss. She had seen a look flash in Aspen's eyes when they were talking about their time on the ranch, and Aspen mistaking her response as a sign she didn't want to be here. "Shit."

It didn't seem to matter how hard she tried, she still managed to screw things up. Shaking her head, she pushed herself off her stool and poured herself another cup of coffee. She was just adding creamer when Aspen made her way back to the kitchen.

"Did you leave me any?" Aspen asked with an accusing smile.

Lex shook the pot guiltily. "No, but that pot was stale anyway. How about I make you a fresh pot and bring it out? And, maybe you will actually take my offer to help."

"Maybe." Aspen smiled sweetly. "You bring the coffee, and I'll consider it."

Lex watched her walk out. She was wearing a thick fleece and worn jeans that hugged her in all the right places. She almost laughed out loud at her brightly-colored rain boots. That was one of Aspen's many quirks, and it always made her smile. Truth be told, everything about Aspen made her smile. Looking back, she couldn't remember what exactly had driven her away in the first place. Failure over not being able to conceive. It seemed rather childish now. Of course, Lex had never been able to deal with her failure in a constructive way.

She cocked her ear and heard the coffee pot pushing the last few drops of coffee into the pot. She pulled a travel mug out of the cabinet and filled it almost to the top with steaming coffee. She added a touch of creamer, and two scoops of turbinado sugar. She gave it a quick stir and popped the lid in place. She quickly located her coat and boots and stepped outside with Aspen's coffee.

As she approached the barn, she could hear Aspen's soft voice carrying towards her. She tip-toed silently, trying to make out the words.

"Well, girl, what do you think of this weather? It's going to be a cold winter. I'll be wishing there was someone here to warm me up."

Lex smirked and swallowed a chuckle. In her mind, she immediately volunteered to be Aspen's blanket. *Stop it,* she thought. *You have someone at home that wouldn't be too thrilled with you even thinking that.* She was surprised when another thought answered. *Yeah, but she did give you permission to do whatever you needed to do to get over*

Aspen, including you know. Lex shook her head. *Yes, I know what you know is, and I'm not sure how that will help get over her.*

Lex rolled her eyes and pushed the voices to the back of her mind. Yes, she knew that technically Cass had given her permission for one last time with Aspen. She thought it would help Lex get over her. Honestly, Lex was worried it would just remind her that she would never get over her. Sleeping with Aspen would only serve to further complicate an already complicated situation. *Let's just forget we have that option, shall we?*

She stepped into the barn and cleared her throat. "Hey, did I hear someone order coffee?"

Aspen took the cup with a grateful smile. "Thanks."

Lex shivered. "Cold in here."

"Yeah, a bit. Aunt Ginny had heaters installed with the remodel. I think we are going to have to turn them on. They don't mind it too cold out here, but if the water freezes, they can't drink it and that's not good."

Lex pulled a pitchfork off its hook and started towards Tarra's stall. "I hope they have a better tolerance for it than me."

"They do, you baby." Aspen teased. She rubbed Reba's nose. "Don't you? You can tolerate a little cold, can't you?" Reba whinnied in response. "I already did Lacey's stall. Once I finish Reba's, I'll get them fresh water and turn on the heaters. Don't worry, girls, we will get you warmed up soon."

Lex watched Aspen's profile a moment longer before she shoved the pitchfork into her own piled of straw and started shaking it out. "So, when is Aunt Ginny coming back?"

"It's supposed to be this weekend. She's bringing Mom up for the Thanksgiving holiday." Aspen paused and turned to Lex. "I guess you will be spending the holiday back home."

Aspen's somber tone tugged at Lex's heart strings. She planned on spending it with her family, since Cass and her family usually traveled for Thanksgiving. "I was going to go home, but I…"

"Oh, that will be fun. I remember the Tataris family holidays were anything but boring." Aspen went back to filling Lacey's water bucket. She wasn't sure what had made her think Lex would be staying here for the holiday, but she had to admit she was disappointed that Lex wouldn't be with her. There were flashes in this whole arrangement that reminded her so much of their own marriage. Holidays were split between their families, and Aspen had to admit that she missed the time spent with Lex.

"Yeah, tons of fun. Nothing like listening to Ma get on Nicky because he hasn't made an honest woman of whoever the flavor of the month is."

"That and she is always pushing for some grand babies."" Aspen meant it as a joke, but the silence that met her comment stilled them both. Too many memories came pouring into the room and floated around them hauntingly.

Lex finally broke the uncomfortable silence. "Well, what can I say? The Tataris's know how to live it up."

They finished cleaning the stables in silence, each one all too aware of their proximity to the other. Each one's thoughts far away from the task at hand. Both lost a million miles away, in a different time, a different place and both feeling the pang of a reality that wasn't the one they had dreamed of.

Lex hooked her own pitchfork back on the tool rack and dusted her hands off on her pants. "Anything else?"

"Nope." Aspen patted Reba's neck. "That's it for now. Let's get inside and check on the dough."

The sun was cresting over the mountains when Aspen plopped a giant roll on Lex's plate. She moaned appreciatively. "God, they are just as good as I remember them. I can't seem to say enough how much I have missed your cooking."

Aspen felt herself blush. Lex had always loved her cooking, and to this day, it still warmed her heart to be able to cook for her. That was one of the ways she had shown Lex that she loved her, giving truth to the old adage about the way to a woman's heart. "Glad I haven't lost my touch."

"I'm sure you won't ever lose your touch." Lex winked suggestively and ducked as Aspen sent a towel flying toward her head. "So, what are you up to today?"

"I thought I would wander down to the house and do some sketches." Aspen hadn't committed to it yet, but when Lex said she would be working to meet a deadline, she thought it would be a perfect way to kill time. "I haven't picked up my charcoal in weeks."

"Mind if I watch?" Lex asked nonchalantly. That had been something they started when they were still married. Aspen would sketch, and Lex would sit and watch.

"Umm, I don't know. I don't want to distract you from your article." Aspen stuffed the last bite of her own cinnamon roll in her mouth. She eyed the plate hungrily. "I really shouldn't, but they were so good."

"Do it." Lex tempted her by holding the plate up under her nose. "You know you want it."

Aspen watched the plate dance under her nose, and she finally broke down and grabbed another roll. "Damn you. I never could resist you."

"Oh yeah?" Lex waggled her brows suggestively. "I'll remember that for future reference."

Aspen looked at her askance. "You always were trouble." She waggled her finger in her direction. "You and your rolls can just stay on that side of the kitchen. I don't need to get you in any trouble with the missus."

"She's fine." Lex said dismissively. "What is it, they say? What happens in Vermont stays in Vermont."

"Not exactly." Aspen reached around and grabbed the coffee pot and divided the last remnants of coffee between the two of them. "Anyway, if you want to hang out at the house today, it's no big deal to me."

Lex's face broke out in a warm smile. "Cool. It will be just like old times."

Aspen met her eyes. Not exactly like old times, she thought. More times than not, when Lex watched her work before, they ended up naked on the floor of her studio. She was pretty sure that was not going to happen this time. "I'm gonna clean up and then we can head down."

"Sounds good. You want help or can I grab a quick shower?" Lex stood up halfway, waiting for Aspen's response.

"Go ahead. I'll put the dishwasher on a delay, so I don't take all the hot water."

"I'll save you some." Lex padded off to her room, her own mind picturing the painting sessions that happened all those years ago. By the time she was undressed and ready to shower, she was contemplating not using hot water at all. Somehow as turned on as she was after picturing Aspen naked beneath her, a cold shower sounded like a much better idea.

Chapter 11

Lex watched Aspen's hand move slowly over the thick paper. She alternated between soft strokes of charcoal and rubbing her pinky over the same spot, adjusting the shadows until they were just like she wanted them. An involuntary smile crept over Lex's face, and she felt warmth spread through her body. Too many moments felt like home, and she relished the quiet times with Aspen.

She directed her focus back to her laptop and frowned at the single line of type. So much for her deadline. She wasn't able to concentrate long enough to even finish a paragraph. She didn't care though. Nothing mattered at all except the need to be near her, the need to feel Aspen filling every part of her soul. It was foolish; she knew. A couple more months and this fantasy would be over, and she would go back to her life.

It would have bothered Lex more if she hadn't fooled herself into believing she needed this. She shouldn't have let herself get so close again, so invested. Somehow, she had convinced herself that she was merely doing what Cassidy wanted. Figuring out a way to finally let go. However, something in the mantra she repeated more often than not didn't ring true. Lex hoped that her heart caught up with her brain and stopped being so damned romantic. This was not a reunion. It was the first step in finally severing the last tie that bound them together.

Finally deciding that she wasn't going to get much done, she closed her laptop and set it on the floor next to her. She swung her legs over the side of the chair and let them dangle, her concentration now fully on Aspen. She watched the picture take shape. She watched the outline of a mother nursing her child fill the page. Aspen shadowed around it again, the light hitting only the profile of the woman, her young child asleep in her arms. It was poignant in a way that made her breath catch.

She waited until Aspen backed away and crossed her arms over her chest to survey her work. "It's beautiful."

Aspen jumped at her voice. She was conscious of Lex as much she was aware of the beating of her own heart. It just was and so was Lex's presence in her life. She had crept inside Aspen and settled in every inch of her body. She had captivated her heart and soul once again, had filled her mind with thoughts of yesteryear. She pushed those thoughts back and shot Lex an appreciative smile. "Thank you."

Lex saw her frown. "What?"

"It's just…" She narrowed her eyes. She rubbed her chin thoughtfully and smudged charcoal on her jaw. "Something's just not right."

Lex stood up and stretched her arms over her head. She covered the distance between them and stopped so close to Aspen that she could feel the heat emanating from her body. "Hmm."

They studied it together like that for several more moments, the lines between yesterday and today blurring rapidly. Too many times before they had gone from this to making love in Aspen's studio, certain that it inspired creativity.

Aspen sighed loudly. "I'm not sure. Something just isn't right here." She pointed to the outline of the woman's breast.

Lex cocked her head sideways and took a step closer. "Maybe a little more shadowy here."

"Maybe so." Aspen made several short strokes with her charcoal and smudged them with her finger before stepping back and studying it again. "Yes, I think that was it. Thank you."

Lex smiled. "Just like old times."

"Not exactly." Aspen laughed ruefully. It wasn't just like old times. It was so far from old times that it made her ache. She was getting too close, allowing herself too much liberty with her feelings. This time with Lex felt too close to perfect, and she knew if she didn't guard her heart better, at the end of the six months she was going to hurt more than the last time.

Lex felt her close off before she even spoke and in her desperateness to keep the connection, she inched closer. She studied Aspen's profile. She chuckled when she saw the black streak on her chin. "You have a little…" Without even thinking; she licked her thumb and brushed it over Aspen's chin.

Aspen felt her touch, and she froze. Lex's thumb was warm and soft, and although she didn't mean the gesture to be intimate, Aspen's heart thundered in her chest. Lex's touch had always done that. She only had to touch her, and shockwaves would rip through her body. She leaned into the caress, and a soft moan escaped her lips. Aspen pulled away a little too quickly. She rubbed her palm over her chin. "I got it."

Lex watched her, a stunned expression on her face. In that moment, she felt more closely connected to Aspen than in all the years with Cassidy. *I am so fucked.* Somehow, that seemed to be the only appropriate response to the burgeoning feelings she was trying hard to keep tamped down. She desperately needed to get this moment under control. She took several steps back. "So, what was the nightmare about this morning?"

Aspen paled slightly. "Nothing."

"You weren't screaming like it was nothing." Lex countered. "It sounded like something."

"Don't worry about it." The words came out more harshly than Aspen intended, and she offered an apologetic smile.

"How long have you been having nightmares?" Lex studied Aspen's face closely, knowing if her answer wasn't truthful, she could tell immediately. Her eyes would give her away.

Aspen shrugged. "A while."

"How long?"

"Since you left." The words were devoid of emotion, but Lex didn't need to hear it. She could see it as plain as day and the admission broke her heart again.

"I'm so sorry, A." Lex felt the need to pull Aspen into her arms, but she fought it. She could see from the look on her face that Aspen was trying to stay resolute and offering comfort would not be welcome. "I didn't know."

"How would you?" Aspen's eyes flashed accusatorily. "Kind of hard to know when you walk out and leave everything behind you without so much as a look."

Lex pulled on her pony tail, the only sign that she was emotionally stressed. "I fucked up, A. Everything I did was wrong. I was stupid and scared. That's no excuse. I don't have one that could even begin to make up for what I did to you."

"Not just me. Us."

One word and it encompassed everything about their situation. They had been an *us,* and Lex had taken that from them. She had taken everything that was special to them and pissed it away.

"It's fine." Aspen offered quietly. "That was a long time ago. We are where we are supposed to be now."

"Are we?" Lex challenged her to think about her response. Were they where they were supposed to be? Honestly, she didn't think so. Rather than continue down that path, she asked Aspen about her nightmares again. "Do you have nightmares often?"

Aspen shook her head. "Not too bad. A couple per month maybe. More lately."

Lex felt her heart catch. She opened her mouth to reply, but Aspen stopped her.

"Lex, stop. Don't apologize again. It is what it is. For now, I'll deal with them. Besides, we are only together a little while longer, and then we can move on. Once I get out of this situation, they will stop again."

You mean once you get away from me, Lex thought sadly. Guilt was something she lived with daily. Most of the time, she could bury it but there were times, like now, that it pushed its way to the surface. It was at moments like this that she felt the need for self—recrimination. She could normally beat herself up better than anyone. Today her guilt was overwhelming. "I'm just sorry. Sorry for everything."

Aspen squeezed her arm. "Enough, okay? I'm a big girl. I handled it this long, and I will continue to do that. Forget about it, okay?"

Lex could only nod in agreement. She wasn't sure that she could open her mouth and not subject herself to a vitriolic diatribe.

"Aspen?" Ginny's voice carried into the studio, and Aspen breathed a sigh of relief. Watching the guilty emotions play on Lex's face was almost too much to bear. Secretly, she knew that Lex had run because of her guilt. She blamed herself for their inability to have a child. Shouldering the majority of the pain and not letting Aspen share in that. Instead, running the other way and breaking them both. Yes, she'd had enough of the guilt. Right now, she just wanted to move on without the pain of yesterday's mistakes between them. Holding onto the past was chaining her down, and she couldn't move on without letting go.

"In here." She shot Lex a smile. "Thanks for the help with the sketch."

"My pleasure." Lex moved away and met Ginny's smile with a big one of her own. "Hi, Aunt Ginny."

"Lex." Like she had so many times before, she pulled the women into a bear hug. "I missed you girls."

"We missed you too, Aunt Ginny." Aspen hugged her hard then pulled away and shot her a questioning glance.

"She's bringing her suitcase in. Lord, you would think the woman was staying for a month and not just a week. I think she brought half her dresser."

Aspen cocked her head. "You know Mom is starving for company. She may just try to move in with you."

"Oh, no." Ginny waived her hand dismissively. "We may be sisters, but too much time together, and we fight like cats and dogs. I think with this week, in addition to my stay there that she will be ready to go. If not, I'm sending her to the bunkhouse."

Lex watched the banter between the two with a whimsical smile. She missed the easy-going chatter that Aspen and her family shared. Her family was too loud. She got a headache anytime she visited. And Cassidy's family, well they were a little too uppity for her comfort, too much money and too many airs for her liking. It was different with Aspen's family. They were warm and welcoming, and she had felt instantly at home from the minute she met them. She did miss Aspen's dad and uncle though. The sports banter was lost on the women. She shook her head and sighed. This was the home she wanted and instead of holding onto it, she had run and found an imitation to fill the void.

"Come on, Lex." Aspen grabbed her hand and pulled her out of the studio in search of her mother. "I know Mom will want to see you."

"I don't know abo..." Lex's words halted in her throat when she stepped into the kitchen and saw Aspen's mom coming through the back door. She had always thought Aspen took after her mother, but after being apart for so long, the likeness was even more noticeable. She swallowed nervously. "Hi."

"Lex." Susan studied her face closely before pulling her into her arms for a hug.

Lex felt her warm arms encircle her and felt immediately relieved. She had expected censure and received welcome. She didn't doubt that Susan would give her a piece of her mind, and she deserved whatever she got. But, to be ensconced in her warmth if even for a second was a welcome respite from the anxiousness she felt.

Susan finally pulled away and held Lex at arms' length. "You didn't say good-bye."

Lex lowered her head guiltily. She looked back up and realized that was all Susan was going to say. Properly chastised, she smiled ruefully. "Just add it to my list of transgressions. You can cut down on my Christmas presents this year."

It had been a longstanding joke in their family that Aspen's parents liked Lex better and her pile of presents at Christmas had always been bigger. Susan narrowed her eyes and gave Lex a stern look. "Don't worry. Your pile of coal is bigger than normal."

Lex's laughter filled the room, and any awkwardness at their reunion melted away. She nodded at Susan's bags. "Can I take those up to your room?"

"Of course." Susan stepped aside and winked at Aspen over Lex's head.

"Thank you." Aspen mouthed the words, silently thankful that her mother hadn't decided to give Lex a piece of her mind. Ginny did a good enough job of that very early on. Lex had slinked away with her tail between her legs after Ginny had finished with her. No doubt, Ginny had filled her mom in on the trip home, and her mother had decided to spare the poor woman another round of abuse. Although, Aspen thought, she probably did deserve it.

Aspen gave her mother a quick hug and smiled. "How was the trip up?"

"Long." Susan leaned in. "Don't tell your aunt that I said this, but lord, that woman can talk. I was trying to read my Kindle thingy you got me, and she just kept talking."

"I would offer to get her a reader, but I'm thinking her driving and reading at the same time is not such a great idea." Aspen hugged her mother again. "I missed you."

"I missed you too, honey." Susan studied her daughter's face and frowned at the sadness that was evident there. "How is the arrangement working out?"

Aspen shrugged. "Oh, it's okay. She's gone a lot so I don't really even see her all that much."

Susan sensed there was more that she wasn't saying. "What about when she is there?"

"Mmm, it's fine. We get along okay. Just like having a roommate I guess. We work around each other easily enough."

Susan opened her mouth to ask another question when loud footsteps from the stairway stopped her. She watched Lex step off the bottom stair and flop down in a chair. "Goodness, Lex, you always were such a loud walker."

Lex smiled sheepishly. "Guess it's the shoes."

Susan's eyes took in her heavy looking Borns and she laughed. "Yes, you did always like the clodhoppers; I remember."

"Is anyone else as hungry as I am?" Ginny had already found her way to the fridge and when they turned to answer her, the only thing visible was her bottom pointed at them from inside the fridge. "I'm in the mood for fried chicken."

Lex rubbed her hands together greedily. "Yes, please."

Susan laughed. "And she hasn't lost her appetite either."

"I would say not." Aspen seconded the observation. "You should see what she can put down. I don't know how she isn't as big as a house."

"If you're anything like me, you won't get so lucky." Susan said with a chuckle and swatted Lex's arm. "One day you will wake up and realize there is a small caboose following you."

"Oh, stop it, Mom." Lex chuckled softly. She tested her old habit of calling Aspen's mother Mom. When she wasn't corrected, she continued. "You look wonderful. I hope I can look that good when I'm your age."

Ginny set a package of chicken on the counter followed by a carton of buttermilk. "Oh, not the *your age* comment. That's like saying your old and have a foot in the grave to women *our age. Lex, I thought you were quite the flatterer, but not anymore.*"

Lex reddened deeply, the laughter breaking out around her. She caught the wink Ginny gave Susan. "Hey, not funny." She shot Aspen a look, begging her to step in, but Aspen merely threw up her hands as if to say you are on your own. "Fine. Laugh it up, ladies. I deserve that."

Aspen stilled, waiting for her mother's reaction. So far, she hadn't given Lex hell for leaving all those years ago, and she wasn't sure if Lex would continue relatively unscathed. She was saved when Ginny held the chicken out to her sister and told her to get to cleaning. "So, how was your stay, Aunt Ginny? Did Mom put you to work fall cleaning?"

Oh, lordy, you know she always does." Ginny said with fond laughter. "I'll be returning the favor, of course."

"I hope so." Aspen watched her aunt pour buttermilk into a bowl and add several shakes of pepper and some hot sauce. "So, what are we planning for Thanksgiving?"

Susan lifted her brow and shot her sister a look. "You want to tell her or should I?"

"Tell me what?" Aspen asked suspiciously. "What have you two women cooked up in my absence?"

"Oh, you know, a little of this and a little of that." Ginny's eyes sparkled with obvious delight. "I talked your mother into a cruise instead of doing the traditional dinner."

"Are you serious?" Lex cocked an eyebrow questioningly. "What about your no water rule?"

Ginny laughed. "Well, I am getting so much *older.*" She couldn't resist the chance to tease poor Lex. "I think it's high time I did something fun."

"That's great, Mom." Aspen offered. "Where are you going?"

"Some place in the Caribbean. Your aunt made the arrangements. All I had to do was pack and show up."

"Wow, Aunt Ginny. I am seriously impressed. Dad tried to get Mom to go on a cruise for years."

Ginny took the chicken from Susan and dumped it unceremoniously in the buttermilk mixture and set it aside. "I always have been a good deal more persuasive than your Father ever was." She shot Susan a look, which was rewarded with a surreptitious smile.

"Whoa, I know that look." Aspen interjected. "What aren't you telling us?"

Lex leaned forward. "Yeah, something tells me there is a story behind that look."

Susan waived her hand dismissively. "Nothing as exciting as you two are thinking; I'm sure. Although, you might be surprised that your aunt got me to traipse around Europe for a summer."

"What?" Aspen's eyebrows shot up. "You never told me about that. When was this?"

Ginny chuckled. "It might surprise you to know that us *old fogies* have a few tricks up our sleeves."

Aspen shook her head, disbelievingly. "So, tell us about this clandestine trip to Europe. When did you go?"

Susan smiled reminiscently. "It was the summer after I graduated from college. We went to Europe. We had rail passes and just went everywhere. Ginny even got me to stay in hostels while we were there."

"Hostels?" Lex frowned. "That's not safe."

"Oh, sure it is." Ginny said dismissively. "They are a lot different now than they were forty years ago. It's a different world now."

"I'll say." Susan seconded. "It really was fine, honey. No need to worry. We made it home safe and sound, and here we are to tell all about it."

"Oh, sure. Forty years later." Aspen shook her head, still unable to believe that her own mother had done something as outside the box as go to Europe for the summer. "What else haven't you told us?"

This time the look that passed between her mother and aunt was almost comical. "Okay, this is totally blowing my mind."

Susan laughed. "Oh, honey, there is a lot that would surprise you about your old Mom. I wasn't always a stodgy old curmudgeon."

"Well, I don't think you are that now." Aspen countered. She looked around for something to occupy her hands, which were wringing together with obvious excitement.

"Here." Ginny handed her the chicken and a bowl of flour. "You can be my sous chef. I'll tell you a story that will knock your socks off."

Grateful for a distraction, Aspen dived into her task; her eyebrows cocked. "I can't get over Mom in Europe. I'm not sure you can top that one." She shot Lex a look, and was rewarded with a barely perceptible shoulder shrug that clearly said *I'm just as thrown as you.*

"You know your uncle was in the Army."

Aspen nodded. "Yes, Airborne?"

"What you don't know is that Neal went A.W.O.L after the first two years."

"What?!" Aspen and Lex's voices combined in a comical half—shriek of disbelief.

"Oh, yes." Ginny continued. "He ran away to Mexico. Even had a girlfriend named Esperanza. Mexico's the reason your uncle wouldn't ever drink tequila."

"What? Why?" Aspen's head was spinning. She knew that her parents and her aunt and uncle had a life prior to them, but she had no idea it was so colored.

"Let's just say he drank way too much nickel tequila and ended up on the floor of the cantina way too many times. After that, just the smell was enough to make him sick."

"Unbelievable." Aspen shook her head, unable to wrap her mind around this new information.

"What about you, Mom?" Lex leaned forward questioningly. "Any other sorted stories in your past?"

"My dear, there are some things a mother never tells." Susan smiled mischievously.

Aspen finished battering the chicken and watched as Ginny started dropping it into a pan of hot oil. The immediate sizzle reminded her so much of being a child, waiting for her mother to cook dinner. She looked at her mom and saw the sparkle there and wondered what stories her own mother hadn't shared. She shook her head, realizing that she may never know. Somehow, she was okay with that. She had always looked up to her mother and believed her to be without guile. She wanted to keep it that way. "So, tell us about the cruise."

Ginny clapped her hands together excitedly. "Show her the brochures."

Aspen laughed at her aunt's excitement. She washed her hands and took one of the colorful brochures her mother handed her. She scanned the pages and had to admit it sounded like more fun than staying home and pigging out on traditional holiday fare. "But what about the too much time together and threatening to send Mom to the bunkhouse?"

Ginny laughed and waived her hand dismissively. "It's a big ship. If I get tired of your mom, I'll just send her to the opposite side."

"Ha!" Susan countered. "I'll just push your aunt overboard." They dissolved into amused laughter.

After several minutes of chatter about the itinerary, Lex's brow wrinkled. "What about you?"

"What about me?" Aspen laid the brochure down.

"What will you do for Thanksgiving?"

Aspen shrugged. "I guess I'll just stay here, pig out on anything and everything unhealthy and watch the parade. I really need to get some more pieces done. This will give me a chance to do that without any distractions."

"No." Lex replied. "You can't stay here alone on Thanksgiving."

"Why not? I'm a big girl."

"You're coming with me."

"Oh no, I am not." Aspen said with a chuckle. "I am not subjecting myself to another Tataris Thanksgiving. I want to fit into my clothes, after all."

"Nope." Lex said with finality. "I refuse to let you stay here alone. You're coming home with me."

A knowing look passed between Ginny and Susan. "That's a good idea, honey." Susan offered. "There's no reason you need to be here by yourself."

"I can't leave the horses." Normally, Aspen wouldn't have minded going to Lex's family's house for the holiday. But it was different now. Now that they were no longer together. It would just be weird. "And I really need to work in the studio."

"It's one day." Ginny pulled the first of the fried chicken out of the pan and set it on a paper towel to drain. "Lex, can you grab a box of those instant potatoes out of the pantry?" Ginny may stick to some of the home-cooked meals, but she loved convenience, and if she could make decent mashed potatoes out of a box with minimal effort then by God, she was going to. "The girls will be fine."

"I shouldn't really." Aspen hesitated. "I haven't told you guys yet, but I have an exhibit in the spring. I don't have enough pieces yet, so this gives me the perfect opportunity to catch up."

"Oh, honey, that's wonderful." Susan squeezed her shoulder affectionately.

"No way, are you serious?" Lex was almost out of her chair. "When were you going to tell me?"

116

Aspen shrugged noncommittally. "It's no big deal."

"It's a huge deal. This is what you've always wanted." Lex pressed. "When did you find out?"

"Last week." Aspen offered. "It's just a small gallery in New York, so it probably won't be seen by too many people."

"I can't believe you didn't say anything." Lex pretended not to be hurt. The past few months had brought them closer, and she wished that Aspen could share things like that with her. Her heart ached knowing that five years ago, she would have been the first person Aspen told and now, after her mistake, the news was shared as an afterthought.

"Really, it's no big deal." Aspen took the box of instant potatoes from her and pulled a pan out of the cupboards. She couldn't take the look of hurt in Lex's eyes. Those brown eyes had been her undoing so many times before, and she needed a distraction before they pulled her in again.

"Well, honey, I'm certainly proud of you." Susan winked at Lex conspiratorially. "I am sure you will have plenty for the show. I don't want you alone on Thanksgiving."

"I agree." Ginny seconded. "Besides, it's one day. I promise you the girls will be fine."

Aspen shook her head in defeat. She couldn't stand up against the three of them. "Fine, but I can only be gone for the day."

Lex smiled exuberantly. "Awesome! I'll let Mom know you will be there. She will cook everything under the sun, you know."

"Ugh." Aspen pictured herself lying uncomfortably on the couch, so full she wouldn't be able to move. "That's what I'm afraid of."

"Well, it's all settled then." Ginny took the last piece of chicken out of the pan and shooed Aspen out of the way. "Go, sit. Tell us about your show."

Over chicken and somewhat tolerable mashed potatoes, Aspen filled them in on the details, all the while questioning her decision to go home with Lex. The pain of not being with her had dulled to a gentle ache, and she wasn't sure she would survive the day unscathed. If not, the next couple of months were going to be even harder than the last couple. *Oh well, it will make for some interesting pieces.*

Chapter 12

"Aspen, you are way too skinny. It's a good thing my Lex brought you home. You need some fattening up."

"Ma." Lex's voice dragged out in exasperation. "She just got here. Can you wait until she gets her coat off before you start shoveling food into her face?"

Aspen laughed at Lex's attempt to save her from the day long food fest. She saw the twinkle in Maria's eyes and knew she was in for trouble today. She felt herself pulled into Maria's arms again for the third hug since she had walked in. "Maria. It's so good to see you."

"Kopela mou." Maria beamed, obviously delighted that Aspen remembered her pet name. "I told Alexis she should have brought you home years ago."

"Ma." Lex's tone was serious, but her mother merely waived her off with a chuckle. She hated being chastised almost as much as she hated being called by her full name. "Aspen, you come in and see Nicky. He heard you were coming and hasn't talked about anything since. You know, he always did have a crush on you."

Aspen caught Lex's eye and winked conspiratorially. Both of them knew that Lex's brother Nicky liked pretty much any female. He was as undiscerning in his taste in women as anyone. He liked to say he found something in all women to love.

Maria led them into the kitchen and immediately smacked Nicky's shoulder. "Sit up, Nicky. We got company."

He met Aspen's gaze, and his whole face transformed into a smile that went from ear to ear, making her wonder if maybe Maria was right, and he did have a crush on her. "Hi, Nicky."

"A, you made it!" He lifted her into the air and spun her around exuberantly "You look great. You should have picked me, A. I never would have left you."

His comment earned him another smack on the shoulder from his mother and a momentary glare from his older sister. "Aww, Lexie, you know I'm just kidding." He turned and gave Aspen an earnest smile. "We did miss you like crazy though. It hasn't been the same without your cooking. Sorry, Ma."

"It's okay, Nicky. You did know your way around the kitchen...with American food." She smiled mischievously. "But, not with our Greek food. No one does Greek like Maria Tataris." She pointed at an empty chair. "Now sit, tell me what you've been up to the past few years."

Aspen felt everyone's eyes on her, and she felt the heat rise in her cheeks. She knew she had better get comfortable fast. Her audience of three was going to grow to about fifteen within minutes. Lex's extended family filled in every empty spot in the house during the holidays.

"Ma, let her be for a few minutes, okay? We just got here."

Aspen shot Lex a grateful look, and she mouthed a silent thank you.

"Yo, Nicky, where's your girl?" Lex grabbed a piece of turkey off the tray and sidestepped quickly, avoiding her mother's swat. "Too many to narrow it down to just one?"

Nick looked at his sister askance. "It's just me tonight, Lexie."

120

"Can you believe that?" Maria wiped her hands on her apron. "My Nicky, he doesn't have a date." She squeezed his chin and shook his face. "Aspen, look at my handsome boy and tell me why he has no girl tonight."

"Ma." Nick's voice raised in a long, nasal whine. "Cut it out, will ya? I told you, I am not dating anyone right now. I want to graduate from the academy first."

Nicky had enrolled in the police academy and was just weeks from graduating. It was an ironic choice for the man who had spent many hours trying to avoid the law. Lex wondered if maybe he was finally growing up to be the man she knew he could be.

"I just don't understand." Maria set three sandwiches down on the table. "Eat."

Lex rolled her eyes. They would be eating in an hour, and here she was shoving food at them. She opened her mouth to respond when Nicky caught her eye and shook his head.

Maria continued unfazed. "You need a woman to take care of you. You aren't getting any younger. You should be dating. I'm not getting any younger, and I am not bouncing any grandbabies on my knees yet."

Lex met Nicky's eyes, and she shook her head from side to side. It was the same thing at every holiday. They knew the speech by heart and if pressed, could repeat it word-for-word. Swallowing a snicker, she took a huge bite of her sandwich and figured she would need to work out extra hard to lose the additional five pounds she put on every Thanksgiving. Lex could feel Aspen's eyes studying them all, taking this annual ritual in with barely concealed amusement. Leaning closer, she met Aspen's twinkling blue eyes and whispered. "You think this is funny?"

Aspen's eyes danced with amusement. "Nothing like a Tataris Thanksgiving." She waggled the sandwich in Lex's face. "No day would be complete without your mom over feeding us and riding Nicky's ass all day."

Lex rolled her eyes. "You know Ma." She held Aspen's gaze a bit longer, looking for something buried in her eyes. "You're okay though? I mean this isn't too much, is it? I know Ma can go a little overboard."

"No, it's fine." Aspen shook her head and finished the last bite of her sandwich. "She makes me comfortable. My little girl, she remembered."

"Of course she did." Lex's smile widened. "Ma always loved you."

"Alexis." Maria's voice filled the room. "You take the tzatziki and put it on the table. Your aunt Irene will be here soon and she is not going to outshine your momma with her spinach and cheese pie." Maria's voice suddenly changed to emulate Irene's nasally whine. *"It's so much better than yours because I put leeks in it.* Humph! Leeks. Thinks it's so good. Nick doesn't even touch it. How Milo eats Irene's cooking is beyond me."

"Ma!" Lex shot her a look and when Maria turned around she feigned innocence.

"What?" Maria shrugged her shoulders. "Milo is a better man than most. Your poppa, he would say to me. Maria, I love you, but you need lessons in the kitchen. Mind you, I don't. But, that is what Milo should tell your aunt Irene."

Nicky chuckled out loud. "Ma, that's your sister."

Maria already turned her attention back to her roasted potatoes. Her only answer was a loud snort.

Lex rolled her eyes. "Seriously, Nicky. How are you still living here?"

Nicky snuck a look in his mother's direction before replying. "Just a few more months. Once I graduate, I'm moving out and getting a place with one of the guys from the Academy."

"Are you serious?" Lex's loud reply reverberated around them. A sheepish look spread over her features, but a glance at her mother, and she knew that there was a definite benefit to her mother getting old. She couldn't hear a thing. She leaned forward and whispered conspiratorially. "You're really moving out? Ma will have a fit."

"I know." Nicky's face broke into a wide grin. "I figured I'd break it to her today."

"What are you three whispering about?" Maria set a plate of feta cheese slices covered with oregano and drizzled with olive oil between them. She ruffled Nicky's hair. "Look at my Nicky. He's going to be a cop. He does just like his big sister and abandons his poppa to run the business by himself. Thank goodness your cousin Peter has a head for numbers. Perhaps, he will give his momma grandbabies, since you two won't take pity on your mother."

"Ma, seriously." Lex let out an exasperated breath. It had been five years since she and Aspen had lost the baby, and she could tell by the pained expression in Aspen's eyes that she didn't need the reminder. She would have gladly given Lex's mom grandchildren. It didn't work out that way and Lex felt the need to protect her still. She found Aspen's hand underneath the table and squeezed it. *"I'm sorry."*

Aspen squeezed her hand back then released it just as quickly. She shook her head to let Lex know she was okay.

"Aspen, you are coming for Nicky's graduation." It was more a statement then a question. To Maria, she was still part of the family no matter what had happened. It was just expected that she would be there.

"Ahh...I don't think that Cass...well what I mean..." Aspen pleaded with Lex to save her.

"She can't, Ma." Lex interjected. "A's getting ready for a show."

Disappointment flashed briefly in Maria's eyes. "Nonsense. You will come. The whole family is going to be there." She squeezed Nicky's chin and shook his head around. "Don't you want to see our Nicky graduate?"

Aspen's face reddened, and she could see from Lex and Nicky's expressions that there was no deterring Maria now that she had made up her mind. She opened her mouth to reply when bells started ringing through the house. *Saved by the bell.*

Lex watched her mother's retreating figure for several seconds before smiling apologetically. "I'm sorry."

Aspen shook her head. "It's okay. I probably shouldn't have come. It's weird for me to be here. I think your mom forgot you are with Cass, and we aren't together anymore."

A pained expression flashed in Lex's eyes before she forced herself to smile. "She never wanted anyone else for me. She always thought you were perfect. She never really got over us breaking up."

Aspen winced. She had never really gotten over them breaking up. Perhaps she shouldn't have come today. It was all too much. They were no misconceptions that they were together. Cass and Lex never spent Thanksgiving with each other, so it was no surprise she wasn't here. But, Aspen's presence probably came as a bit of a shock. She hoped Maria wasn't actually under the impression they were getting back together. "Your mom knows we are getting a divorce, doesn't she?"

Lex colored. "I, uhhh…"

"Lex!" Aspen's mouth dropped open. "You didn't tell her?"

"I couldn't." Lex smiled sheepishly. "She still thinks we will get back together."

Aspen threw up her hands. "You better tell her."

"I will."

"When?" Aspen countered. "God, this is going to be an awkward lunch. You probably didn't even tell her that we weren't back together. You were just going to show up with me and let her believe what she wanted."

The guilt was evident in Lex's eyes. She didn't set her mother straight. The conversation was a bit one—sided anyway. When she had called Maria to let her know that she was bringing Aspen home for the holiday, Maria had been overjoyed. She had even gone so far as to say what her real opinion of Cass was. At the time, Lex knew she should have corrected her, but she didn't. Choosing instead to play make believe for a day. One look in Aspen's eyes and she suddenly knew that was a bad idea. "A, I'm sorry. I'll talk to mom. For now, can you just let it go? I don't want to mess today up. You know how she gets."

Aspen sighed wearily. "Yes, I know." Maria was an outspoken Greek woman, and Lex had no desire to set her mother off today. "You promise you will talk to her?"

"Yes."

"Thank you." Aspen felt her heartbeat return to normal. It was one thing to play house with Lex, but to have her family believe that they were back together was unacceptable. For the time being, though, she would play along. She didn't feel like being the one that broke Maria's heart today. Pulling away from Lex's penetrating gaze, she punched Nicky in the arm. "So Nick, you have a girlfriend for real, don't you?"

Nicky's face reddened. "Yeah, I do."

"Don't want to introduce her to the family yet, huh?" Aspen winked.

"No." Nicky's eyes widened at the thought. "I really like this one and there is no way I'm letting Ma get to her yet."

Lex leaned forward and joined in. "Smart move. You know Ma would have her upstairs trying on her old wedding dress."

"Oh god!" Aspen chuckled softly, remembering the first Christmas at the Tataris house. She was forced to try on Maria's dress and veil. It practically swallowed her. "Yeah, you may not want to bring her home until after you're married."

"Ha, Ma would kill you." Lex warned.

"What Ma will kill you?" Maria walked back into the kitchen.

"Nothing, Ma." Nicky grabbed a slice of feta and stuffed it in his mouth.

125

Maria swatted him on the back of the head. "Don't *nothing Ma* me." She regarded him with a stern expression.

"Nicky was just teasing that he was going to slice off a huge piece of turkey." Lex said innocently.

"Ooh." Maria smacked the back of his head. "I would kill you twice if you did that."

Aspen snickered quietly. The exchange was reminiscent of so many holidays before.

"Your aunt Irene and your cousins are here. We will eat soon. You keep your hands off the turkey." Maria scolded Nicky, but her eyes still sparkled. No matter what happened, Nicky was still her baby and there wasn't much that he could do that would make Maria truly mad. "Take that to the table."

Nicky shot Lex a grateful smile and grabbed the plate off the table. "I'm gonna see if Pop has the game on."

"Lex, you can watch the game. I know you need to write about it later."

"It's okay. I DVR'd it, so I can catch up later." Lex offered quickly. "Besides, it's just the Thanksgiving game. It's not that big a deal."

"Go on." Maria put her hands on her hips impatiently. "Wake your father up too."

Lex started to reply, but her mother waved her off. "Go. I want to talk to Aspen alone."

Lex shot Aspen a look as if to say I'm sorry, there is nothing I can do.

Aspen watched her walk away, praying that she could disappear. She wasn't ready for the conversation that she knew was looming. She tried to stave it off by distracting Maria. "Do you need help with anything else?"

Maria waived her off with a smile. "Sit, sit. I want to look at your sweet face. I haven't seen my girl in too long. Alexis should never have let you go." She shrugged and settled herself beside Aspen with a sigh. "But she's wised up and soon, maybe you will give me a grandchild."

Maria's eyes were filled with such hope that Aspen prayed she couldn't see her face pale. "Mmm…maybe."

Maria studied Aspen's face closely. There was something in her eyes that gave away what she was trying to hide. She squeezed Aspen's hand. "Alexis thinks her momma isn't so smart sometimes. But I know. I can see it in both your faces. You never could hide from me, Kopela Mou. I can see in your eyes that you and Alexis are not back together."

Aspen swallowed the lump in her throat and nodded.

Maria squeezed her shoulder. "It's okay, honey. I know in my heart that you are meant to be together. That much I am convinced of. Alexis, sometimes she gets scared, afraid she will let people down. I can tell she still loves you and if I'm not mistaken, you are still in love with her. No?"

Aspen blinked back tears and smiled wistfully. "That was such a long time ago, Maria. We are so different now." Aspen's heart ached just to say that. "Besides, it doesn't matter. She's with Cass now."

Maria shook her head. "She's just filling a void. All these years later, my Alexis is still in love with you. She can never really love anyone else like she loves you. She doesn't need someone like you, she needs you. She will find her way back to you. A mother knows these things."

"No." Aspen admitted softly. "You might as well know the truth. She's staying with me, so we can file for divorce. She's marrying Cass." Aspen could see how badly the words hurt Maria, and she felt horrible for saying them. After all, she had promised Lex that she wouldn't say anything, but it hurt too much to see the hope in Maria's eyes. "I'm sorry, Maria."

"Don't be." Maria's eyes twinkled behind her frown. "I can see you never really moved on. It's just a matter of time." She didn't allow Aspen to respond. She cupped Aspen's face in the palm of her hand and smiled. "There are some things that a mother just knows."

127

Aspen watched Maria walk away and tried to push her words to the back of her mind. She didn't want to think right now. Today, she just wanted to be happy. She took a deep breath and plastered a smile on her face. She would think again tomorrow.

Chapter 13

Aspen groaned loudly and shut the car door behind her. "I'm going to go take care of the girls."

"Want help?" Lex shoved the keys in her pocket and started to follow Aspen to the barn.

"Nah, I'm okay. I'll take care of that, if you want to get a fire going." A cold wind blew around them, and Aspen shivered uncontrollably. She hesitated for a moment, nearly changing her mind then stopped. The look on Lex's face was almost too much. The day was perfect, too perfect. Dinner at the Tataris house reminded her too much of being married. Her conversation with Maria had stirred up so many feelings from the past. Surrounded by all of Lex's family, Aspen had allowed her mind to wonder and where her thoughts were headed was not somewhere she would allow herself to return. That was the past, and this was now. They were living with each other as a means to an end, a way for Lex to sever the last remaining tie that held them together. She needed to put some space between them before her mind started convincing her it was anything but business. "Hey, get Guinness some food, too."

"Okay." Lex watched her walk away, not sure how to take her refusal for help. It was almost as if Aspen couldn't stand to be in her presence any longer. She had seen a cloud pass over her face, and wondered what had happened between dinner at her family's and now that had caused the sadness in Aspen's eyes. She almost walked into the barn after Aspen and made her take help. Instead, she shook her head and started toward the house. She stepped inside and looked around the house she had shared with Aspen for the last few months. It was warm and homey. Something she couldn't say about the loft she shared with Cassidy. It had seemed alright before. Now, in her mind, it seemed sparse and unwelcome. It was so unlike the bunkhouse, which had quickly enveloped them and tucked them into a little fantasy world to which she was rapidly becoming attached.

Lex filled Guinness's bowl and watched his little nose sniff excitedly then tear into the food with wild abandon. "Buddy, you don't know how good you have it." She scrubbed her hands over her face and let out a loud sigh. She knew Aspen would be joining her inside, and she wanted to have the fire built before she got down. She would be cold, and Lex knew she would need to warm up. Within minutes, the kindling took and a warm fire crackled in the fireplace. Pleased with the results, Lex stood up and stretched out her long legs. There were two other traditions that had evolved from their marriage. The second, and the one that her body ached for, was totally out of the question. The first was mostly harmless and Lex was pretty sure she could talk Aspen into repeating that one.

By the time Aspen joined her, Lex had already switched her jeans out for comfortable sweats with Red Sox emblazoned down the leg. She was sitting Indian style on the floor in front of the fireplace rubbing Guinness's soft belly and listening to him growl in his sleep. She felt Aspen's eyes burning into the back of her head before her eyes settled on the bottle of Citron vodka sitting on the floor in front of her. She met Aspen's eyes and smiled. "I figured we could do one of our old Thanksgiving traditions."

Aspen cocked an eyebrow, and a smile played in the corners of her mouth. "Oh, you did, did you? And, which of our traditions did you have in mind?"

Lex waggled her eyebrows suggestively, and Aspen could feel her face heating up. She shook her finger in Lex's direction. "Uh—uh. I am pretty sure Mrs. Lex would have a problem with that one."

"Hmm, maybe so." Lex smiled cryptically then pointed down the hall. "Go change."

"Aye, aye captain." Aspen sent her a mock salute and giggled at the middle finger Lex shot in her direction.

"Women." Lex muttered playfully to no one but herself. She was thirty-three and for the life of her, still hadn't figured out all the wonderful intricacies of the fairer sex. It didn't matter that she was one herself. That fact only made her understand more the many facets that made up half the world. She would probably go to her grave as confused as she was today. There was one thing she was sure of, with absolute resolution, was she loved the woman just down the hall. She hadn't been able to get Aspen out of her system. She weaved in and out of every fiber in her body, making Lex ache with delicious wanting. She knew after spending six months with Aspen, she would either have purged her from her thoughts or have to accept that their souls would be forever joined. The only downside to that was loving someone she could no longer have.

Quiet footsteps broke through her ruminations. She felt Aspen settle down beside her. "Hey."

"Hey, yourself." Aspen studied Lex's face, watching the flames dance in her eyes. There was a winsome sadness in them that spoke to her own soul. She had done a good job of putting a box around her former life and tucking it up on a shelf, no longer feeling the hollow ache that had plagued her for the months surrounding their break up. However, now, in the closeness of the room and the look in Lex's eyes, she felt herself pulled along by an unseen hand, voices from the past beckoning to her. She felt a shiver run through her, and she forced herself to look away before the pain and longing in her chest made her do something she would no doubt regret. "What's our poison this year?"

Lex sensed the wall going up. She wanted to tear those walls down, but it wasn't her place. Her life was with someone else now. *Get a grip, Lex. It's business; it's not personal.* Except it was personal. It took on a life of its own, breathing hope into even the darkest corners of her soul. She shook her head, trying to banish the feelings of hope that had taken root and were threatening to divest her of her last shred of resistance. "Lemon drop shots."

"Wow." Aspen smiled automatically. It had been a long time since they had done those. She felt a tremor run through her body. She remembered all too well the Thanksgiving that they had done lemon drop shots. It was their first Thanksgiving together, the year they had met each other's family. It was awkward for both of them, as they put their best foot forward and tried to win over the family of the woman they loved. By the end of the day, both of them needed a drink and a reminder of why they had thrown themselves to the wolves in the first place. And, there was born the tradition of doing shots and spending the evening listing the things they were each grateful for.

Lex watched the emotions play on her face and knew Aspen remembered that first Thanksgiving. She felt her heart catch. She had always been able to read Aspen's face and know exactly what she was thinking. Her eyes were truly the window into her soul. Lex saw love and pain and hunger flash across her eyes. They still reminded Lex of a stormy sea. She felt something tug at her and without the strength to fight it, she reached out and brushed her thumb along Aspen's jaw line. Lex could feel her tremble beneath her touch. "I never forgot that night."

Aspen leaned into her caress, allowing herself a momentary stroll down memory lane before she sat up and pulled away from Lex. "Yes, well, that was a long time ago.

A lot has changed since then. And, I'm sure we both have a great deal we are thankful for now."

Lex nodded. "Yes, we do."

Aspen leaned back, her palms on the floor behind her. "I'm thankful…"

"Wait." Lex put her hand on her arm to stop her. Electricity shot up her arm, and she pulled her hand away quickly. She could feel her heart pounding in her chest and when she went to pour their first shot, her hands shook. She wasn't sure how, but she managed to fill their shot glasses and only lose a couple of drops. She set the bottle down and grabbed Aspen's hand, exposing her wrist.

Aspen tried to pull away, but Lex gripped her hand tightly and shook her head. "Like old times."

"I don't know, Lex." The heat from Lex's skin on hers was humming through her body, and she wasn't sure the close contact was a good idea. Her conversation with Lex's mom was still fresh in her mind, and it gave her pause. If she were truly going to move on with her life, it started here. She needed to be able to be around Lex and stay unaffected. This was as good a time as any to start.

"Please." The look in Lex's eyes coupled with the ache in her voice almost did Aspen in. She resisted the urge to pull away, playing down the quickening beat of her heart. Lex felt her relax. She took a lemon wedge and rubbed it over Aspen's wrist slowly, sending shivers racing up and down Aspen's spine. Lex could feel the electricity as it coursed through their bodies and left her fingers tingling. She sprinkled sugar over Aspen's wrist. Barely breathing, she repeated the gesture on herself. She picked up her shot glass and gestured to Aspen's glass. "You go first."

Aspen picked up her shot glass. She shivered, still feeling Lex's skin against hers, even though they were no longer touching. "Hmm." The sound was somewhere between a breath and a moan and Lex smiled. There was something about Aspen's voice that she loved. It was sexy in a sweet, innocent way, much like Aspen. The noises she made always sent Lex's body into overdrive. The first few months they had been together, Lex had spent hours just listening to her talk. Hell, she could have read the dictionary and found a way to make it sexy. "Okay. I'm thankful that my mother is finally getting out and having a life." She swallowed her shot then slid her tongue along her wrist, savoring sugary sweetness mingled with the tart bite of the lemon. She set the glass down with a quiet thud. "Your turn."

"Umm." Lex cocked her head sideways and stared into the fire. There were a thousand different things she could say. Right now, in her fantasy world, everything seemed right. "I'm thankful the Sox finally broke the curse of the Bambino and won two World Series." She smiled sheepishly and threw her shot back, the contents warming her body from inside out. She poured the next round of shots and handed Aspen a lemon wedge, not sure she could touch Aspen again without taking more. "Next."

Aspen grabbed her glass. She needed a few more before she could calm down. This little tradition was opening her up and making her more vulnerable than she wanted to be. "Okay, I'm thankful that I'm finally getting to put my art out for the public." Aspen downed her vodka and licked her wrist, feeling the tart juice pucker her taste buds and twist her face into a comical scrunched up look.

Lex chuckled softly. "You're adorable." She caught the sideways glare and laughed even harder. "What? You never could do the lemons without total face contortions."

"I'm glad you think I'm so funny." Aspen feigned indignation. When they had been married, Lex would normally kiss her right now and tease her about tasting something sweet to counter the tartness of the lemon. Instead, they suffered through an awkward moment of silence where both remembered all too well the electricity that they had once shared. Now it only simmered below the surface, an ever-present reminder of how their bodies called to one another. "Lex, I can't…"

Lex put her hand on Aspen's arm to silence her and nodded once in understanding. She was silent a beat longer, before she resigned herself to what she needed to say next. "I wanted to say I'm thankful that I got to spend Thanksgiving with you." She emptied her own glass before Aspen could object. She saw Aspen look at her questioningly. "What? That's what I'm thankful for."

"Why do you have to be so sweet?"

Lex shrugged. "I don't know. I guess you bring out the best in me."

Aspen cocked her eyebrow. "Is that so?"

"Yes." Lex couldn't answer any differently. She did feel like Aspen made her want to be better. It was unfair to compare the two women, but Cassidy had never inspired improvement. Lex was content with the take it or leave attitude. Not in a cavalier, uncaring way. More in a *what you see is what you get* way, and so far that suited them just fine. However, now, she wondered if it was enough anymore. "You always did. I guess somewhere along the way, I got lost. I'm just reminded lately of how far off course I got."

"You're not off course." Aspen added quickly. "You're just on a different course." She could see the far-off look in Lex's eyes, and she felt a small tinge of fear and knew she needed to turn the conversation around before Lex pulled her back in. She looked away from Lex and inhaled deeply. She wished putting distance between them wasn't so hard.

After several seconds, Lex knew Aspen was closing off, and she desperately wanted to keep the connection they had. She handed Aspen another lemon and waited while she rubbed the juice over her wrist and sprinkled it liberally with sugar. She repeated the process on her own wrist and waited for Aspen to say what she was thankful for. The alcohol was starting to warm her stomach.

Aspen tapped her lip thoughtfully. "I am thankful I'm starting to find myself again." She lifted her wrist to her mouth, but Lex grabbed her arm and held it softly. She pinned Aspen with her gaze, and before she could resist, Lex slid her tongue over Aspen's wrist. Aspen stilled, the feel of Lex's tongue on her skin made her heart beat furiously. She closed her eyes and gave herself to the moment, her stomach fluttering wildly. She lost herself in the space between reality and her dreams, feeling her body tighten with pleasure. *God, it would be so easy. If only...* The *if only* brought her hurtling back, and she pulled her hand away with undisguised quickness. Her blue eyes narrowed almost imperceptibly. "You shouldn't have done that."

"I'm sorry." Lex at least looked contrite, but the deep flush of her skin and her shallow breathing gave her away. She had been more turned on by that small gesture with Aspen than she had ever been with Cassidy. She shouldn't compare them and honestly, she had tried not to, but it was becoming increasingly difficult lately. She leaned back against the couch and willed her heart to slow down. It took even longer for her breathing to return to normal. She felt the need to explain herself. "A, I'm sorry. I shouldn't have done that."

"No, you shouldn't have." Aspen's voice was stern, but she couldn't hide the tremor in her voice. "You're with Cassidy. This is the course you chose."

"Then why does it feel like I'm hopelessly lost?" Lex asked quietly. "Why have the last few months with you given me more clarity than I have had in years? It's like all this time away from you; I've been looking at the world through a dirty window, all the while thinking that the view was just fine. But then I'm with you, and you clear everything up for me. It's like seeing things clearly for the first time in years. I don't question my choices or where I want to go. I don't feel unsure of where I am in the world."

"Lex, it has nothing to do with me." Aspen said quietly. She didn't want to feel anything more than she already did and Lex's admission made her heart ache. What she wanted, no needed was to make it through the next two months with her heart intact, and Lex was making it very difficult. "You are just getting to a point in your life where you know what you want, and you can finally allow yourself to see it."

"I do know...with one hundred percent certainty." The answer was right in front of Lex. It was what she wanted all along and had fooled herself into believing she didn't need it. She needed Aspen. She needed to love her and to be loved. However, loving her wasn't enough. She needed to spend her life loving her. She needed to hold her, to feel their bodies pressed together, to let her body show Aspen everything she felt inside. "A, I need..."

"Lex, don't." Aspen saw the look of longing in her eyes. It went beyond any physical hunger she had ever seen in Lex's eyes. What Aspen saw mirrored there was her own need. It was like her body's need for air or water. Her body, heart and soul would always crave Lex. They were joined, soul mates who had been created for each other, each other's perfect match. They would always call to each other, but Aspen knew they could never be together. Too many hurts pulled them apart; too much life had been lived, until now, when they were side by side they no longer fit together. No matter, how much they tried, the spaces between them were too much to overcome. Or at least they were for Aspen. "I can't go back there. Too much has happened. I'm not the same woman you left all those years ago."

"I'm not either." Lex knew that if there was any way that they were going to move forward, she needed to prove to Aspen that she had changed. "I've grown up too."

"Aww, honey. I know you have. That's the thing, we have both grown up. We just grew up in different directions." Aspen wanted to believe the sage advice she was doling out, but a quiet voice deep inside kept reminding her how good it had been and how wonderful it felt to be with Lex again, if even for a short time. She took a deep breath and tried to keep some of the resolution that five years had forced her to have. "You can't turn back time or act as though it didn't happen. You taught me how to love and even more so what I deserve. Well, what we both deserve. So now, I'm going to take those memories and tuck them back away. I am going to take the lessons we had and let myself live again. It's what I need to do to survive."

Lex tugged on her pony tail nervously. "So there's absolutely no chance for us again?"

Aspen felt tears stinging her eyes. This was either her chance to follow her heart, risking everything on someone who had hurt her so much. Or it was her chance to finally say good-bye. She felt her heart rip in two as she knew she would follow her head and not her heart. "No, Lex, there isn't."

Pain flashed in Lex's eyes. "You know I might actually believe that if I didn't see this." She reached over and cupped Aspen's cheek in the palm of her hand and wiped a single tear away with her thumb. Her gaze held Aspen. "Tell me you don't love me."

Aspen leaned into the caress, wishing she could make her body understand what her head was saying. The heat radiated between them, and she felt her body tremble against Lex. Four words—that was all she needed to say. Four words that would free her, and she couldn't make her mouth say them. They screamed at her from inside her head, and she prayed Lex would hear them. The battle that waged between her heart and her mind sent shivers down her spine. The tears she once held at bay were slowly cascading down her cheeks and as Lex gently wiped each one away, Aspen felt her heart shatter.

Lex could see the struggle in Aspen's eyes. It broke her heart. Had Lex been strong enough, the last five years never would have happened. Tonight would have been like every other Thanksgiving they had shared, and they would have already been in bed showing each other how grateful they were. However, fear and failure made her run. Now, five years later, she didn't want to run anymore. She wanted to stay and face life with Aspen beside her. She just needed to break through to Aspen's heart and show her. "I'm sorry."

Before Aspen could even register the whispered apology, Lex narrowed the distance between them. Aspen felt Lex's soft lips against hers, and she melted. Hours, days, years disappeared until the only time that mattered was this moment. Aspen's strength left her body, and she gave herself to Lex. She opened herself, and Lex's tongue slid between her lips and brushed against hers, sending shockwaves down her body. She felt the warmth of Lex's palm caress her cheek softly and the rightness of the moment singed her sensitive skin.

Lex felt Aspen lean into her kiss, and she slid her palm around the back of her neck and pulled her even closer, her tongue exploring every inch of her sweet mouth. All the memories came pouring into her head, waves of history flooding her senses. This was what felt right to her, felt like her home. All the years away from Aspen had only sharpened her need until she was acutely aware that there would be no other place in the world except for beside Aspen. Giving herself to the kiss, she poured everything she was feeling into their union and hoped that Aspen could feel what Lex's body was telling her.

Aspen shuddered against Lex, the first of many as they shared what seemed to be an infinite kiss. Lips melded together in sweet passion, tongues dancing in perfect rhythm as their bodies remembered the rightness of their mate. Aspen's body searched for Lex's, and her hands traced down the ripples in her arm, slowly memorizing the soft planes in her forearm. She felt her breasts brush against Lex's, and a low moan built deep inside her. Aspen's body was on fire, an ache so acute that she couldn't breathe from the pain of it. She felt her chest tighten and her stomach clench with a longing that was deeper than any she had ever felt before. The torment broke through the haze, and she pulled away guiltily.

Lex felt the cool air hit her lips, and she missed Aspen immediately. She didn't need to see the agony in her eyes to know she had pushed too hard. Tears welled in Aspen's eyes and Lex's reached to wipe them away.

"No." Aspen shook her head and clenched her fists. This wasn't what she wanted, at least not the way Lex was giving it to her. Her feelings were leftover from years of wanting, and she couldn't allow them to reign free. She pulled away from Lex like a wounded animal looking for safety. She saw Lex start towards her, and she moved further away. "No, please don't." She scrambled to her feet, pausing when she saw the hurt in Lex's eyes. A part of her wanted to give in and fill the aching void in her soul, but the part of her that had ached all those years knew it would be temporary and walking away a second time would hurt her more than she could take. She pushed Lex's hand aside. "Don't touch me…please. Just let me go."

Lex opened her mouth to reply. She could see fear making Aspen's body tremble, and she knew that she had caused it. Tonight, five years ago—it didn't matter; Lex had taken everything they had shared and tossed it aside. Aspen didn't owe her anything, and here she was, sharing her life so that Lex could divorce her and move on. Nevertheless, here was Lex still taking everything and giving her nothing in return. The selfishness of it hit her squarely in the gut, and she shuddered with the weight of it. Suddenly, she understood the gravity of her actions. "I…I'm so sorry, A. I didn't know. I didn't mean to hurt you."

Aspen watched the emotions play across Lex's face, and she knew that Lex had finally realized what had made her leave and what made her take something that wasn't hers. She couldn't deal with it though. She had spent the last five years making a mess of her own life, and she didn't need the anguish of trying to figure someone else out, especially someone that had hurt her so bad. The hurt of abandoning Lex made her heart ache, but this was her time to heal. She had started on this journey to figure out how to let go and holding onto a past that had shattered her in pieces wasn't going to help. Aspen had to look to her future; she had to let herself live. Seeing the look on Lex's face made her realize that this time, she needed to be the one to say good-bye. That was the only way she was going to move forward. She slid back down to her knees and cupped Lex's face. She smiled wearily. "I have to let you go, Lex. I can't keep holding onto yesterday. The images, the feelings, those are the things that are etched into my soul and will never go away. I will always love you, but I won't let myself be with you again. It hurts too much."

Lex's lips trembled softly. She let out a deep breath. As much as she wanted to fight Aspen, she knew she was right. They would always love each other, that much was a given, but too much had happened between them to go back. "I know you're right, even if my heart tells me it's crazy to try to live without you." Even as she said the words, she felt her heart split in two and knock the wind out of her. She couldn't describe the sheer agony she felt. Tired and broken, she smiled through her tears. "I won't ever love anyone like I loved you."

"I know." Aspen whispered softly. "Love her better than me."

Lex winced. "I don't know if I can."

"Yes, you can." Aspen put her hand over Lex's heart. "You have the capacity for great love. You just have to put her first. Love her more than you fear yourself. That was always our problem. I realize that now. You were too afraid to give me all of you. Don't make the same mistake twice. Don't be afraid to love, Lex. All the great loves hurt; that's how you know it's real."

"But she doesn't make me hurt like you do." Lex couldn't explain the feeling she was having. Never good with words, she struggled to find the ones she needed right now. She put her hand over Aspen's and clasped it to her chest. "No one does. Everything inside me tells me this is right. I can be what you need."

Aspen shook her head. "Lex, this isn't what I need anymore. Being here with you has made me realize that I stopped living all those years ago. Even up until a few months ago, I would have let you back in, but I can't now. I'll always cherish what we had. You are such a special woman. However, I have to make my own life now, find my own identity. I can't let myself be defined by what we were. I have to let go. I am letting you go."

Lex heard the finality in her tone, and she let out a sigh. She knew there was no more she could say or do to change Aspen's mind. "I don't think you will ever know how sorry I really am."

"Oh honey, I know." Aspen smiled. "Promise me that you won't give up on yourself again."

"I won't." Lex said wearily. "So this is really good-bye."

"Yes." Aspen nodded. "This is really good-bye. Or maybe it's a hello to something better. Either way, what we had was yesterday." She pulled her hand away and cupped her palms against Lex's cheeks. She wasn't fighting the tears anymore; she let them stream down her face. She pulled Lex to her and captured her mouth against hers. It was a sweet and gentle kiss, the hunger from earlier all but gone. This was their good-bye kiss.

Lex felt Aspen's lips tremble against hers, and she crumbled a little more. She could feel the good-bye in her kiss, and it broke her heart. She moved against Aspen, all the love she felt poured into this bittersweet kiss. When Aspen broke the caress and pulled away, Lex could see something new in her eyes. "I love you, Aspen."

Aspen smiled a sad smile, her eyes a mix of sorrow and determination. "I love you always." She pulled away and stood up in front of Lex, her hand caressing her cheek one final time. "Goodnight, Lex."

Lex watched her walk away, her fingers brushing her still swollen lips. However she thought tonight was going to go was the complete opposite of where she sat now, her broken heart aching in her chest. She wasn't sure how she would face the next couple of months seeing Aspen all the time, aching for her and not being able to have her. If she thought walking away before hurt, nothing could have prepared her for the anguish she was feeling now. Somehow, she had to figure out how to get to tomorrow and how to move past the tiny world she had carved out for them a second time. Easing back against the couch, she stared into the dying embers of the fire and let herself cry. With every tear, she bid farewell to everything that was and opened up a place for everything that could be and by the time exhaustion took her body captive, she was ready for tomorrow. She just had to figure out a way to convince Aspen that their tomorrow was meant to be shared together.

Chapter 14

Aspen grabbed Ginny's bags from the trunk and shut it with a resounding thud. She smiled at the glowing tan on her aunt's face. "So you had a good time?"

Ginny's smile widened. "We did." They were gone two weeks, opting for a longer cruise. "I've developed quite a fondness for fruity drinks with little umbrellas in them."

Aspen chuckled heartily. "Oh lord, my aunt is turning into a lush." She followed Ginny up the steps to the porch and waited while she unlocked the door. "How was Mom?"

"Oh, you know your mom." Ginny smiled cryptically. "She's her normal chipper self as always. Surprisingly enough, we actually got along great. Probably, the first time ever she's behaved herself."

Aspen's eyebrow cocked in disbelief. "My mother behaved?" Shaking her head, she carried the bags inside and deposited them in the kitchen. "I've never known Susan Lane to behave and it's worse the older she's gotten."

"I think she's just lonely and really misses your dad."

"What?" Aspen asked incredulously. "She said that?"

"Not in so many words." Ginny turned to fill a teapot and put it on the stove to heat before taking off her scarf and settling into a nearby chair with a sigh. "You know she never talks about anything."

"Oh boy, do I know." Aspen scoffed loudly. "She's the queen of keeping things to herself."

"From what I gathered, she is tired and lonely. I don't think she wants to keep the farm by herself anymore. It's just too much, and the winters in Maine are a lot worse on her old bones than they used to be."

The comment made Aspen pause. "You suppose she is thinking about selling?"

"I know she is." Ginny added quickly then pushed herself out of her chair with a slow groan. "I think I concur." Catching Aspen's look of shock, Ginny patted her arm softly, trying to console her. "We aren't young anymore and with Neal and your daddy gone, it's so much to keep the farms running."

"So you're going to sell too?" Aspen leaned back in her chair, the news rendering her speechless for several seconds. She hadn't given much thought to the fact that her mother and her aunt were getting older, and maybe they didn't want all that responsibility anymore. Her mother didn't farm, only rented the land out to local farmers. Nevertheless, she was in her sixties and probably ready to slow down.

Ginny poured hot water over a bag of Chamomile tea and handed the cup to Aspen. "I've been thinking about it. I know how much you love this place, honey, but it's just too much. The girls, not so much. I love taking care of the horses. It's the land and the house and the barns. It's a lot for me to try to keep up. Old man Riley's been asking about buying my acreage for a couple of years now. His son wants to expand their farm, and this would be a good start."

"Wow." Aspen dunked her tea bag, her mind reeling from the announcement. She had expected tales of their cruise together and instead her aunt was telling her that both she and her mom wanted to get rid of their farms. To say she was shocked was an understatement; bowled over would be a better statement. "But you love the ranch. This was yours and Neal's dream."

"It was our dream. It was different when he was alive. Your uncle took care of everything. Now that he's gone, I can't do it myself anymore."

"We can hire some people." Aspen offered. "You could rent the land out like Mom and pay someone to take care of the girls." She just couldn't accept the idea of both homes she had grown up in disappearing overnight. There was so much history here, and she didn't want to let go of it. "What about the girls? Will you sell them too?" Aspen's voice trembled slightly. She was the reason her aunt had kept the horses in the first place. She knew it was selfish to hold her aunt to this place just for her, but it was one of the last places that she had felt safe and sheltered. It was fear that kept her from letting go.

Ginny nodded. "I'm afraid so. Mr. Riley would take them too." She caught the look of fear that passed over Aspen's features. "It's okay, honey. His son Jonathon has helped me a couple of times over the past few years. He's good with them. He will take good care of them. I bet he'd even let you come by and see them anytime you want."

"It just wouldn't be the same. I know I'm being selfish." Aspen reached over and squeezed her aunt's hand, and her eyes held her gaze, looking for answers in her eyes. "You're sure about this?"

"I am." Ginny smiled as tears formed in her eyes. "It will be hard to let go, but I need to. I'm not getting any younger and lord knows I can't do this forever. Your uncle passed before he could slow down and rest. I don't want that for myself."

"I understand." Aspen sipped her tea as pictures of her life spun through her mind. "I guess you and Mom have a plan?"

Ginny chuckled softly. "Of course we do, honey. You know us too well." She shook her head and looked at the ceiling. "We are thinking about getting a place together...in Florida."

146

"You and Mom?" Aspen stared at her in disbelief, her incredulous tone raising several octaves. "Move in together? Where in Florida and why so far away?"

"As much as that shocks you, yes." Ginny leaned back in her chair and sighed. "It's about time your mom and I started getting along. We were thinking Melbourne. There are some really nice retirement villages down there. We're both ready to relax and at least that will give me space to hide when I get fed up with your mom. I can tell you I haven't felt as good as I did the two weeks in the sun in a long time. The warmth was good for these old bones."

Aspen snorted. "Old bones, ha! I hope I am in as good a shape as you in thirty years."

"Thank you, sweetie. I wish I felt as young as you think I am."

"So your minds are made up? There's no talking you out of it?" Aspen searched her aunt's gaze even though she knew her answer already.

Ginny nodded. "Your mom and I had a lot of time to talk, and it's the first thing we have agreed on in years."

"You know I can honestly say this is the last time I'm letting you girls go anywhere together. You come back with all these harebrained ideas." Aspen started laughing. "I just don't know what to do with you."

"Well for starters, when you come to visit, you can take two old ladies shopping. Goodness knows; we have no fashion sense at all, and we will need someone young to carry all those bags." Ginny's eyes twinkled mischievously.

Aspen looked around, her eyes memorizing nooks and crannies she already knew by heart. "I'll miss this place."

"Me too." Ginny set her empty cup on the table. "We shared a lot of memories here. It will be hard not coming down those steps every morning and watching the sun coming up over the hills."

Aspen watched a single tear roll down her aunt's face, and she squeezed her hand again. She was fighting tears herself, but knew she needed to help her aunt through the difficult transition of saying good-bye to her life here so she could start making new memories. "I won't miss the cold floors."

Ginny half—cried and half—laughed. "Bless you, honey. You are right about that."

"And the stairs always creaked." Aspen actually liked the old creak in the stairs. When she had stayed here as a child, she had always known when her aunt was up and making breakfast. She never slept with her door closed in case she missed the sound of the old house as her aunt made her way to the kitchen.

"I won't even know what to do with myself not snowed in for half the winter."

"I'm just trying to picture you and Mom holding a daiquiri in one hand and a shuffleboard paddle in the other."

Ginny guffawed loudly. "Humph. I'm not that old yet." Wiping her face, she stood up, went to the window over the sink and stared at the ranch. "I'm going to call Mr. Riley today and let him know in the spring; he can have her."

Spring seemed so soon to Aspen, and she sucked in a breath. By then, she would leave all of this behind for the last time. Sure, she could visit, but it wouldn't be the same. She knew saying good-bye was going to be nearly impossible. Letting go of the girls might just push her over the edge. Joining her aunt, she put her head on her shoulder exactly like she had years before. "I guess I should call Mom and find out her timeline."

"She is going to sell sooner than later." Ginny said quietly. "I'm going to drive out for a few weeks and help her get everything together."

Aspen swallowed the lump in her throat. It was all happening so fast. Everything in her world was being taken away. She could be rational and accept that what her aunt and mother were doing was the best idea for them all, but her heart hurt just thinking about it. She didn't want to let go.

This was her life. The ranch, the farm in Maine, all of it made up a big chunk of who she was. Forget that the woman that made up the rest was all but gone. It was almost too much to stomach. She needed to wrap her head around it. "I guess I should pack up the rest of my stuff at the farm."

Ginny wrapped an arm around her and hugged her tightly. "You can keep it here for now."

For now? That could be as little as three months. Aspen had avoided finding her own place after she moved back from New York. She had struggled there for several years, barely getting by on the few pieces she sold and random part—time jobs. She knew she needed to find her own place, but at the time, she had been in no condition to be alone. Fortunately, her mother had plenty of room and had tolerated her company. As much as she didn't want to move out for good, Aspen knew she needed to. How else would she be able to keep moving forward if she kept taking steps backward?

Ginny saw her niece struggling, and she leaned over and captured her in a motherly hug. "Honey, you will be fine. I know it seems like everything is getting pulled out from underneath you right now, but this might just be the push you need to get you back out in the world."

Aspen snorted loudly. "Yeah, I know. It just feels shitty right now. I know I can't have you and Mom as crutches forever. It was just so easy to pretend I was fine when I could hide out from the world. This whole thing with Lex has opened up wounds that I am having trouble healing."

Ginny sat back down. "How was Thanksgiving?"

Aspen shrugged. "Fine, I guess. It was sad in a way. I loved seeing her family, but it was a huge reminder of what we used to have. It did help me make some decisions." Aspen's mind played the last week's events in her head. She'd had plenty of time to reflect on her decision after Lex's admission. There were moments she wondered if she made the right choice of if she should have followed the strong tug in her heart. Lex made it easy though. The morning after their kiss she had met Aspen with nothing but a jovial smile and no word of what had transpired before. Simply thanked her for breakfast and left on her next road trip. Either she had realized that Aspen was right, or she had gotten really good at hiding her true feelings. Aspen hoped it was the former.

"Oh that's good, honey." Ginny's brow furrowed with concern. The emotions that had played across her niece's face had ranged from near tears to a wistful smile. "Unless they weren't good decisions."

"They were." Aspen chuckled. "Lex...she..." Aspen's voice trembled and she looked away from her aunt, collecting her thoughts.

"Shhh, honey, it's okay." Ginny rubbed circles around Aspen's back, trying to soothe her as she had when Aspen was young. Her heart broke for her niece. She could see she was caught between a love she couldn't let go of and a life she needed to live. "We can talk about this later."

Aspen shook her head and swiped the back of her hand over her nose. "I need to say this now and shut the door behind me." Taking the Kleenex her aunt offered, she swiped at her eyes. "Basically, Lex told me she wanted to give us another try."

"How do you feel about that?" Ginny could see from the tears that kept threatening to fall that whatever decision she had made had hurt her anew.

Aspen shrugged. "How could I feel? Up until a few months ago, I would have given anything to hear Lex say those words."

"But now?" Ginny watched Aspen fiddle with the edges of the Kleenex, deeply affected by just having a conversation on the subject.

"Now I have to think of me." Aspen's chin lifted with renewed pride, something Ginny hadn't seen in years. "I can't keep pouring salt over an open wound. I'll never heal that way. Right now, the most important thing for me is to finally think about myself. Somewhere out there is a life I've

150

hidden from, and it's time for me to let myself live it. For the first time in years, I realize that I have been frozen by fear, and I can't let it cripple me anymore. You and Mom selling is just another sign that it's time to let go. I wasn't sure how this six months with Lex would go. I even regretted saying yes to the whole thing, but now I'm glad I did."

"Oh honey, that's wonderful to hear." Ginny matched her niece's positive tone. If anything, she knew she needed to support whatever decision that Aspen made. "Maybe, just maybe, you will find someone to make you forget about Lex."

"No." Aspen shook her head. "I don't want to forget about her. I will always love Lex. There will always be a part of me that stays with her. Forgetting isn't going to make me whole again. What I had with her made me who I am today and I wouldn't change that for the world. Would I go back and change the outcome? Maybe. I don't know. I can't think that way anymore, always asking myself what if. The one thing this has taught me is that I can't stop living no matter what happens. If I do find love again, there's nothing that guarantees it will forever. I know that there's a chance that I'll find it and lose it, but at least now I will let myself be open to it."

Ginny laughed quietly. "What did Lex's mom put in that turkey? I'm not sure what to do with this new you."

Aspen's eyes danced mischievously. "Is there anything that can be done with me?"

"Most certainly not!" Ginny exclaimed. "You wouldn't be my niece if there was. I must say this new outlook suits you. I haven't seen you this alive in a long time."

"Hmm." Aspen sighed thoughtfully. "The thing I realized was that I miss the old me. I'm tired of looking in the mirror every morning and asking myself if I'm okay to face the day. That's no way to be. The only downside is my art has suffered tremendously."

The comment made Ginny snort loudly. "Leave it to you to think of that at a time like this."

Aspen smiled guiltily. "I have to. I have my first real show in four months."

"Honey, don't you fret. I've seen the pieces you have picked out for the show. No one can mistake your talent."

"That's just half of what I'll need. I have to come up with twelve more pieces before March." Aspen looked around the kitchen. "I'm gonna miss this place. The studio here has always been my favorite. It's too bad I..." Her voice trailed off as a thought started to form in her head.

"It's too bad what?" Ginny saw the gears turning in her niece's head, and she couldn't guess where her head had gone.

"I just had the craziest idea." Aspen stood up and paced the kitchen. "What if...what if I bought this place?" She saw the shocked look on her aunt's face. "Not the land, Mr. Riley can have that. Just the house and the barns, and of course the girls."

"Aspen, you can't be serious." Ginny watched her niece's face harden with determination.

"Yes, I am serious. And why not?" Aspen asked stubbornly. "This is my second home. Certainly, they don't need the barns, and even if they do, that's not a problem. As long as I can keep the house and the girls can stay."

Ginny shook her head. "I'm not going to sell this place to you. I'll give it to you."

"No." Aspen exclaimed defiantly. "I will buy it from you. I need to do this for myself."

"I can see there is no talking you out of it."

"No, there isn't." Even as she said it, Aspen was doing the calculations in her head. It would certainly be cheaper than her rent in New York, and she had managed to make that...barely. Between the pieces that she sold monthly and getting a job in Burlington, she should be able to afford the place. She thought she had a good idea of what her aunt would sell it for. "Besides, that will give you and mom a place to come back to when it gets too hot in Florida."

"It would have to get pretty warm down there to get your mom back up here. She actually said that she may park her butt on a chair and never move again, the heat felt so good on her bones. You might have to come visit us."

"Well that's a given." Aspen's smile widened. "So, we are really doing this?"

Ginny pulled her into a hug. "We are really doing this."

Aspen folded herself into the hug. She had always felt secure in her aunt's arms, sometimes more so than her own mother. Ginny saw her through the darkest of her days with tremendous strength. Aspen felt a renewed sense of life coursing through her veins. For the first time in years, she actually felt alive. It was a feeling she welcomed whole-heartedly. She knew that when she woke up tomorrow and every day after that, she was going to welcome the new day. She was done with letting her yesterdays hold her back. She was going to live for today. Most importantly, she was going to live, and the thought made her happy for the first time, in as long as she could remember.

Chapter 15

Aspen pulled the last box out of her closet and stacked it on the floor next to a growing pile of items she was going to donate. She didn't have much left at her mom's house besides a few odds and ends, and nothing that she wanted to keep. It was mostly clothes and other items that she had accumulated throughout her school years. A couple of glances in old yearbooks convinced her that she was certainly glad she had outgrown her obsession with big hair. There were several boxes from her and Lex's place. She had packed them hastily and hadn't looked at them since.

Flopping down on the bed with a sigh, Aspen pulled a box marked living room out and pulled the strip of tape off the top. Her hands stilled on the box flaps and she willed her breathing to return to a normal pace. She wasn't sure what she would find, but knew it would be poignant reminders of her and Lex. "God, Aspen, just breathe. It's stuff."

Two more deep breaths and she pulled the lid open and flinched, half-expecting something to jump out and attack her. When it didn't, she stilled visibly. She knew this was just another step in moving forward. She knew there would be no giant leaps; instead, she was content with each baby step she took. Her mother had been surprised at first when she explained her plan to buy the ranch. When she explained her reasons, her mother had reluctantly agreed that perhaps it was the best thing for Aspen.

Shaking her head, she pulled the packing material out of the box and set it on the bed next to her. The wooden frame caught her attention, and a quick glance told her this was the box containing pictures from the living room. She pulled the first frame out and flipped it over slowly. It was a picture of her and Lex on their wedding day. They were married at the ranch. All their family and closest friends witnessed the blissful union. Only a handful had been around to witness the end.

Aspen's eyes roved over the picture and the corners of her mouth curved into a sad smile. She wore a simple white gown. Lex had worn a black vest with a silk button-down and tuxedo pants. The photographer had taken most of the pictures with the hills behind them, but this picture she had captured in a moment that neither one of them were paying attention. Aspen was resting on the steps of the porch, and Lex had leaned over the railing and kissed Aspen on her temple. Aspen could only see Lex's profile, but the smile on her own face told the story of how happy they had once been.

She traced her finger over Lex's jaw line and she felt a shiver run down her spine. When they were together, she had spent hours watching Lex. Her face was perfection in Aspen's mind. Her golden skin and chiseled features always took Aspen's breath away. Even now, she couldn't look at Lex without an aching tug in her heart. Aspen studied the picture for several more seconds before setting it aside with a sigh of finality.

The next few pictures were ones of her. A small bouquet complimented her dress with tasteful simplicity. Her eyes were what pulled her to each picture. Her blue eyes shone more then. She looked happier than she could remember. Now when she looked in the mirror, her sad eyes taunted her at every glance. Not much longer, Aspen thought. She knew she wanted to be happy again and for the first time in a long time, Aspen knew she would let herself be.

She pulled the next picture out and when she flipped it over, her body froze. It was one of her drawings, one she had done before they were married. A simple sketch of Lex's profile, her hair loose from its normal ponytail, framing her face in one of Aspen's favorite moments. They had just made love, and Lex had collapsed against the couch; her fingers poised at her mouth, memorizing the feeling of her tingling and swollen lips. Aspen had studied her, and her stomach fluttered as she remembered the electricity she felt when Lex had innocently tasted the after-effects of what she had done to Aspen.

In and of itself, the drawing evoked raw emotion, but combined with the memory that had come rushing back into Aspen's head, and she was gasping for air. Warmth spread through her veins, and a welcome tingling teased at her extremities. She brushed her fingers over her lips, and she could almost feel Lex's lips against hers. She took several deep breaths and stared at the ceiling, praying that eventually her mind and body would forget what it felt like to be touched by heaven. It was almost more than she could take.

Aspen wasn't sure how long she sat there waiting for the world to right itself again. She only knew that when her breathing returned to normal, she had decided this would be the centerpiece of her showing at the gallery. If any piece would evoke the emotions that she was trying to encompass, this was the one. She took another long look before she set it down beside her. She started putting the pictures back in the box, not able to endure revisiting her past anymore. She taped it securely and pushed it next to the other boxes. She eased off the bed and stretched her arms over her head with a low moan.

"Did you get it all packed up?" Susan's head popped around the corner. She eyed the stack of boxes and laughed. "Never knew someone that held on to everything. You're so sentimental like your father."

Aspen took the cup of tea she held out and sipped it gratefully. She let her gaze fall on the stack of personal effects she had accumulated in her thirty plus years and smiled ruefully. "Considering all the stuff I've come across, this is a small pile in comparison. Besides, most of these are going to the shelter. It's mostly old clothes and such." She nudged a box with her toe. "This is the only one that is coming with me. I've got to get a truck and pick up the rest of my stuff from storage. Aunt Ginny is leaving most of the furniture at the ranch, so I don't really need much."

Susan rested her hand on her daughter's and forced her to look her in the eye. "Are you sure this is what you want, honey?"

Aspen nodded, but didn't say anything right away. After several silent moments, she exhaled softly and smiled. "Yes, this is good for me. Aside from Lex being there, this is the first time in years I actually feel hopeful. I need something to focus on. The ranch and the girls are perfect for me."

"Even with all the memories?"

Her mother meant the wedding, in particular, but there were hundreds of other still shots that were nestled in the corner of her mind. Aspen knew she needed that connection to her past in order to move towards her future. "Especially with all the memories. Besides, the studio is perfect for me." She flipped her hand over and squeezed her mom's reassuringly. "This is good for me, Mom. Don't worry so much."

"I'm trying not to." Susan confessed. "I know you were much closer to your father, but I want you to know, I love you very much. I worry about you being so far away. What if it gets to be too much?"

"Mom, stop." Aspen pleaded with mock exasperation. "I'm thirty-three years old. I think I can take care of myself. And if I can't, I'm adult enough to know when to pack it in."

Susan saw the determination in her daughter's eyes and knew that the one thing she had passed along was her stubborn will, and once she dug her heels in, there was no need trying to change her mind. She put her hands on her knees and pushed herself up, her knees popping loudly. "It will feel good to get these old bones out of the cold." She cupped her daughter's cheek and smiled. "I know you will be fine. But if you ever need your mom, your aunt and I will have plenty of room."

"Thanks, Mom." Aspen watched her mother's retreating form, and she smiled to herself. Her mother had shown more emotion in those few seconds than she had in all the time Aspen had been alive. Stoic to a fault in matters of the heart, Susan was a rock, even when her father passed. However, today, Aspen had seen a side that touched her deeply and in that moment, she loved her mother even more.

Aspen wasn't sure how long she sat watching the door before a loud ring made her jump. She pulled her phone out and checked the caller ID. "Lex."

"Hey."

Lex's voice seemed oddly flat and Aspen fought the urge to pry. It wasn't her business anymore what Lex's mood was and what had made her melancholy. "What's up?"

"I was just checking to see what your schedule was. I'm leaving the apartment, and I wanted to see if I should pick up stuff for dinner."

"Mmm." Aspen glanced at her watched and mentally calculated the time it would take to pack the few remaining boxes and make the trip back to the ranch. She figured on at least three hours, which would put her there at roughly the same time as Lex. "Sure. Why don't you pick up stuff for pasta puttanesca. I feel like Italian tonight."

Lex smiled into the phone. She had been gone two weeks this trip and her mouth watered at the thought of Aspen's home cooking. "Want me to grab a bottle of Ruffino Chianti?"

Aspen chuckled out loud. The name alone made her smile. It was the bottle of cheaper wine they had indulged in at the beginning of their relationship when they could barely afford to eat. Years later, a ten dollar bottle of wine seemed so childish. For some reason, she thought it sounded perfect. Something so simple seemed to calm her more than she had been in years. "Sure, that sounds perfect."

"'Kay." Lex paused then took a deep breath and pushed forward. "I can't wait to see you."

"Lex." Aspen tried to ignore the flutter in her stomach at Lex's admission. She knew that there would always be something between them no matter how much time passed. She just didn't need a constant reminder. "You only missed my cooking."

Lex took Aspen's hint and agreed. "I have been starving the last two weeks."

"Then we had better get you fed." Aspen stood up and stretched, holding the phone away from her mouth when she yawned. "I guess I will see you around six."

"Yeah." Lex sighed. "Can we talk tonight?"

"Lex, we always talk."

"I mean about important stuff."

"Oh." Aspen had hoped to avoid any discussion about their kiss. After not mentioning it for the last few weeks, she figured Lex had accepted that she was moving on. "I'm kind of tired. I was hoping to eat and then go to bed early."

"I see." Lex's voice plummeted. She wasn't sure what she expected Aspen to say. There were so many thoughts running through her mind, and she needed to voice them before it was too late. She wasn't sure why she couldn't just walk away; give Aspen the peace she asked for. Maybe because in the five months, they had been living together, she had fallen more in love with her than she was the first time, if that was possible. It was painfully apparent that Aspen wasn't going to make this easy on her. "Then I guess I'll see you tonight."

Aspen opened her mouth to object then shut it quickly. They did need to talk tonight. She hadn't told Lex about the ranch yet and for some reason, she felt the need to share this piece of information with her. "I'm sorry. We can talk over dinner. I have something to tell you too."

Lex exhaled softly. She felt a small weight lifted off her shoulders. She wasn't sure what outcome she wanted, but at least she would get to tell Aspen her news. "Alright then, I'll see you in a couple of hours. And, A?"

"Yes."

"Thank you." Lex felt the corners of her mouth curl into a smile.

"Sure." Aspen grabbed the tape and pulled a strip over the top of the last box. The sound of packing tape echoed through the phone, and she heard Lex's chuckle. "Sorry, last one."

"It's okay; I'm gonna stop and get gas anyway. I'll see you later." Lex heard Aspen's good-bye and ended the call. She stared at the phone in her open palm as if it were Aspen's face, a myriad of emotions storming through her mind. Tonight was her *do or die* moment. Tonight, she would lay her heart on the line and pray that Aspen would give her another chance.

Chapter 16

Aspen chopped garlic and slid it into a pan of hot olive oil, the sizzle sending an immediate aroma of pungent spiciness into the air. "How was your trip?"

Lex sat at the island, spinning her glass between her hands and watching Aspen make dinner. "Good. Long, but good." She licked her lips nervously. "How was everything here?"

Aspen spun around and smiled cryptically. "Good. That's part of what I have to tell you." She grabbed a can opener and opened a can of diced tomatoes while she spoke. "Mom and Aunt Ginny are moving."

"What?" Lex's voice rose incredulously. She sat in stunned silence, trying to process the news. "When? I mean, well, I'm not sure what I mean. I'm shocked."

Aspen watched Lex's face contort comically, and she laughed. "I was too." She turned to fill a pot with water and put it on to boil. "I had no idea they were even thinking about leaving."

Lex watched as Aspen added the tomatoes, capers, anchovies, Kalamata olives and a dash of oregano and crushed red pepper to the pan and gave the mixture a quick stir. "So, how did this all transpire?"

"I wasn't there for the conversation. I guess they decided on the cruise." Aspen added pasta to the boiling water and added a dash of salt. She dusted her hands off on her apron. "Ginny said that she felt better on the boat than she had in years. I guess the cold is really getting to her arthritis. She and Mom decided to sell and move to Florida."

"But they don't even get along." Lex was still wide-eyed.

"I know, right." Aspen chuckled. "Ginny said it's a retirement village with enough space that she can get away from Mom anytime she feels like strangling her." Aspen gave the sauce a quick stir, added a pinch of salt then pulled a strainer out of the cabinet. "Mom already put her place on the market. She should sell pretty quickly."

"So they are pretty serious?"

Aspen shrugged. "So it would seem. They are planning to move down in the spring."

"Spring?" Lex shook her head. She was having a hard time wrapping her head around Aspen's news. Although, she had been gone for over five years, the ranch felt like a second home. They had spent so much time here as a couple, even married here. Letting it go seemed like letting a huge part of her life go. Everything she held dear was disappearing. Conveniently, she forgot the part where she walked away, turning her back on everyone and everything behind her.

Aspen watched Lex's face darken, and she knew exactly where her mind had gone. The ranch was the last piece of their lives together and selling it would close the door on everything they had known. "Lex, it's okay."

"No, it's not. Everything about this place feels right, and if it goes away, it's almost like all the memories go away with it." Lex knew that wasn't the case, but it felt like it. "What happens when this is gone?"

Aspen saw the heartbreak in her eyes and knew Lex didn't mean the ranch itself, but what it represented. "I meant it's going to be okay. I'm buying the ranch."

The look on Lex's face was priceless and had it not been so emotionally overwrought; Aspen might have laughed. "I couldn't let it go either. Ginny is still selling the land, but the house and the barns are mine."

Lex visibly brightened, the initial shock of everything finally wearing off. "You are?"

"Yes." Aspen handed Lex a wine opener and nodded at the bottle. She poured the pasta into the strainer, gave it a couple quick shakes to get rid of the water and added it to the tomato sauce.

Lex opened the bottle and poured two glasses. "Can you afford it?" After college, she had always had a pretty decent income, content to let Aspen follow her dream of being an artist. Now, she worried that Aspen wouldn't be okay.

"Yes, Lex." Aspen cocked her head and shot Lex a wry smile. "I'll be fine." She grabbed the handle of the pan and tossed the pasta in the air, mixing it in the pan with a deft flick of her wrist. "Ready?"

"Yes." Lex moaned loudly. The aroma of the food was enough to make her mouth water, and her stomach growled in agreement.

"Then let's eat." Aspen filled two plates and sprinkled grated parmesan cheese over both. She handed Lex her plate. "Living room?"

"Sure." Lex grabbed her plate and wine glass and followed Aspen, surreptitiously admiring her tight bottom. It was all she could do not to moan out loud when her mind pictured cupping Aspen and pulling her close. "So you're really gonna do this, huh?"

Aspen licked sauce off her finger and nodded. "Yes, Ginny and I already drew up the paperwork. I'm working with a mortgage broker in town to get the loan. He said everything should be fine."

"And you're sure you will be okay?" Lex's brow furrowed with concern. She smiled ruefully when she saw Aspen glare. "I know, sorry. You're fine. It's none of my business anyway."

"No, it's not." Aspen chuckled, lightening the mood. "But since you are being so nosy, I will be fine. I've got enough in savings for the down payment, and I'm getting a part-time job at a gallery in Burlington. Between that and what I make on the pieces I sell, I will be okay."

"Okay." Lex stuffed an enormous bite into her mouth and moaned loudly. Her face broke into a huge grin. "Man, I haven't had this in so long. Damn, it's good."

Aspen lowered her face and blushed. "Thank you, it's nothing really."

Lex touched Aspen's arm softly, forcing her to meet her gaze. "It is something. Stop doubting how wonderful you are, okay?"

"I can't help it." Aspen's voice broke slightly, and Lex's heart sank. "You know how it is."

"I do." Lex couldn't hold Aspen's gaze any longer. She did this. She had taken a beautiful, confident woman and altered her so immeasurably that, five years later; she still believed she didn't deserve praise. "I'm so sorry, A. I fucked up royally. You're such an amazing woman. I wish I could make you see yourself the way I do."

"Oh, so I can see how easy it is to leave me." Aspen said acerbically. "No thank you."

"I didn't mean…"

"Don't worry about it." Aspen forced a smile that didn't even begin to mask her pain. She gestured at Lex's plate, still full of spaghetti. "Let's just eat and try to enjoy tonight, okay?"

Lex sensed Aspen shutting down and knew she had pushed too far. "Yeah, sure." She tried to eat, but the hunger that she had two minutes before had been replaced by a solid rock of guilt sitting in the pit of her stomach. After several more attempts, she set the plate down on the coffee table and grabbed her glass.

"Not hungry?" Aspen eyed the plate with feigned nonchalance. She knew very well that neither of them was hungry anymore. Her own stomach was an unsettled ball of nerves.

Lex shook her head. "It was good. I just can't eat right now."

"Me neither." Aspen set her plate down beside Lex's and sighed loudly. "I guess we are never going to get this right."

Lex's laughed nervously. "No, I suppose not." She twirled her glass in her hand, losing herself in the dancing light of the fire.

Aspen studied Lex's profile, soft amber light illuminating the angles of her face. "You wanted to tell me something?"

Lex turned at the question and tried to smile, but it wouldn't come. "Yes, but it can wait." Her nerves were raw, and she wasn't sure that this was the time to bring up her news. She had already managed to ruin what was an otherwise pleasant evening and one of the last ones they would be spending together…if things continued as they were now.

"Lex." Aspen put her hand on Lex's arm. "I'm sorry. We can still salvage this night. You can talk to me about anything."

"Even about Cass?" Lex asked quietly.

Aspen swallowed the lump in her throat. She knew she needed to be Lex's friend, at least for now, no matter how hard it was to hear about her shared life with another woman. After the divorce, they could go their separate ways. Aspen nodded her ascent. "Especially about Cass." She pulled her hand away, wrapping her arms around her knees and holding them to her body. She rested her chin on her interlocked arms and waited for the dark feeling she knew would come.

Lex could hear the tremor in her voice, and her heart clenched painfully. She wanted to gather Aspen into her arms and hold her until the hurt was gone, but she resisted the urge to touch her. "This past few days with Cass I tried to listen to what you said. You know about loving her better than you."

Aspen blinked back tears. "Yes?" She urged Lex to keep talking. She needed to hear this to heal.

Lex swallowed loudly, her mouth suddenly very dry. "I spent the weekend looking at our life together-our place, our friends, everything that we shared, and I came to one huge conclusion. I can't love her better than you." Lex paused, gauging Aspen's reaction and when she didn't say anything, Lex plowed forward. "I've spent the last three years fooling myself. I tried to give myself to Cass, but all these years I've held part of me back. The part of me that I gave to you so long ago."

Aspen squeezed her knees more tightly. She felt her self-control starting to unravel. The hopeful expression on Lex's face unsettled her even more. She opened her mouth to reply when Lex stopped her.

"I...it's not fair to Cass to stick around when I can't give her all of me. I ended it with her, Aspen. I want...no, I need to be with you." Lex's stomach clenched nervously. "I want another chance with you. I want to prove that I can love you like you deserve to be loved. I fucked up and I know I don't deserve your love, but I can't stop from wanting you. I can't stop loving you."

Aspen blinked back tears. She heard the words, felt them in her heart, but something held her back. Fear, anger, hurt, pride, maybe a little of all of those mixed together. Everything Lex was saying she had longed to hear...five years ago. Now, as much as she wanted to forget the time that had passed and let Lex in, she couldn't. The words sliced through her soul with so much pain that she trembled. She couldn't let herself be hurt again, no matter how much she still loved Lex.

"Please say something." Lex's eyes pleaded with her, desperation haunting her face. "Please say we have a chance. I know we can make it work this time."

Aspen shook her head. "I can't, Lex. I'm sorry. You need to move on."

"I can't." A single tear streamed down Lex's cheek, and she made no motion to wipe it away. "I can't let go of you. I can't move on. Aspen, please."

"Please?" Aspen asked sarcastically. "Please what? Please don't walk out on you. Please don't turn my back on you. Please don't rip your heart out. What, Lex? Tell me what you would like me to do to make you okay." The hurt was too much to control any longer, and it fueled her anger. "Why couldn't you say that to me five years ago? I know I said I was okay with this, but I'm not. I'm working to get past it and move on with my life, but for now, it fucking sucks. It's too late, Lex and I think it pisses me off that you would come back and say it to me now."

"I know I messed up; I will regret that to the day I die. But please don't punish us both. I love you, and I'm pretty sure you still love me." Lex's eyes pleaded with Aspen. "We can be something wonderful."

Aspen shook her head, her lips quivering with emotion. "We were something wonderful, Lex. We had something magical. Now, we have the memory of that." Aspen felt herself calming down. She couldn't stay angry at Lex, not when she had decided to move forward with her life. If she stayed upset, she was letting the past control her, and she refused to do that. She grabbed Lex's hands between hers and forced a smile. "I'm honored, Lex. Really, I am, but this isn't what I want anymore. I think there's something wonderful waiting for me, and if I keep looking back, I'll never see what's in front of me. Cass may not have been the one for you, but I'm not either…not anymore."

"I respectfully disagree." Lex interjected quietly. She almost wished that Aspen's anger would have stayed near the surface rather than the sudden calm that had overtaken her. At least then she had a chance. Now Lex knew she had made up her mind and no amount of talking was going to change that.

"It's okay." Aspen smiled. "We've been known to do that, disagree, I mean. But this is my life, and I have to live it my way. You know we got to a pretty good place, you and I and I'd like to go back there. We are good as friends, Lex. Let's just work on that."

Lex's chin dropped to her chest. *Friends.* It wasn't exactly where she saw this conversation going tonight; actually, it was pretty much the opposite of where she wanted it to go. She glanced up and saw the determined set of Aspen's jaw and knew she had lost. She nodded her ascent. "I would like that." Even as she said the words, she knew she was lying. She didn't want to be Aspen's friend. She wanted to be her lover again. It wasn't the do-over she wanted, but it was a start. A start she felt like she could work with and build on, and when the time came, she would try again to convince Aspen that they belonged together. For now, she would concede defeat. For now.

"Thank you." Aspen smiled sadly. She knew that even though she was moving on, there was a huge part of her that Lex would always have. They were destined to be in each other's lives, one way or another. Their hearts would be forever bound, like twin stars pulled from the sky, sent to separate corners of the world. That she knew with all her heart, and she accepted the truth of it with quiet resignation. She wouldn't fight that, but she would protect her heart from ever hurting that way again. She was silent several moments before she chuckled softly. "Guess I ruined dinner."

Lex shook her head and smiled. "Yeah, I guess you did. Nice going." She rubbed her stomach and groaned. "And damn, it tasted so good too."

Aspen leaned back against the couch and sighed. "Popcorn?"

"Sure." Lex leaned back against the couch and nudged Aspen's shoulder. "We're gonna be okay, aren't we?"

Aspen didn't respond immediately, playing their lives in her head before she answered. She knew they would be okay.

It was going to be a strange transition to a friendship between them, but it was a change they needed. "Yeah, we are going to be okay."

Chapter 17

"Yes, Mom. I will be fine." Aspen rolled her eyes. Ever since their decision to move, her mother called her almost daily to check on her. Initially, it was a welcome change. However, now, after forty-five minutes on the phone, for the third time that day, Aspen had had enough. "You guys enjoy the holiday in the warmth."

"Will Lex be there?" Susan asked quickly. "I don't want you to be alone."

"Mom, seriously, I'm fine." Aspen sighed loudly. "Besides, I'm not certain what Lex's plans are. I'm sure she will be spending Christmas with her family."

"I'm sure you could tag along." Susan made the suggestion with a hopeful tone. She felt somewhat guilty that they had picked now to check out retirement villages in Florida, but the idea of spending a week away from the frigid winter temperatures had been too enticing to pass up.

"I'm not tagging along to someone else's family Christmas. Can you please just accept that I'm an adult, and I will be okay? Please." Aspen's tone bordered on exasperation, and she hoped her mother didn't pick up on it. She meant what she said. She was actually completely fine with spending Christmas alone. It wasn't like they did much for the holiday anyway. Now that she was an adult, they didn't exchange presents. There wasn't anything they needed, and if they wanted something, they just bought it.

"Okay, okay." Susan laughed. "I won't push anymore. I know you will be fine. I'll leave you alone, but if you need us, just call."

"I will." Aspen smiled into the phone. "I love you, Mom."

"I love you too, honey. I'll call you on Christmas morning."

"Okay, bye." Aspen hit end on the phone and laid it on the counter. She shook her head, unable to keep the amusement off her face. Her mother could be so annoying sometimes, but it was nice to know that she cared as much as she did.

"You could come home with me for Christmas, you know."

"Huh?"

Lex sat down across from Aspen. "Mom wouldn't care."

"You heard that?" Aspen leaned down on her elbows and laced her fingers together. She rested her chin on her hands and smiled at Lex. "No offense to Maria, but one holiday was enough this year."

"You sure?" Lex searched Aspen's face for an answer. Finding none, she waited silently.

Aspen nodded and took the opportunity to study Lex. She was dressed in an old black turtleneck, and Aspen was momentarily thrown off by how beautiful she looked. It took her several seconds to respond and several more before her traitorous heart stopped pounding out of her chest. "Yes, I'm sure." Although, when she said it, it was followed by a brief moment of doubt. It would feel good to spend time with Lex. They only had a couple of weeks left before they could begin the divorce proceedings. Plus, the end of the football season meant playoffs and that meant Lex would be gone more than she was around. Aspen pursed her lips with renewed determination. This was her time, and she needed to spend it her way. "I'm going to finish a few more pieces. March is right around the corner, and I still need ten more pieces for the show."

"Okay." Lex accepted her no with disappointment. It had been a week since their talk and while she didn't expect Aspen to change her mind, she had at least hoped that there would be a sign that their friendship might develop into something else. Sadly, Aspen was nothing more than friendly, no hint of any romantic interest at all.

"Besides, someone needs to stay and look after the girls. Soon enough, they are going to be all my responsibility." Aspen fiddled with the edges of a kitchen towel before throwing it down in mock exasperation. "What? Why are you staring at me?"

Lex shrugged. "Because you're beautiful. Is it a crime to stare?"

Aspen blushed. "It is if I'm the object of your stares. Go make yourself busy. I'll get dinner started."

"Sure thing, boss." Lex smiled wryly then spun on her heel. She picked up her overnight bag and headed to her room. Before she rounded the corner, she looked over her shoulder and shouted back in the kitchen. "Remind me to tell you about the job offer I got."

"'Kay. Hey, how does grilled cheese and basil tomato soup sound?" Aspen had already started taking the beginnings of the meal out of the fridge when she thought to ask if it was okay. It shouldn't matter since she was the cook, she should have the pick of what they ate, but here she was still deferring to Lex on decisions as minor as dinner.

"What?" Lex came around the corner and plunked down on her customary stool.

"I was just asking if grilled cheese and soup were okay. But then I decided it was good." Aspen smirked at the look of disbelief on Lex's face. "Hey, when you start playing chef, you can make the menu."

"What?" Lex's mouth dropped in shock. "The steaks I made were killer."

"Oh yeah, they were wicked good." Aspen teased in her affected Maine accent. "But you still have no say in the kitchen."

"And this is where I'm supposed to be sad I don't get to cook all the time?" Lex waggled her eyebrows teasingly. "Sorry, you know I'm much better on this side of the kitchen than where you are. If it were up to me, we would have lived on bologna sandwiches, pop tarts, beef jerky and the occasional filet."

"Oh, lord." Aspen dropped a bit of basil in the tomato soup that was warming on the stove then started layering slices of Havarti on sourdough bread. "You'll just have to eat what I put in front of you."

"For now?" Lex asked quietly. "That's only three more weeks, unless…"

Aspen stilled, her body suddenly rigid. "Lex, we talked about this."

"I know." Lex's defeated tone spoke volumes. This wasn't the choice she would have made, but then Aspen wouldn't have chosen to leave all those years ago. "You just want friendship."

Aspen felt her chest tighten. She busied herself with dinner. She couldn't turn around and face the look in Lex's eyes. There was too much heartbreak between them and the sooner she moved on the better. But that thought didn't make it any easier to face the woman she had loved for so long. She flexed her hands, willing the tremors to stop. It would do her no good to fall apart right now. It took her several minutes to calm down and even longer for her breathing to return to normal. When she finally turned around, there was a glass of wine waiting for her on the island, and Lex had moved to the living room to give her some space.

There were no words between them as they ate. They merely stared at the fire, wrapped up in their own thoughts. Aspen wasn't sure how long they sat there before she broke the silence. "So tell me about this new job."

173

"Oh yeah." Lex smiled, and her brown eyes danced excitedly. "I'm coming off the road."

"Seriously?" Lex had freed her hair from her standard ponytail and it flowed around her face, framing her elegant cheek bones and accentuating her golden skin. Aspen felt her breath catch again, lost in her beauty. She knew she was staring, but she couldn't help it. If Lex noticed she had chosen to let it pass without a comment.

Lex could feel Aspen's gaze locked on her face, and it made her stomach jump excitedly. She knew at that moment; she could have reached over and captured Aspen's lips against hers. She could see the emotion boiling just below the surface and knew with only the slightest bit of insisting; she could make Aspen's hers again. But it wasn't fair to take what she was almost certain Aspen didn't know she was offering. Being so close and yet so infinitely far away hurt her deeply, and she dragged her eyes away, breaking the intimate moment they had shared.

Aspen felt the exact second that the connection was broken, thankful that Lex had the strength to turn away. At that moment, she didn't trust herself to do the right thing; at least what she hoped was the right thing. However confused she was before, this new gray space they shared was even more bewildering. She knew that Lex wanted her back but her fear of getting hurt was keeping them apart. It was sad really. The two of them had always been able to talk, but sharing their fears and working through them together, that was a different thing all together. Neither of them had been able to put those feelings on the table and each time it had driven them apart. She shook her head. It would do no good to beat this horse into the ground. She had made up her mind, and she was determined to stick to her choice, no matter how devastatingly handsome Lex looked with the firelight dancing on her face. She rubbed her palms on her jeans and laughed nervously. "What are you going to be doing now?"

Lex drained her wineglass and set it down on the coffee table. "I'm going to be a staff columnist for ESPN magazine."

Aspen didn't need to hear the excitement in her voice or see the twinkle in her eyes to know that this was a big deal. She could tell just from the energy brimming right below the surface. "That's awesome! I'm so proud of you. Are you okay not traveling all the time?"

"Yeah, I think so. Cass..." Lex stopped but Aspen's hand on her arm prompted her to continue. "Cass always wanted me off the road, but I never wanted it before this."

"Well she will be super excited." Aspen's voice trembled.

"A, we aren't together anymore." Lex said quietly, her eyes searching Aspen's for her response.

"I know." Aspen pulled away physically and emotionally. "I think you should try to get her back."

Lex didn't reply. She leaned back on the couch and crossed her hands over her stomach. She stared at the ceiling for several beats before she turned her head, and her gaze pierced into Aspen. "Tell me why."

"Well, she loves you for one." Aspen ticked off on her fingers. "Two, she puts up with you."

Lex's laughter filled the air. "And I'm so hard to put up with?"

"You can be." Aspen smiled wickedly. "You can be such a bear when you're about to blow your deadline."

"Mmm." Lex nodded in agreement. "That's true. What else?"

"You love her." Aspen offered quietly. This one was hard to say. It was strange to be talking about another woman, as though they were locker room buddies, but she needed to try to define the relationship.

"Do I?" Lex asked quietly.

"You did before this." For some reason, Aspen felt the need to push Lex away again. It felt safer to have her with

175

Cassidy then single. That was too dangerous in her mind. It opened way too many doors that she didn't want opened.

Lex shrugged. "Maybe, maybe not. Perhaps I was just looking for someone to fill the void."

"That's a horrible thing to say." Aspen laughed as she said it. "You wouldn't have asked her to marry you if you didn't feel something."

Lex snorted loudly. "I didn't exactly ask her to marry me. Cass is...well Cass is a take charge kind of girl. She said we are getting married, and that was that."

"Mmm, romantic." Aspen teased. "I can see why you are dying to get her back."

Lex smacked Aspen on the leg. "Quit it, you! She's a nice girl...most of the time."

"Sounds like it." Aspen felt herself relax. This part felt better. She finally admitted that perhaps they could be friends. She would take their history, and all the feelings that they shared and lock them up in a tiny box and hide them as far away as possible, tucked somewhere in the darkest recesses of her mind. That was how she would deal with them; at least for the next few weeks. Once the divorce was final, they could go their separate ways; have a few awkward conversations before finally drifting apart. She swallowed the lump in her throat at the thought of one last good-bye. It was almost more than she could take. "I forgot how picky you were."

"Hey." Lex feigned offense. "I'm not picky. I just got spoiled by the best." Lex picked at a thread on her jeans distractedly. "So what about you?"

"What about me?" Aspen crinkled her brow.

Lex was silent for several more seconds, her thoughts seemingly occupied by a wayward thread. "Are you going to start dating again?"

Aspen gasped loudly. "What are you saying? That I don't date? That I sat around this whole five years and waited for you?" Her eyes twinkled, belying the sarcasm in her voice.

"Touche." Lex smiled ruefully. "Just making conversation…since you won't take me up on my offer. Figured I would see what your type was."

Aspen looked at Lex askance, stopping short of rolling her eyes.

"Okay, okay, I know that I'm your type." Lex's tone was self-deprecating. "Man, you don't set your bar very high, do you?"

It was Aspen's turn to punch Lex. "Shut up!" She looked away shyly. "You were the most amazing woman I've ever been with."

"But?"

Aspen lifted her brow and gave Lex a sideways glance. "Really?" This time she did nothing to hide the sarcasm.

Lex chuckled softly. "Sorry, this friend thing is a bit weird. I'm trying, but I'm not sure yet how to be around you."

"Be normal, silly." Aspen teased. "Pretend like we are friends and always have been."

"Oh, and just ignore all our history?"

"Or at least pretend to." She caught the look that Lex shot her and laughed. "What? Lesbians do that all the time. Why do you think everyone is friends with their ex? Or at least acts like it." Aspen got up and grabbed the wine bottle from the kitchen. "I have a feeling, we might need this."

Lex waited while she refilled their glasses. She grabbed hers and took a sip while she ruminated on what Aspen had said. Sure, most of the women she knew were *friends* with their exes. But could they really be just friends? She seriously doubted it, but knew she would try just to keep Aspen in her life. "Seriously though, what would your type be? In case I want to fix you up."

"Don't you dare." Aspen laughed sarcastically. "I do not need you fixing me up."

"Fair enough." Lex winked and smiled saucily. She missed this part of their relationship sometimes more than anything else. The easy-going banter they shared. She missed just being with the woman who had captured her heart and her mind all those years ago. Nothing and no one ever felt like it had with Aspen. She was special and Lex knew she would never be able to forget the bond they shared. "Just for fun then."

Aspen swirled the liquid in her glass as she gave some consideration to Lex's question. Did she really know what her type was? Had she given any serious thought to it? Honestly, she probably hadn't even considered dating anyone for the last five years. She had lived them all in a fog, and truthfully she didn't know what she would look for in a woman. Sad, really; that she let so much time go by locked up in her past. She finally chuckled wryly. "God, I really don't know."

"Blonde? Brunette? Maybe a spicy redhead?" Lex continued to tease. "Maybe you like the artsy type. Purple hair, flighty, forgets to eat."

"Quit it!" Aspen smiled despite herself. "Are you calling me flighty? And the purple hair was an accident, and you know it!"

Lex's laughter filled the small room. "It was cute, though."

"It was so embarrassing!" Aspen buried her head in her hand and shook it from side to side. "That was the last time I ever considered coloring my own hair."

"Thank God." Lex pulled away from the hand that came flying her way. "Hey, I'm just kidding. Never could stand up to the left hook."

"Damn straight, and don't you forget it!" Aspen leaned back against the couch, smiling anew. "You know I've never really thought about a type. I think I just go on whoever attracts me. You know I'm a sucker for a beautiful smile."

Lex's smile widened until she had the most ridiculous, toothy grin on her face. At first glance, she looked like the joker. She held it as long as she could before dissolving into laughter.

Aspen snorted loudly. "Oh God, that was the most unattractive thing I've ever seen. Talk about creepy."

"So you're saying that you're not attracted to this?" Lex gestured to her face and pasted another smarmy smile on her face.

Aspen doubled over; her arm wrapped around her waist. "Seriously, you have to stop. I can't breathe."

"Or this." Lex waggled her eyebrows suggestively, all the while posturing in the most ridiculous poses she could think of.

Aspen's breath came in short gasps as she struggled to stop laughing. When she finally got herself under control, she shook her finger at Lex. "If this is your way of getting me to tell you my type, I can now say any woman who is the complete opposite of you."

Lex's mouth dropped in shock, and despite her best efforts to feign indignation, she couldn't keep the smile off her face. "It's cool. I know you want me."

Aspen lost herself in laughter this time. She had to admit this felt good. Just being with Lex with no pressure for anything else was a huge relief. Maybe she would be able to survive the next three weeks. "Yes Lex, I can't help myself. You're just so damn irresistible."

"Mmhmm, totally irresistible." Aspen winked, tempering her sarcasm. "The one thing I always wanted was someone who was a diehard romantic like my uncle Neal. I miss him."

"He was something special." Lex smiled nostalgically. "I'll never forget our wedding video."

"Oh, I know." Aspen agreed quietly. "I didn't even realize he spent all those months taking pictures and putting it together. When "In Your Eyes" by Peter Gabriel started playing, I don't think there was a dry eye in the house."

Lex shook her head. "I know. He caught moments with us that I didn't even remember. He captured our love perfectly."

"Yes, he did." Aspen laughed quietly. "God, I just remembered something I hadn't thought about in years. It was one summer; I think I was eight maybe. It rained all spring and half the summer. You know Aunt Ginny is a sun person, and the rain was taking its toll on her. I think Uncle Neal was fit to be tied that year. Aunt Ginny was so moody that summer, even to me. One day she was bitching about the weather and not getting to have any picnics. Unbeknownst to her, my uncle set up a picnic on the lawn, even went as far as putting up this huge umbrella. When he told her, he was taking her on a picnic and showed her the spot, I thought she was going to lose it. He just smiled obligingly and walked out in the rain by himself. It took her a few minutes watching him make a fool of himself for her in the rain just to give her a picnic before she moved. By the end of it, they were laughing and dancing in the rain. He was such a fool for her."

Lex smiled. "That's a sweet story."

"He loved her so much." Aspen ran her finger along the edge of her glass. "I guess I want someone like that; a woman who will stand in the rain and make a fool of herself for me. A woman who is willing to do anything to show me she loves me. Is that asking too much?"

Lex sipped her wine and shook her head. "I don't think so."

"Well, anyway." Aspen sighed loudly. "What about you? Now that you and Cass aren't together…"

"Mmm, I don't know." Lex shrugged. "I haven't really thought about it. Cass wants to meet and talk things over. I get the feeling she isn't walking away without a fight."

"You know she doesn't seem all bad. You should give her a chance." Aspen said it so nonchalantly that she surprised herself. She wasn't sure if she would be able to disconnect and talk about this part of Lex's life without pain.

180

It seemed, at least for now, that she could compartmentalize the Lex and Aspen history enough to at least carry on a conversation. "I am sure she really loves you."

Lex nodded, but didn't reply.

"Be honest with yourself, Lex." Aspen cautioned. "Do you want to make the same mistake twice? Why do you keep running from love? That's the thing you need to think about."

"I know." Lex said quietly. "I do love Cass. It's just different and all this time together reminded me that sometimes you find magic. I don't think that happens twice."

"It won't if you keep holding on to the past and not letting people in." Aspen set her empty glass down and turned to face Lex again, pulling her legs onto the couch. "Tell me something good that you love about her."

Lex eyed Aspen in disbelief. Was she really sitting here discussing her current girlfriend, well ex-girlfriend, with Aspen? "Can I just say this is a bit weird?"

Aspen chuckled softly. "Umm, yeah, you can. Is it bad?"

"No." Lex shook her head quickly. "Just weird." Lex stared into the fireplace, her hand pulling on her hair despite not having it in a ponytail. Her mind wandered several moments before she finally answered. "Cass is so focused on what's going on in her world, almost to the point of being self-absorbed."

Aspen snorted. "I said give me something good."

"I am." Lex rolled her eyes. "Patience, my dear. Everything is right here in Cass's world." Lex gestured with her hands directly in front of her face, accentuating the narrow space right in front of her eyes. "Especially when she has a new clothing line coming out, but there is always a part of her that is sweet and considerate. She invariably leaves something in my bag when I'm traveling- a note, some small token of her love. She never forgets that."

"Okay, that's a start."

Lex smiled. "It's a small one, but yes, it's a start."

"What made you fall in love with her in the first place?" Aspen asked softly. It made her heart ache to ask the question, and she wasn't sure she could hear the answer, but this was part of healing and moving on, and she needed both.

Lex chuckled softly and ran her hand over her hair. "Cass is different than anyone I've ever met. She's pure energy in this small package. When she walks into a room, you can't help but notice her. She sort of pulls you in and holds on tight."

"I can see why you fell for her." Aspen's voice trembled, and she hoped Lex hadn't picked up on it. "She sounds very special."

"A, it's not like that." Lex searched Aspen's face, holding her gaze. "I'm not even sure the moment I fell in love with Cass. It was like we met and then one day we had moved in together, and then we were in love. There was no defining moment, it just was."

"How is that different than falling in love normally?" Aspen pushed for an explanation despite her better judgment.

"It wasn't like with you." Lex dropped her gaze, unable to look into Aspen's eyes any longer. "When I saw you for the first time, my world exploded. I felt life pouring into my soul, electricity scorching every fiber in my body. You reached in and filled every part of my being without even trying. With you, I fell in love the second I saw you and my heart knew it would be forever yours."

"Oh." Aspen couldn't respond. She couldn't breathe. She had known better than to ask a question that she already knew the answer to. How could she not? She had felt the same magic that Lex did.

"Magic doesn't happen twice, A." Lex touched her arm softly. "If you're lucky, you get to keep that feeling. If not, you take what you can get. Some people don't ever get to feel what we felt. I should be happy I got to burn bright for a moment."

"I don't know what to say to that." Aspen was at a loss for words. She did what she normally did when she was overwhelmed emotionally. She sat silently for several moments, biting back tears.

"Aww, honey." Lex tried to soothe Aspen, rubbing her arm absentmindedly. "I didn't mean to make you sad. You asked a question and I just ended up here. I can't lie. I love Cass, but nothing, and I mean nothing, will ever compare to what I had with you. I didn't realize at the time what I was giving up. I was young and stupid and scared. I took for granted that I may never get that back. I know you want me to move on and for you, I will try. I just couldn't live with myself if I didn't at least let you know that everything about us is indelibly inked on my soul. You will always hold a piece of me in your hand."

"I know." Aspen whispered between tears. "I think that is the part that is so hard, keeping you with me every day-at least that part of us. That's why I have to put you away. I need to be friends. I can do that. I can talk about Cass and what makes you guys tick. I just can't talk about us."

"Fair enough." Lex sank back against the couch. It was several moments before she spoke again. "I'm guessing that doesn't include locker room chats about our sex life."

Aspen shook her head and smiled. She knew exactly what Lex was doing, and she silently thanked her for that. "Umm, not yet. Maybe one day, but for now, let's just keep it out of the bedroom."

"Yes, dear." Lex teased. Unable to contain it any longer, she stifled a yawn.

"Tired?"

"I guess so." Lex laughed around another yawn. "It just hit me."

Aspen smiled. "Go to bed, Lex. I'll see you in the morning."

Lex hesitated for a moment before the look on Aspen's face made her stand up. She stretched her arms over her head and yawned loudly. "Thank you."

"For?" Aspen looked up from the couch and held Lex's gaze.

"For this, for everything. I know asking you to do this was pretty shitty."

Aspen shook her head and smiled. "It needed to be done, and this was the best way. I should be thanking you. It's a step that we both need if we are going to move on."

"Yeah, I know." Lex turned to go then stopped midstride. "Anyway, I just wanted to thank you."

Aspen nodded and watched Lex leave the room and close the door before a single tear escaped and rolled down her cheek unchecked. Her strangled reply whispered so softly that she couldn't even hear it. "You're welcome."

Chapter 18

Aspen jumped at the sound of footsteps on the wooden floor. "Hello?"

"Hey, it's just me." Lex shouted from the kitchen.

Aspen couldn't contain her smile. She set her charcoal down and dusted her hands off before going into the kitchen. It was Christmas night, and she had expected to spend it alone. "What are you doing here?"

"Came home early." Lex shrugged out of her coat and returned Aspen's wide smile. She held a container towards Aspen. "Mom sent leftovers. We knew if you were here alone you wouldn't eat."

Aspen's jaw dropped. "What? I take care of myself."

"Mmhmm." Lex snorted loudly. "You have a tendency to forget to eat. I figure you probably haven't eaten today."

Aspen's stomach growled, and she smiled ruefully. "Okay, maybe I haven't eaten today."

"Exactly." Lex took the lid off the Tupperware and put it in the microwave to warm.

"So you left your family on Christmas to bring me leftovers?" Aspen cocked an eyebrow at Lex, her eyes twinkling with amusement.

"Maybe." Lex's cheeks reddened under her golden skin. "Actually, the storm is hitting earlier than they predicted, so I headed back early. I didn't want to get stranded on the road or worse yet, be stuck at Mom's house for the next couple of days."

Aspen laughed and grabbed a fork out of the utensil drawer. "I totally understand that." She dove into the leftovers hungrily. "How's the fam?"

"Good." Lex smothered a smile. She had always known Aspen to go all day without eating when she was busy working on her art. It never failed, when it finally dawned on her that she hadn't eaten, she would attack food with animal ferocity. Tonight was no different. "Mom says hi."

"Hi back." Aspen stopped shoveling food in her mouth long enough to point at a package on the counter. "It's from Cass; I think."

Lex eyed the package warily. She had spoken with Cass several times since she had broken off their engagement. She had pled with Lex to get back together and so far Lex had resisted. She still had some thinking to do. She did love her, but knew it wasn't with the same intensity as Cass loved her. Lex was finally starting to accept that she and Aspen would not get back together, but that didn't mean she needed to stay with Cass.

"Have you talked to her?" Aspen asked the question casually though her heart beat erratically. She may have decided to keep Lex at arms' length, but for some reason, it felt good that Lex hadn't gone running back to Cass.

Lex nodded and turned the small package over and over in her hands. "A couple of times."

"And?" Aspen set the fork down and leaned back in her chair. She sensed that Lex wanted to talk about something, maybe Cass was it. "I'm sorry. It's none of my business."

"It's fine." Lex shrugged. "There isn't much to talk about. She still loves me, and she wants to get back together."

Aspen stilled. She wanted to ask if they would, but she knew she should respect Lex's privacy. They were working on the *just friends'* thing, but it was still new and there were still boundaries she wasn't sure she could cross.

"I'm not sure what will happen." Lex confessed. "There is a part of me that loves her, but I'm not sure that's enough

186

anymore. It's hard to be reminded how wonderful it can be and think about settling for something less. That's not fair to me, and it sure as hell isn't fair to Cass."

"Maybe once you get away from here, there won't be as many reminders."

Lex eyed Aspen dubiously. "It's not the ones I can see; it's the ones I can feel. Some things you just can't forget."

Aspen looked down, unable to meet Lex's penetrating gaze. The honesty and the heartbreak she saw there was too much to take while her own heart was still so fragile. "I know."

Lex resisted the urge to reach across the table and take Aspen's hands in hers. She knew she couldn't safely touch her and not want more. Parts of their relationship now, however friendly they felt, were too much like being married again. The easy banter, nights spent enjoying each other's company; they were all intimate in a manner that was so different and yet so similar to a lover's caress. Lex accepted that there would always be a shared intimacy with Aspen, no matter how far apart they were. Aspen had once told her that she was *her person,* and Lex knew that would last forever.

"So." Aspen put her hands on the table and pushed herself up. "We're getting a storm?"

"Yeah." Lex shook her head, the moment between them passing as quickly as it had come, and it left her body cold. "I guess they are saying it could dump as much as a foot in some places. It's a clipper system so it's moving fast, but it's packing a punch and temps are going to drop into the single digits overnight. Do we need to do anything here?"

Aspen shook her head. "I've got the girls taken care of for the night. They should be fine." No matter how distracted Aspen got, she never forgot the horses. It was second nature to her to care for them, even before herself. "The house should be fine."

"Okay." Lex yawned and stood up. "I'm more tired than I thought. You want to head up to the bunkhouse?"

"Not yet." Aspen picked up her dish and fork and washed them quickly. "I want to finish this last piece before bed."

"Want me to wait?" Lex asked hopefully.

Aspen would have liked her company, but she could see the exhaustion in Lex's eyes, and her heart went out to her. "No, thank you though. You will just distract me."

Lex opened her mouth to object, but saw the twinkle in Aspen's eyes and knew she was teasing her again. "Yes, dear."

Aspen shivered at Lex's husky tone. She had always been a sucker for Lex's sexy voice, but when Lex was tired, it dropped an octave; Aspen hadn't been able to resist it. Aspen wrapped her arms around her chest protectively and smiled. "Go to bed, Lex. I'll be fine."

Lex smiled and yawned again. "I'll see you in the morning."

Aspen watched her leave and breathed a sigh of relief. Just the way *dear* had rolled off Lex's tongue sent chills through her body. She could feel the aftershocks of electricity, and she shivered unconsciously. "Damn." She swore softly and shook her head. Retreating to the safety of her studio, Aspen marveled at the hold that Lex still had over her body and wondered if she would ever feel that with another woman. So far, she hadn't. But then in all fairness, she didn't give herself the opportunity to find out. Maybe one day, she thought. Maybe one day.

A sudden gust of wind rattled the windows and sent a shiver down Aspen's spine. She looked at her watch, and it dawned on her that it had been hours since she sent Lex home to bed. She stared at the picture in front of her and suddenly realized that her latest piece was also of Lex. This pose was from Christmas night. She could see the soft amber glow highlighting Lex's cheeks, and she had captured the mischievous twinkle in her eye. The shadows accentuated her defined cheek bones and her hair dancing around her face gave her a definitely sultry look.

Aspen brushed her finger over her lips, smudging the charcoal across them until the fullness and shadow matched the memory that was forever etched in her mind. Another shiver stole through her body and this time it had nothing to do with the chill outside. She laid the charcoal down and stepped back, her eyes taking in the entire piece. Lex's hair cascaded down the fluid planes of her neck and Aspen tried to push images of her lips on Lex's soft skin to the back of her mind. Once this show was done, she vowed she would never sketch Lex again. It was far too painful and kept too many emotions bubbling near the surface.

A cold wind shook the house again, and Aspen realized the storm was close. She needed to check on the girls one more time and make sure they were warm and settled in. She pulled a thin shell over her sweater and hoped it and her wool hat would keep her warm on the short trek to the barn. She opened the door, bracing against the bitter cold that swirled outside. She had to lean forward to counter the frigid gusts of wind that were pummeling her body. She swore loudly and wrapped her arms around her body, mentally ticking off the steps to the barn. Normally, it wasn't a bad walk, but tonight, surrounded by cold and darkness and battered by the wind; it felt like miles.

When she finally made it, she hauled the door open and took a moment to relish the warmth inside. She heard one of the girls nicker softly, and she felt a smile creep over her face. Lacey was generally the skittish one. Aspen found her waiting at the edge of her stall. She rubbed the bridge of her nose softly. "What's a matter, girl? Storm got you a little unsettled?"

Lacey snorted softly and flicked her head.

Aspen nuzzled her cheek against Lacey's nose. "I know, girl. You hear the storm. It's not too bad. Just some snow. Will you keep an eye on your sisters?"

Lacey nickered deeply as if to say yes. "That's my girl." Aspen reached into her pocket and pulled out a sugar cube. She held her palm out and let Lacey nibble it off her hand. "Good girl. You just needed some reassurance." Aspen smiled at the slow snort and patted Lacey's neck. "I'm gonna get some sleep, but I'll check on you girls in the morning." Lacey whinnied letting her know it was okay to go.

Aspen checked the heat and made sure it was set on forty-five degrees. She resisted the urge to turn it up any further, knowing it was better to keep it cooler. She cocked an ear and listened for the exhaust fans humming at the back of the barn. Satisfied everything was okay; she eased the door open and braced for the icy punch that she knew would take her breath away. She took one more deep breath and pushed herself into the cold.

It took Aspen no time at all to cover the thirty or so steps to the bunkhouse, but when she closed the door behind her, her teeth were still chattering. Aside from the wind, the house was quiet. Lex would have fallen asleep hours ago. A small part of her wanted to go crawl into bed next to Lex. She wasn't craving sex per se, but she did miss the warmth of Lex's body holding her at night. She missed tucking her body against Lex's and those strong arms encircling her through the night. Tonight was one of the nights that she would have lain in Lex's arms all night.

Shaking her head, Aspen pushed those traitorous thoughts to the back of her mind and shrugged her coat off. She hung it on a rung by the door and put her hat on a hook next to it. Normally, she liked the quiet, but tonight it did nothing but let her mind wander, and it wandered places it shouldn't. Aspen growled softly. She didn't want to think about what once was and what might have been. She needed to stop living her life with what ifs and regrets. All that did was root her firmly in the past. She needed to be in the present and look to the future. Otherwise, she would be forever haunted by the life that could have been, if only...

190

"Shit. Enough already." Aspen tugged her boots off and padded to the kitchen. She needed a stiff drink, but settled for a hot cup of tea. She sipped it and let her eyes wander around the bunkhouse she called home for the last five and half months. By silent agreement, she and Lex had kept their discussions away from the short time they had left and what would happen after they filed for divorce. The divorce wouldn't be final for several months after the filing, but Lex would no longer need to live there. There wouldn't be much need for keeping in contact during the waiting period and Aspen thought it might be better that way. It would be simpler to move on once she didn't see Lex regularly. At least, she hoped it would be easier.

Another gust of wind and Aspen heard the first tings of the icy snow hit the window. She pulled the curtain back and watched the frozen pellets hit the ground in the dim light from the porch lamp. Snow was one thing, but the ice falling combined with the drop in temps was going to make for some treacherous conditions. She shivered and wrapped her arm around her body, feeling the warmth of the tea beginning to settle her down. She stifled a yawn and realized she was tired after all.

Aspen let the curtain fall back in place, put her cup on the island and made her way to her bedroom. She quickly changed into her pajamas, brushed her teeth and slipped into bed, exhaustion finally overcoming her. As she lay there, feeling her heartbeat slow and her breathing even out, she listened to the tiny bits of icy snow pinging off the window remembering a time when things weren't quite so complicated and praying that one day it would be blissfully simple again.

Chapter 19

"Lex, wake up." Aspen shook Lex's shoulder, trying to wake her from a deep slumber. She knew she was dead asleep from her quiet, even breathing. She felt Lex stir beneath her hand then still again. "Lex. Wake up."

"Huh." Lex groaned softly, not quite awake and not entirely thrilled with being pulled out of a deep sleep. She scrubbed her palms over her eyes, allowing them to adjust to the dark. Seeing Aspen's form, she bolted up and grabbed her hand. "Aspen? What's wrong?"

"The power's out. I'm not sure how long now." Aspen shivered and resisted the urge to jump under the warm covers. "I need to go start the generator in the barn."

Lex pulled the covers aside and swung her legs over the edge of the bed. She rested her elbows on her knees and yawned loudly several times. "I can go with you."

"No, it's okay." Aspen started towards the door but stopped when Lex grabbed her wrist. "I'm fine."

Lex cocked an ear and listened to the howling wind. "I'm not letting you go out there alone. Give me two seconds to throw some clothes on."

Aspen nodded and left her to change. She felt her way into the kitchen and pulled a flashlight out of the utility drawer. Using the light, she located several candles and a lighter. She lit one and left it on the island. The remaining two she lit and placed them on the mantle, the small light flickering and illuminating the living room in a soft glow. She would start a fire once the girls were taken care of.

"'Kay, I'm ready." Lex joined her in the living room and pulled her coat on. Jokingly, she nodded towards the kitchen. "I'll take my coffee in a travel mug."

Aspen rolled her eyes, but laughed softly. It was already chilly inside the bunkhouse, and with the only generator hooked up to the barn, it was bound to get colder before the electricity came back on. "Funny."

Lex pulled a stocking cap on and shoved her hands into her gloves. "Ready?"

Aspen pulled the door open, and a gust of wind hit her squarely in the face. "Ah, no."

Lex narrowed the gap between them and caught Aspen's hand in hers. "Don't worry, sweetheart. I'll hold you tight so the wind doesn't sweep you away."

Lex smiled, and Aspen could see her eyes twinkling in the moonlight reflecting off the snow. Her husky voice sent warm shivers down her spine. She pulled her hand away quickly. Even through gloved hands, Lex could still make her body react like no other woman. "Just walk in front of me and block the wind."

"Yes, dear." Lex nodded and saluted curtly. She covered Aspen's hand with hers and pulled the door all the way open. "After you."

Aspen swallowed loudly. Too much contact was warming her body very quickly. She said a silent thank you when the wind hit her full force and all but knocked the wind out of her. A little extra warmth wasn't so bad after all.

The short distance from the bunkhouse to the barn seemed triple its normal distance and Aspen felt like they were actually being driven backwards by the wind. The icy ground beneath them compounded the problem even more. After what seemed like an eternity, Aspen pulled the door to the barn open and she and Lex stepped into the welcoming safety of the barn.

Aspen flashed the light towards the three occupied stalls, not surprised at all to see Lacey's forlorn face watching her hopefully. Tarra and Reba were asleep and blissfully unaware of the storm around them. Aspen stroked her palm over Lacey's nose and leaned in close. "Still can't sleep, huh girl? It's a bad storm; I know." She let Lacey nuzzle against her for several more minutes then laughed when Lacey sniffed at her pocket. "What is it that you're after, missy? Do you think I brought treats?"

Lacey threw back her head and snorted softly as if to say she knew that Aspen had brought her something. She pawed quietly and nickered at Aspen.

Aspen chuckled softly. "You know me, girl. Here you go." She pulled several cubes of sugar out of her pocket and let Lacey nibble them out of her hand. Satisfied, Lacey nudged Aspen's shoulder softly to say thank you.

Aspen patted her neck and smiled. "Alright girl, Lex and I have to work. We're gonna get the generator on so your water doesn't freeze."

Lex chuckled softly.

"What?"

"Nothing." Lex smiled wryly. "You always carry on conversations with them?"

"Maybe." Aspen felt her cheeks redden, and she smiled shyly. "It helps calm her down."

"Mmhmm." Lex smothered another smile. "Come on, let's get the generator on and get back to the bunkhouse."

Aspen bounced the light around the barn as she led them to the back and the generator. "In case you hadn't figured it out yet, this is the only generator on the property."

Lex nodded. "I gathered as much from the snow flurries in the house."

"Hey." Aspen stopped short and leveled her gaze on Lex. "It's not that bad. We can make a fire when we get back."

"Honey, I'm just messing with you." Lex laughed and nudged Aspen. "Tell me how to turn it on."

"Seriously, you've never used a portable generator before?"

Lex smiled sheepishly. "City girl, remember? When the power goes out, we just find a hotel."

Aspen rolled her eyes. She stopped at the small generator tucked in the back corner of the barn. "This part you're gonna love." She flashed Lex a devilish smile and opened the cap to check the gas level. Satisfied it was full; she muscled the back door open and gestured for Lex to pull the generator outside.

The wind hit Lex, and she started coughing. "Yeah, tell me when I'm going to love this again."

Aspen's laughter echoed into the night. "Bring it over here." She nodded towards a small make shift shelter and waited while Lex situated it on the concrete pad.

"Mmhmm." Aspen cleared her throat loudly.

"You need to turn it around."

"What?" Lex stared at her incredulously.

"You need to make sure the exhaust isn't pointing at the barn." She twirled her finger in a circle.

Lex grunted loudly and flipped it around. She took the cord that Aspen held out to her and plugged it in. "Okay." "It is just like a lawn mower." Aspen smothered a smirk. Lex had always been lost when it came to anything even remotely related to power tools. She shook her head and knelt down in front of the generator. She flipped the ignition switch on, opened the choke and yanked the pull start. The generator started up with a satisfying growl. She slid the choke to full and pushed herself up. "And that's how you do it."

"Humph." Lex rolled her eyes and stuck out her tongue. She shivered, and Aspen pushed her towards the door.

"Don't you know enough to come in from the cold, silly?" Aspen teased between her chattering teeth. With the lights back on in the barn, the walk back to the girls was made with relative ease. She flipped the flashlight off and slid it into her coat pocket. She stopped once more at Lacey's stall. "Alright, Lacey girl, everything is okay. I'll be back in the morning to check on you."

Lacey whinnied softly and nodded her head.

"Good night, girl." Aspen stroked her nose one last time. "Ready to go?"

Lex nodded. "Yes, I'm freezing."

"Come on, you baby. I'll make you some hot chocolate." Aspen spun on her heal then shot Lex an expectant look. "What?"

"Well, I just wondered if you realized that the power was still off. How are you going to make hot chocolate?"

Aspen's mouth dropped open. "What? The power's out?"

"Shut up." Lex punched her in the arm. "Just for that, I'm locking you out of the house." Lex tore out of the barn and started running up the slight incline. It was mere seconds before Aspen caught up to her and started to pass her by.

"Slow poke." Aspen ran as fast as she could, given the icy conditions. She bounded up the steps and yanked the door open, slipping out of the cold.

Lex joined her a second later. "Damn, it's cold outside. I think I may take your mom and Ginny's lead and move to Florida. This crap is for the birds."

Aspen laughed. "Not me. I like having seasons. You can keep that heat all to yourself."

"Even with an ice storm and no power?" Lex cocked an eyebrow, almost daring Aspen to disagree.

"Yep, even with the cold." Aspen nodded towards the living room. "Can you start the fire? We are gonna be spending the rest of the night out here."

"Sure." Lex smiled and hesitated.

"What?"

"I was just going to say if I'm going to be stranded with no power in the middle of winter, I'm glad it's with you." Her dark eyes held Aspen's in the dim candlelight.

"Me too." Aspen said it without thinking, but quickly realized she meant it. She fell silent, returning Lex's gaze. Feeling an all too familiar pull, she dropped her eyes. "Hot chocolate."

Lex sensed her wall go up and felt the loss immediately. She watched as Aspen turned away and busied herself at the stove. Shaking her head, Lex could only accept regretfully her part in ruining what they once had. She made her way to the fireplace and within minutes, had a small fire started. She could feel the heat immediately. She walked back to the kitchen. "Need any help?"

Aspen had already turned on the gas and used a match to light the burner. She stirred chocolate into the milk, trying to judge how much she needed. "Nope, got it. You can grab the sleeping bags out of the hall closet and a couple extra blankets. Even with the fire, we will need the added warmth."

"Sure thing, boss." Lex smiled to herself and shuffled off to complete her task. When Aspen handed her a steaming cup of cocoa some minutes later, Lex was seated on top of her sleeping bag. She layered several blankets on the floor for insulation and padding. Several more were piled next to their sleeping bags, in case they needed them. "Thanks."

They sipped their hot drinks in relative silence, staring into the fire. Aspen stole a glance at Lex's profile. The ambient light from the fire illuminated her angular features. She was still breathtaking. Aspen felt her heart skip a beat, and she pulled her gaze away quickly. Tonight was not the night to start thinking about Lex that way.

"What are you thinking?" Lex sensed Aspen's gaze, but she didn't turn around.

"Nothing." Aspen lied quickly, but the slight tremor in her voice gave her away.

"Liar." Lex set her empty cup on the table. She leaned back on her elbows and stretched her long legs out in front of her, casting a sideways glance at Aspen. "I always know when you get quiet that you have something on your mind."

Aspen sipped her hot chocolate and set her cup down before she finally mustered up the courage to be honest. "I am going to miss you."

Lex smiled sadly. "I'll miss you too." She could have said more, could have offered to stay if Aspen wanted. At this point, it wouldn't take much. She had already been thinking about next week. The six months would be over, and their divorce paperwork would be filed. There was no need for her to stay there any longer. Aspen had made it clear she was ready to move on and staying only hurt Lex more. "I forgot how much I love being around you."

"I know, Lex." That was all Aspen could say. She wouldn't allow herself to feel any more than that. She had caught glimpses of her future, or maybe it was her past reflected in her eyes, and she thought she remembered the woman looking back at her finally. She was losing the hollow look that had haunted her for so long. It was time for her to let go of her past. "Thank you for keeping me company. It's been nice having you around."

"Nice?" Lex managed a sarcastic laugh. "I figure you are ready to boot my ass to the curb. I've been nothing but a pain."

Aspen giggled. "Maybe a little."

"Hey!" Lex objected quickly. "You're supposed to deny that."

"Am I?" Aspen waggled her eyebrows. "Aw, poor Lex, doesn't feel loved."

Lex's bottom lip jutted out. "Picking on me when I'm down."

Aspen's laughter filled the tiny room. "You baby. You're fine." She shot Lex a satisfied smile and set her empty cup on the table next to hers. A yawn built up, and she tried to hide it behind her hand. "Excuse me. I'm getting a little sleepy."

"I'd say." Lex chucked softly. "I guess we should get some sleep while we can."

Aspen nodded and slid into her sleeping bag, pulling it up to her chest. She watched Lex get situated and smiled to herself. "Having trouble?"

Lex smiled sheepishly. "I'm too tall."

"How are you too tall?" Aspen queried. "Those bags are made for everyone."

"Well obviously, you gave me the kid sleeping bag."

"Oh yeah, how do you figure?"

"Well duh." Lex pointed at the Strawberry Shortcake figure on the front her hers.

Aspen snorted loudly. "That's funny."

"Is it?" Lex looked askance at Aspen and rolled her eyes. "I can't sleep like this."

"So trade me." Aspen was already zipping hers open and squirming out of it.

"Okay." Lex muttered quietly.

"You are such a baby." Aspen giggled once again. Lex reminded her of a petulant youngster, and it made her smile to see that side of her again. She slid into Lex's abandoned sleeping bag, feeling her own toes pressing into the crease. She tried to pull the cover up over her shoulders and grimaced when it would go no further than her breasts. "Ugh."

"Uh-huh." Lex murmured softly. She opened one eye and shot Aspen a sarcastic look. "Who's the baby now?"

Aspen glared at Lex. "Bitch." She tried to bend her knees and shorten herself to fit. After several minutes of exasperated groans, she sighed loudly and flopped backward against her pillow. "I take it back. I can't do this either."

Lex didn't say a word, but a small snicker escaped her lips, and she was rewarded with a punch to her side. "Ow!"

"You deserve that, you turd."

"I did?" Lex rubbed her side and groaned loudly. "So what do you want to do?"

Aspen shook her head. "There's just one thing to do. Get up."

"Yes ma'am." Lex sent Aspen a mock salute, her eyes twinkling behind her stern expression. She slid out of her bag and unzipped it all the way open. She stood up and waited while Aspen opened her own sleeping bag and stood up next to her. Lex spread her bag out over the pallet she had already made and Aspen opened hers over the top of it.

Aspen got under the covers and settled down on her side. She punched her pillow a few times before she put her head down. "Don't get any ideas."

Lex snorted. "I was just going to tell you the same thing. Don't try to take advantage of me."

Aspen giggled. "I wouldn't dream of it."

"Damn." Lex swore softly, a smile playing on her face. "Good night, A. Sweet dreams."

"Good night, Lex." Aspen pulled her knees to her chest, curling them against her. She could feel Lex's heat already even though they weren't touching. It felt good after all those years. It was the last thought she had before she drifted off to sleep.

Chapter 20

Aspen's scream pierced the darkness and pulled Lex from a deep sleep. She bolted up, her mind suddenly awake. "A, wake up." Lex shook her gently. The dream was a bad one. Lex hadn't heard her scream like that in a while. "Aspen, honey, wake up."

Aspen stirred slowly, her mind hurtling back from the dark place that had taken her captive. Her body was rigid, and her breath came in shallow gasps. "Lex?"

"Shhh, honey, I'm here." Lex scooted next to her and pulled her head on to her shoulder. "It's okay."

Aspen shivered against Lex's body, trying to draw from her warmth. She felt so cold, so empty. Her dream was so real, and it scared her more as her subconscious continued to play still images from the depths beyond. She felt Lex's arms tighten around her, and she allowed Lex to hold her. "I'm sorry."

"Don't be." Lex's voice rumbled quietly. She pulled Aspen as tightly to her body as she could, leaving no space at all. "It was a bad one?"

Aspen could only nod. She could still see the visions. She knew Lex was waiting for her to share the dream, knowing that talking about it would help. She burrowed her head into Lex's shoulder and let herself be comforted for several more minutes before she could finally speak. "It was so real. You were there."

"I figured." Lex knew that Aspen's nightmares usually revolved around her. Her heart ached for the pain that she had caused her. Her hand rubbed lazy circles on her arm, and she dropped light kisses on the top of her head. She could still hear the wind howling outside, and she silently thanked the short sleeping bag that had put them in the make-shift bed together. "Wanna talk about it?"

Aspen nodded against Lex's arm and wrapped her arm around Lex's midsection. "It was our wedding day, and everyone was here. We had a little boy named Henry. He looked just like you. He was beautiful." Aspen felt her throat tighten, and she leaned further into Lex.

"It's okay, honey." Lex's voice was low and soothing. She could hear just how much the nightmare had affected Aspen. "We don't have to talk about it."

"No." Aspen shook her head. "I need to. The ceremony was small and intimate just like before. Henry walked me down the aisle. He seemed so real, Lex. His dark hair and sweet beautiful, brown eyes. He had your features."

Lex felt her tense. "Shh, it was just a dream."

"God, it was so real. She came after you, and you left with her." The tremor in Aspen's voice was unmistakable. "You took Henry and left."

"Who came, A?" If it was possible, Lex pulled her even closer. "Who took me away?"

"I couldn't see her face, but I know it was her." Aspen's strangled whisper was barely audible over the wind. "It was Cass."

Lex stilled and when she shivered, it had nothing to do with the cold. "It was just a dream, A. I'm right here. See?" She tilted Aspen's face towards her so she could see that Lex was right in front of her. In the pale glow of the fire, she saw the tears in Aspen's eyes. No matter how much time had passed, it was still the same heartbreak. "Fuck, A. I'm so sorry. I'm here now. I'm with you."

Aspen nodded solemnly. Her eyes searched Lex's face, and the last visions from her dream taunted her from her subconscious. The tears started again.

Lex felt her heart drop. She rubbed Aspen's cheek. "Please, baby, don't cry. I'm here; I'm here." Lex pulled her close again and kissed her cheek. "Shh, shh, it's okay."

Aspen felt the soft kisses on her cheek and Lex's strong arms around her. She shivered as the darkness held onto her body. She told herself that it was just a dream, she was here with Lex and that she wasn't leaving her. She repeated the words over and over again, but the fear was still there. As long as she still held onto her life with Lex, she would always dream about her leaving. She needed something to pull her from the dark place. She needed a way to let go. Without thinking, she lifted her head and her lips found Lex's. She felt immediate warmth effuse her body.

Lex stilled immediately, suspended in time. The feel of Aspen's soft lips on hers catapulted her back in time. It felt so foreign and, yet, so perfect. She stifled a moan as Aspen's soft lips slid along hers. When Aspen's tongue pushed softly inside her mouth, Lex broke the kiss and tilted Aspen's face away from hers. She held her gaze, searching for the answer to her unasked question.

Aspen's blue eyes locked onto Lex's for several beats before she nodded. "I need this tonight. Please, Lex."

Lex's heart clenched painfully. Lex could see good-bye in Aspen's eyes, but the fear of losing her again wasn't enough to stop her body from wanting this one last night. She couldn't talk, couldn't breathe as the ache of wanting Aspen built in her chest. Unable to say the word yes, her hand found the back of Aspen's neck, and she pulled her head down. This time when her lips met Aspen's, she didn't swallow the moan.

Aspen explored Lex's mouth, her tongue teasing and dipping between her lips. She pulled her bottom lip between hers and sucked gently, feeling the electricity from her touch tingling in her body, a pleasant ache starting to pulse in her stomach. When her tongue brushed Lex's, she groaned softly and increased the pressure. For the first time in years, she felt her body starting to come alive.

Lex was still reeling from the kiss, and she resisted the urge to run her hands under Aspen's shirt. She longed to feel Aspen's soft skin beneath her fingertips. Lex wouldn't initiate the contact. Tonight, Aspen would be in control. She reveled in the feel of Aspen's tongue against hers, teasing and exploring gently. Aside from the kiss that she had stolen weeks before, Lex had forgotten the feel of Aspen's mouth on hers. The tingling low in her belly let her know that her body didn't forget the magic between them. The want was like none she had ever felt before.

Aspen's mouth plundered Lex's with reckless abandon. Her body ached to crawl inside Lex's, and she fought the urge to push inside her now. No, tonight, she needed to savor the feel and taste, to imprint Lex on her soul permanently. This would be her final good-bye, and she needed to let her body feel perfection one last time before she tucked this part of her heart away in a safe place. The taste of Lex's lips on her tongue was achingly bittersweet and as her hands joined her mouth in sweet exploration, she felt the last tear escape and slide down her cheek.

Lex trailed her thumb across Aspen's face, gently wiping away the last of her tears. She pulled away from Aspen long enough to capture her face in her hands and kiss the soft skin of her cheekbones. She needed to slow down, to savor the moment, not to rush to the end in her haste to join their bodies together one last time. She didn't need Aspen to say this was the last time; she could feel it in her kisses, see it in her eyes. As much as her heart broke just thinking about it, Lex knew she needed this more than life itself. She rubbed her thumb over Aspen's bottom lip. Her heart nearly collided with her throat when Aspen sucked her finger into her mouth gently and swirled her tongue around it.

Pulling away, Aspen shot her a sad smile. "Please say yes."

Lex could only nod her assent. She swallowed the lump in her throat, pushing the ache inside her chest to the back of her mind. Lex had never known pain like she felt tonight, and she marveled at how quickly the need for Aspen's touch filled every inch of her body and pushed reason aside. She slid her hand around Aspen's neck again and pulled her face down; their lips meeting in a blissful abandon. No longer wanting to rein her needs in, Lex teased Aspen's mouth with her tongue, needing to taste her once more.

Their tongues danced together, memorizing the taste and feel and remembering what they once shared. Lex ran her hands along Aspen's back, longing to feel her skin beneath her palms. Though Aspen said this is what she needed tonight, Lex still fought the urge to take what was being offered, waiting for Aspen to give her body to her.

As if knowing what anguish Lex was fighting, Aspen slid on top of her and broke their kiss. "Touch me, Lex. Please."

Lex needed no more invitation than that. Her hands moved underneath Aspen's shirt with practiced ease, and she splayed her palms on Aspen's soft skin, accepting that just the feel of the sweet caress was enough to set her loins on fire. She moved slightly to ease the ache between her legs, and when she did, Aspen settled between her thighs. The pressure was perfect torture, and Lex reveled in it. Rather than trying to settle her body down, she let her hands rove over Aspen's skin and brushed her thumbs along her breasts, remembering the feel of her supple globes balanced in her hands. She pushed her hand between their bodies and ran circles around Aspen's nipple with her thumb, teasing it to a taut peak.

Aspen felt her body respond immediately to the soft caresses. Her body quickly remembered the sweet ache that Lex made her feel with just a touch. She deepened the kiss, their tongues mingling together in practiced rhythm. She felt desire pool between her legs, and she moved against Lex, increasing the pressure on her already sensitive clit. Her hands found Lex's small breasts, and she moaned loudly when her nipples hardened beneath her touch. "God, I missed this."

The ache in Aspen's voice seared Lex to her very core, and her body arched in response. She felt Aspen cup her breast and her own hands stilled, unable to concentrate. It was like this so many times. Aspen would barely touch her, and her body was on fire. At times, it was too much, and she gave herself over to her own needs, but tonight she fought for control. She needed to give more than she received. She needed Aspen to know that despite their good-byes, her heart was Aspen's forever. Lex put her hand over Aspen's and held it on her heart. She let her feel the rapid beat against her palm and the rise and fall of her chest. "You always drove me crazy, sweetheart. That will never change."

"I know." Aspen rested her forehead on Lex's and kissed her lips gently. "It is the same for me." She nibbled Lex's lips softly, brushing her tongue over them. "I need you inside me." She pushed Lex's hand inside her pants. "Make love to me, Lex."

Lex moaned into Aspen's mouth and pushed her hand inside the waistband of her panties. She teased her lips apart and rubbed her clit softly. She coated her fingers with moisture and slipped inside Aspen's body, reveling in her warmth. "God, Aspen. You feel so good." Lex held still as Aspen's body pulsed around her. She kissed Aspen softy. She pulled her hand away and wrapped her arms around Aspen, rolling her over on her back. "I love you, A. I always will."

"I know, Lex." Aspen stilled and felt her heart well up in her chest. "I can't hear that tonight. It's too much. Can you just let this be enough?"

Lex choked back tears and smiled sadly. The word yes escaped in a strangled whisper. She leaned over and kissed

Aspen softly. She could feel Aspen's body trembling beneath her, and Lex ached to console her. Tonight, she would have to let her body ease the pain. She slid her hand underneath Aspen's shirt and rolled her nipple between her thumb and forefinger, urging it to harden from her touch. Her tongue pushed against Aspen's, every fiber of her being so intently focused on this single frame in time. Every hello, every uttered word of love, every heartbreaking good-bye poured into this act of love, a solitary moment of passion so achingly acute in its rendering that Lex couldn't hold back her tears, and she relished each one as they splashed onto Aspen's cheeks and professed her love.

Aspen's heart broke in two, ripped apart without even a word. She held onto Lex with fierceness she didn't know she possessed. She knew she would have to hold her tightly before she could let her go. Letting her in completely was the only way Aspen knew to say good-bye. With Lex, it was all or nothing, no matter how much it hurt. She held her a moment longer before her need to touch replaced the ache in her heart. Her hands roamed over Lex's back, feeling the hard muscles beneath her palms. She returned Lex's kiss with reckless abandon, her need to feel alive outweighing all other thought. Her tongue tangled with Lex's, and she felt her stomach jump wildly. "Please, Lex."

Lex moaned and kissed her hard once more. She slid down Aspen's body and pulled her shirt up, exposing her soft mounds. Her eyes darkened at the sight of her dark nipples against her creamy-white skin. Lex flicked her tongue over the soft peak then sucked it into her mouth, swirling her tongue around it gently. She nipped it with her teeth and felt it stiffen against her tongue. Her palm slid over Aspen's other breast and felt it harden beneath her hand.

Aspen's body was on fire. The feel of Lex's mouth on her nipple was enough to drive her wild. She arched her hips against Lex, and her clit jumped at the pressure. Once again, she guided Lex's hand inside her pants and pushed against her palm. She deepened the kiss and when Lex brushed over her clit, Aspen felt heat building deep inside her.

Lex slid her palm over Aspen's clit. She swirled her fingers over her lips and coated her soft folds with slick warmth. She slid her fingers inside Aspen's body, pushing as deep as she could. She waited several seconds before pulling them out only to plunge them in again, her thumb sliding over Aspen's clit. Lex could feel it pulse against her, and she quickened her strokes.

Aspen's tongue danced with Lex's, and her hips arched wildly, trying to pull Lex in as far as she could go. She could feel her muscles start to contract around Lex's fingers, and she pushed against her hand. She wrenched her mouth away from Lex's. "I need more, Lex. I want to feel all of you." Aspen reached down and yanked at the waistband of her bottoms, trying to tug them over Lex's hand. "Get these off of me."

Lex chuckled softly. She pulled away just long enough to work Aspen's pants down over her hips and off her legs. She tossed them over her shoulder and settled her weight in between Aspen's thighs, sliding her body along her clit.

"Baby, you're killing me." Aspen admitted in a strangled voice. She arched her hips and wrapped her legs around Lex's waist, pulling her into her body. She leaned up and whispered in Lex's ear. "Make love to me like you used to."

Lex's heart melted. Aspen was giving her everything, opening up her entire body to Lex; she was hers for the taking. She hesitated, wanting to make sure that this was what Aspen really wanted.

Aspen sensed her uncertainty and she bit her collarbone softly. "Now."

Lex felt her last wall fall away. It was time to make Aspen's body hers and in doing so, Lex would let go of every bit of herself, unable to protect what was no longer hers. She knew long before tonight that her heart would always belong to Aspen, no matter how far apart they were. She kissed

Aspen's neck gently, planting kisses along her collarbone and down her chest. She stopped long enough to swirl her tongue over Aspen's nipple and pull it between her teeth softly. She kissed the soft skin along her abdomen and down her hip, stopping to tease the mound between her legs.

Aspen's body tingled with every kiss, and her hips arched off the floor when Lex's mouth found her lips. Her hips bucked wildly when Lex ran her tongue over her clit and sucked it between her lips. Her body quickly remembered the deliciousness of Lex's touch and with several deft strokes of Lex's tongue; Aspen was ready to come out of her skin. Her teeth clenched, and her breath caught in her throat. "Baby. I need you inside me."

Lex smiled against her lips and slid her tongue along her swollen folds before delving inside her and tasting her sweet nectar. Lex swirled her tongue inside of Aspen's body as she tasted her with short, teasing strokes, bringing her closer and closer to the edge and holding her there. She slid her hand under Aspen's bottom and pushed deeper and deeper with every stroke. This was as close to heaven as Lex had ever been, as close to tasting perfection as she had been allowed, and she savored each sweet second.

Aspen's clit pulsed painfully, and the ache between her legs built until she couldn't breathe. She arched into Lex, trying to assuage the overwhelming need. When she thought that she could take no more, Lex slid two fingers inside her and started to move with her. Her lips sought Aspen's clit and sucked it gently, her tongue swirling around it deftly. Soon, their rhythm pushed Aspen to the edge and held her there. It was sweet torture to feel the aching anticipation as Lex slowly pushed her over the precipice and stroked her body to wave after wave of pulsing energy, leaving her body trembling with sated exhaustion. When she could finally move, she pulled Lex up beside her and held her there. The need to hold her close was as acute as the need to make love just minutes before. "Are you okay?"

209

"Mmhmm." Lex kissed her forehead. "I'm perfect." For one brief moment, she meant it. It was the moment between making love to Aspen and the good-bye she knew would come. Lex wrapped her heart around those few precious seconds and pulled them close to her. She would hold on as long as she could; knowing the heartbreak that would come was more than she was prepared for.

"I'm sorry." Aspen could almost hear the sound of her heart shattering as she lay there enveloped in warmth. The cold outside had nothing against the chill that she had felt these many years and would soon feel again. It was too much to think about and for the second time that night, she forgot herself and pulled Lex's mouth to hers. She would take Lex's pain away if only briefly. Sliding her hand between Lex's legs, she closed her eyes against the visions that danced in her head and lost herself in the heat of Lex's body.

Chapter 21

Lex shivered and pulled the blankets up to her chin, trying to hold in her warmth. She didn't need to feel the cold spot beside her to know she was lying in their makeshift bed alone. She lay there staring at the embers dying in the fireplace and wondered if she had dreamt last night. A tenderness between her legs let her know that the visions that danced in her head were very real. This realization brought a new wave of sadness.

Sighing loudly, Lex threw off the covers and the chill of the room nearly took her breath away. She could hear the wind howling around the house and knew that without electricity, the fireplace was going to provide little warmth against the bitter cold outside. Struggling with the layers bunched around her, Lex fought to pull her jogging pants on to ward off the cold.

She knew Aspen would be outside with the girls. She fought the urge to join her, but her need to see her outweighed the fear of the impending chill. Lex had to see her face. She wanted to know where Aspen's head was this morning. Last night had been a shock and no doubt this morning she would see regret in Aspen's eyes, but Lex needed to see it. It would help her start to heal.

Lex glanced in the direction of the kitchen. The first muted rays of light were peeking through the curtains. Perhaps if she came with a peace offering, she would be better received. She smiled sadly and set about lighting the gas stove with the matches Aspen had left sitting on the counter. She poured cold milk into a pan and waited while it came to a gentle boil. She found two travel mugs and stirred hot chocolate into the milk before filling the mugs to the top and capping them off. Lex threw on a coat, hat and thick gloves and took several deep breaths before opening the front door and beginning the cold trek across the yard.

Aspen jumped at the sound of the door opening behind her. She saw Lex and forced a smile. "Hi." She turned away quickly, hoping to hide her red-rimmed eyes.

Lex took one look at Aspen, and her heart broke. "Hey." She covered the distance between them and held one of the mugs out. "I made you something warm."

Aspen put her hand out and took the mug, her eyes never leaving Lacey. "Thank you."

"You're welcome." Lex shuffled her feet uncomfortably. She wasn't sure how to act this morning already, but seeing Aspen's tears made it all the more difficult. "I, umm, about…" Lex stuttered helplessly. She felt powerless, and her vulnerability scared her. For the first time in months, she realized that this was what it must have felt like for Aspen all those years ago. Watching her life get ripped out from under her and having no power to stop it.

"I'm sorry, Lex." Aspen's strangled whisper hung between them, making the silence even more deafening. Finally turning, Aspen forced Lex to look at her. It was obvious she had been crying a while, and she did little to hide it. "Last night shouldn't have happened. It was a mistake."

Lex shook her head. "I'm glad it did. I needed to hear you say good-bye, feel the end with something other than my head to believe it."

Aspen smiled sadly. "It was selfish of me to take that from you. It just makes today harder than it needs to be. Last night made me realize that I can't move on with you here."

"So don't move on." Lex pressed her, knowing the answer but silently hoping that she could change it. "I love you, Aspen. Can't you feel that?"

Aspen swiped at a fresh tear and started shaking her head no. "I can't. I just keep hearing good-bye. I barely survived you leaving the first time. I don't think I would survive the second time if I let you in, and then you decide to leave when it gets too hard."

"I'm not going anywhere, A. Being here with you has made me realize that my heart is and always has been yours. No matter where I go or how much time passes, I will always love you." Lex set her mug down on the rail and grabbed Aspen's shoulders, pulling her close. "Know this, if I leave today, it's because you walked away. I can't promise you perfect. I'm old enough to know that doesn't exist. What I can promise you is I am yours forever. I can't leave you. You will have to say good-bye this time."

Aspen couldn't look at Lex without her heart breaking. The tears in her brown eyes were more than she could bear. She pulled her gaze away and stared at the floor between them.

"Please say something." Lex pleaded with Aspen. Her heart hammered in her chest, and she swallowed the sick feeling that was gripping her stomach.

"I don't know what to say." Aspen stepped out of Lex's grip and rested her arms on the railing, her hand brushing Lacey's nose. Lacey nuzzled the side of her head and whinnied softly. Aspen knew what she needed to do to move forward, and yet, saying the words out loud made them so painfully real. She opened her mouth several times before she could force enough air into her lungs to form the words. "I can't live like this. Last night was amazing. It was the first time I've felt alive in years."

"But?" Lex licked her lips nervously. She could sense Aspen's indecision, and she refused to make it any easier to say farewell.

213

"But as wonderful as last night was, this morning, I knew that it was time. Last night was magical, Lex, and I want to thank you for letting me touch you again."

Lex frowned. "You can stop this, A. We can have another chance. I know how badly I messed up, and I won't leave you again."

"How can you be sure?" Aspen chuckled softly, the irony of the situation too bittersweet to ignore. She wasn't a vindictive person, but she wasn't a fool either. "Lex, I love you. I know now I always will. We had our chance. These past months, I realized that I have no defenses against you. You tear all my walls down. I can't be that vulnerable. I have to learn to be whole again if I'm ever going to face the world without worrying that I'll get hurt."

"A, I won't hurt…"

Aspen put her finger on Lex's lips to silence her. "Please, I need to say this while I can."

Lex held her gaze and finally nodded her ascent.

Aspen pulled her finger away. She absentmindedly rubbed the tingling skin, all too aware of the effect Lex had on her body. "I've tried to tell myself a thousand times that there is a whole world waiting for me, I just have to get out and let myself live. If there is anything you taught me in all of this, it's that I can let go of the past."

"That's not exactly what I was hoping you would get from all of this." Lex replied sarcastically.

Aspen furrowed her brow and shot Lex a mock glare. "You know what I mean. Whatever will happen tomorrow, I have to put all of this hurt behind me. I can't keep living my life holding onto you. All this time, I've been turned around the wrong way, looking at everything I left behind. I have missed so much. I'm finally realizing how much, and I'm ready to change that."

"You mean you're ready to dump me for good." Lex's sarcastic tone hung in the air.

This time the glare was for real. Aspen felt some of the anger from the past taunting her, and she pushed it back down before she spoke again. "No, I mean I'm ready to say good-bye to what we used to be. Good-bye to all the hurt and pain that I held onto for so long. Lex, I love you. I always will, but I need to walk away. I need to live my life for me and not for anyone else. You came here looking for closure, same as me. This is it. Go home, Lex. Live your life."

"What if this is the life I want?" Lex's eyes held Aspen, pleading with her to listen to her heart, knowing that no matter what Aspen said, she was still in love with her.

Aspen stepped closer and took Lex's hand in hers. "You can have this life, just not with me. Besides, why would you want some emotionally scarred shell of a woman? We would be broken, Lex, and maybe it wouldn't catch up with us this year, or even next year, but one day it would. I don't want to be back here five years from now, wishing I had the balls just to let go." Aspen pushed up on her tip-toes and kissed Lex's lips softly. When she pulled away, a sad smile played on her lips. "Last night was perfect and I want to have that be my last memory of us. Can you just give me that?"

Lex swallowed the lump in her throat, unable to speak. She finally nodded slowly. She knew from the look in Aspen's eyes that she was serious. Lex couldn't say anything to change it. Pulling away, she swiped at her eyes, pushing back the tears that threatened to spill from her eyes. She propped her arms on the railing and rested her chin in her hands. She wasn't sure how much time passed before she was able to speak. "So what happens now?"

"I guess I file and then we wait. In six months, we will be divorced. We will have to go to the courthouse for the divorce hearing. Since you slept with…since we have been separated, and you were living with someone else, it should be pretty simple. I'll let you know if we need to do anything in the meantime. Otherwise, we go our separate ways." Aspen's tone was solemn and without emotion. This was where she could remove herself and treat it like business. It was when she let her heart into the mix that things got complicated, and she was tired of complicated.

Lex laughed sardonically. "It all sounds so sterile, like we are just acquaintances."

"I'm sorry." Aspen tried to soften the harshness of it all. "This is what you wanted, Lex. I know that changed for you, but this is why we came here. I hate to use this phrase, but it seems fitting. It is what it is."

Lex scoffed loudly and shook her head. "I didn't imagine it would suck this bad. I'm a thirty-four-year-old divorcee."

"No, you're not." Aspen teased, trying to lighten the somber mood. "You won't be that for another six months. Then you will be a thirty-four-year-old divorcee."

"Oh God." Lex muttered sarcastically. "That makes it even worse."

Aspen laughed softly then smiled, searching Lex's face. "Will you be okay?"

Lex shrugged. "Mmm, who knows? But I have to be, right?"

"Yes." Aspen reached over the fence and grabbed Lacey's pail, needing to redirect her heart and her mind. She could feel Lex's pull over her, and she wanted to put some distance between them, knowing she had to stay strong. "Come on, last time to muck the stalls. I know you wouldn't want to miss your last chance."

Lex laughed and followed Aspen's lead. "Yeah, I can honestly say I won't miss shoveling shit."

Aspen snorted loudly. "Isn't shoveling shit an everyday thing for you?"

"What are you saying?" Lex sucked in a breath, feigning offense. "That I'm full of shit?"

"Well, your eyes are brown." Aspen nudged Lex's shoulder playfully, pushing her off balance.

Lex regained her balance and nudged Aspen back, almost sending her to the floor.

Aspen smiled wickedly and grabbed a handful of oats, threatening to toss them straight at Lex.

"You wouldn't dare." Lex's eyes narrowed slightly, her body ready to react.

"Wouldn't I?" Aspen scrunched her face up and shot Lex a saucy smirk. Without warning, she stepped back and sent the oats flying.

"That's it!" Lex grabbed a handful of hay and chased after Aspen. Catching her, she tossed the hay over her head and backed away quickly.

"Ooh, you're gonna get it now." Aspen scrunched up her face and started towards Lex, knocking them into a pile of hay.

"Oomph." Lex exhaled loudly when she hit the ground, catching Aspen in her arms. She searched Aspen's face before breaking out in a nervous laugh. "We're gonna be okay, aren't we?"

Aspen's eyes welled up slightly, and she cupped Lex's cheek in her palm, planting a bittersweet kiss on her lips. Pulling away, she smiled sadly. "Yeah, we are going to be okay."

Chapter 22

Lex's brown eyes scanned the crowded restaurant and settled on Cass just seconds before she waived Lex over to the table. Weaving her way through tables, Lex had to smother a smirk. She and Cass were so very different from the other couples celebrating Valentine's Day. She shot Cass an apologetic smile and pulled her into her arms when she reached the table. "Hi."

"Hi, yourself." Cass held her a second longer, relishing the feel of Lex's strong arms around hers.

"Sorry I'm late. Traffic was a bear on the freeway." Lex settled in her chair and rested her elbows on the table, regarding Cass thoughtfully. "You look good."

"You look good, too." Cass's smile didn't reach her eyes, though she tried. "How are you?"

Lex looked out the window, averting her eyes from Cass's searching gaze. She watched the snow falling gently outside, contemplating her answer. Was she good? She really didn't know anymore. It had been a month since she had seen Aspen and most mornings she still woke up missing her. Lex met Cass's eyes finally and smiled wistfully. "I'm okay, I guess. How are you?"

"Mmm, fine." Cass's voice trembled, belying her words. She busied herself with her napkin, needing to compose herself. Seeing Lex was harder than she thought it would be. She still hadn't gotten over the breakup, and this impromptu meeting had seemed like a good idea at the time, but now she was starting to regret the idea.

"You're lying, Cass." Lex reached across the table and covered her hand. "I'm sorry for everything."

"I know." Cass looked down at her lap and took several deep breaths. "So are you and Aspen back together?"

Lex pulled her hand away and shook her head. Her eyes were haunted and sad. "No."

As much as Cass wanted to exult in the news, she could see the fresh pain in Lex's face, and her heart broke for her. No matter what happened, she wanted Lex to be happy, even if it meant she was happy with someone else. "What happened?"

Lex shrugged. "She didn't want me."

Cass could tell from her tone that it wasn't as simple as that, but she didn't push. "If you need to talk about it, I'm here."

"I know." Lex shot her a grateful smile. "You shouldn't be so nice, considering…"

Cass shot her a sarcastic look. "You mean considering you ripped my heart out, stomped on it and gave it back to me."

Lex laughed nervously. "Yeah, something like that."

"I'll live." Cass waived her hand dismissively. She opened her mouth to speak again, but paused when the waiter appeared at the side of their table, setting glasses of ice water and warm bread between them. Having eaten here before, both women knew what they wanted and placed their orders quickly. Cass watched him retreat from the table then rested her chin on her hands. She wanted to be calm and collected and not let Lex know that she was still as affected by her as she was, but now, looking into her brown eyes, Cass was lost again. All her unaffected reserve was nowhere to be found. "What about us, Lex? Is there any chance for us?"

Lex smiled sadly. No matter what had happened with Aspen, she couldn't get back with Cass. It wasn't fair to either of them. Cass deserved better than someone whose heart was miles away. "I'm…"

Cass reached across the table and squeezed Lex's hand. "It's okay. You don't have to say it. I can see it in your eyes." Cass pulled her hand away and shrugged, ignoring the tears that pooled in her eyes. Her laugh was self-deprecating. "Guess I just like to punish myself."

"We don't have to do this, Cass." Lex leaned forward and held Cass's gaze. She felt tremendous guilt for all the empty promises she had made and for the years she had stolen from her. If Lex could take them back, she would.

"No, I need to." Cass swiped at her eyes. "I needed to be able to say my good-byes too. It's kind of sad, you know. It's been months, and I still wake up thinking it was all a bad dream. That you will be coming home from a trip, and we'll make love just like old times. Then I wake up and feel the empty space beside mc, and I know it's a real-life nightmare." She dabbed at her eyes again. "God, I'm a fucked-up mess. Pining after someone who doesn't even love me."

Lex felt her heart drop into her stomach. "Come on, Cass. It isn't like that. I love you."

"You're just not in love with me." Cass laughed sarcastically. "I should be happy that you're miserable too, but I'm not. In some twisted way, I am sad for you. I never wanted anything except to make you happy. I think I always knew that you would break my heart one day. I tried to make up for that by holding on too tightly. In the end, it just made us both miserable."

"I know." Lex's voice was so quiet that it was almost lost in the low din of the crowded restaurant. "I want the same for you. I'm sorry I wasn't the right one for you."

Cass smiled sadly. "Me too." Needing to get herself under control again, she grabbed a slice of bread and buttered it, handing it to Lex. If there were anything that she could do to take her mind off her pain, it was taking care of Lex. She had always felt the need to nurture her. It was the closest thing to mothering instincts that Cass would ever have.

"Thank you." Lex took a bite and chewed quietly. "So what's next?"

"I didn't know until now." Cass smiled wistfully. "I wasn't sure before, but now I know."

Lex cocked an eyebrow. "What do you mean?"

"I got offered a job in Paris with Dior." Cass was smiling now, and for the first time it actually reached her eyes.

"Are you serious?" Lex's smile matched Cass's. "That is awesome!"

"I know." Cass shook her head in disbelief. "I'm going to be working with some of the most amazing designers in the fashion industry."

"That's wonderful, really." Lex sipped her water. "I'm so proud of you, Cass. Were you honestly thinking about not taking the job?"

Cass nodded. "That's why I needed to see you first. I thought if there were any chance that we would get back together, I would stay. But that's a moot point now, so…"

"Ahh, Cass. You shouldn't make decisions based on me." Lex felt a new wave of guilt wash over her.

"I know." Cass shrugged. "But I can't help it. I'm still in love with you. Call it wishful thinking." Composing herself quickly, she smiled. "Honestly, I'm relieved."

Lex's jaw dropped in mock horror. "Hey!"

"Sorry." Cass smiled indulgently. "I really, really wanted it. You just made the decision a lot easier."

"Well, I'm glad I could help." Lex laughed disparagingly. "I'm happy for you, Cass. You deserve it."

"Thank you." Cass met Lex's eyes and for the first time in months, she started to feel like tomorrow wasn't going to be so bad. She was actually looking forward to it. "I'm still in shock. I mean, it's Dior. That's the big leagues. Everything I worked for has led up to this."

"It's great, Cass." Lex was beaming now. Despite not being truly in love with Cass, Lex did love her, and she honestly wanted her to be happy. "When do you start?"

Cass waited for the server to set plates of steaming food on the table and make sure they were alright before she answered. "They want me to be there in April. That gives me time to get everything moved over. They are paying all my moving expenses and putting me up in an apartment in Paris. I figured I would get there in March, so I had time to get used to the city before I started."

"Wow, that's fast." Lex exclaimed around a bite of juicy filet with Bordelaise sauce.

"It is, but they want me to help with the fall fashion show. It's big, Lex. This isn't New York anymore." Cass ate several bites of her green curry shrimp. "I'm kind of nervous."

"You shouldn't be." Lex offered supportively. "You are amazing."

"I'm good. I don't know about amazing." Cass laughed softly. "But I'm going to have fun trying."

"Look, they wouldn't have offered you the job if you weren't amazing. Like you said, it's big."

"True." Cass smiled gratefully. "Thank you, by the way."

"For?"

"For dumping me." Cass smiled, letting Lex know she was teasing. "I would have stayed here otherwise."

"And I would have made you go." Lex countered. "I would never hold you back. Cass, you're bigger than this town and greater than we ever were. Even if we had been together, I would have done everything in my power to get you to take this job."

"I know." Cass set her fork down and sipped her wine. "Do you think there's a chance that we could still be friends?"

"Really?" Lex was surprised by the question. That seemed to be all she had lately. Everyone wanted to be friends. She hadn't expected Cass to make such a request given their history, but maybe Lex was the one with the issue and not everyone else. It gave her pause.

"Yes." Cass eyed Lex suspiciously. "Why not?"

"I don't know." Lex shrugged. "I guess I figured you would want to put all this behind you."

"Despite the fact that I wasn't what you wanted, I still love you and enjoy spending time with you." Cass shot Lex a winsome smile, making her beautiful face light up once more. "When I'm missing American food, I need someone to go on an Angelo's run with me."

"Well, far be it from me to keep you from your favorite Italian dive." Lex chuckled softly. For the time being, it seemed as though Cass was going to be okay. Now, she just needed to figure out how to be alright herself. If Cass could smile and look forward to tomorrow, maybe Lex could figure out a way to do that too. Mentally checking herself, Lex decided tomorrow she would figure out a way to be happy again. "So, does this apartment have room for company?"

Cass smiled excitedly. "Yes!"

"Good." Lex returned her smile. "I think when Ma finds out you're in Paris, she will make me take her over there."

Cass snorted loudly. "Oh lord, Maria loose in Paris. That could be dangerous."

"I think I'm more afraid for them then I am for Ma." Lex waggled her eyebrows. "My apologies to the French."

Cass laughed out loud. "God help us."

Lex studied Cass's face as they finished dinner. She knew that Cass would be okay, and she hoped that one day she would be too.

Cass watched Lex for several more minutes, memorizing her face. "Can I say something and you not take it the wrong way?"

"Sure." Lex said hesitantly. "I guess."

"If she still loves you which, I suspect she does, fight for her." Cass's tone was serious, and she pinned Lex with her gaze. "Years from now, don't look back on this and regret giving up."

Lex shook her head. "Sometimes, love isn't enough and I have to accept that."

"Sometimes a woman just needs to be reminded how much you love her." Cass squeezed Lex's hand.

"I told her." Lex replied sadly.

"Show her, Lex." Cass wasn't sure where she got the strength to offer advice. In a way, it was a comfort looking out for Lex one last time. "I saw what walking away did to you the first time. Don't make the same mistake twice. If it doesn't work, let her be the one to walk away."

Lex looked down at the table and rubbed her temple. She ran her hand through her hair and sighed loudly. "I think it's too late for that."

"Lex." Cass leaned forward and caught Lex's chin in her hand, forcing Lex to look her squarely in the eyes. "Promise me."

Lex swallowed the lump in her throat. Her emotions wouldn't allow her to speak, so she nodded in agreement. Lex would at least let Cass believe in happy ever after, even if she herself had lost faith.

Chapter 23

"Guinness, please." Aspen shooed Guinness out of the way and put the last stack of dishes away and dusted her hands off on her jeans. "That's everything."

Ginny picked up Guinness and hugged him to her chest, turned a circle in the kitchen and smiled. "I can't believe everything fit."

"I can." Aspen laughed and kissed her aunt on the cheek. "You left almost everything in the house."

Ginny smiled sheepishly. "I wanted to make sure you were comfortable. You really didn't come with that much."

"The bunkhouse is comfy enough. I could have moved a lot of that over and still had too much." Aspen put her hands on her hips and sighed loudly. "You think Mom is done yet?"

"Probably not, you know your mom." Ginny rolled her eyes and set Guinness down so he could scamper through the apartment and sniff every single corner thoroughly. "If she would have let us help, she could have been done hours ago. She sold off most of everything she had on the farm. I don't think she took up more than a couple of feet in the moving truck. I guess we can check on her. I'm getting a bit hungry myself, and I plan on taking advantage of all restaurants here. "You joining us?"

"I guess." Aspen shrugged. "I hadn't really given it much thought."

"Well, missy, you better start thinking about it." Ginny narrowed her eyes and gave her niece the once over. "When was the last time you ate?"

"This morning before my flight."

"Honey, you left yesterday, remember?" Ginny frowned. Her brows furrowed with concern. She grabbed Aspen's hand and pulled it towards her face, inspecting her fingernails. They were smudged with the telltale staining of her charcoal pencils. She squeezed her hand and gave her another once over. "Please tell me you're taking care of yourself. You look as thin as a rail."

Aspen felt her cheeks redden, and she pulled her button-down shirt around her more tightly, hiding her thin frame. Truth be told, she was so busy finishing pieces for her show and trying not to think about Lex that she didn't remember to eat as much as she should to stay healthy. "I'm eating."

Ginny looked askance at Aspen. "I love it down here, but don't think I won't march my happy ass up there to make sure you are taking care of yourself."

"I know." Aspen looked down at her feet. "It'll be better once the show is over."

"That's still a month away. You will waste away to nothing by then." Ginny pursed her lips and forced Aspen to look at her. "Promise me you will start taking better care of yourself."

"I know." Aspen mumbled. "I'll do better. Promise."

"What are you promising?" Susan stepped into the kitchen and eyed them suspiciously.

"Nothing. Just that I would visit often." Aspen shot her a smile, silently hoping she bought her lie.

"Humph." Susan scoffed at the answer, but let it drop. "You ready to eat? I'm starved."

Both Ginny and Aspen hastily agreed.

"Well, come on then." Susan said impatiently.

"Yes, Mom." Aspen shot her aunt a look and rolled her eyes. Little did her mother know that they had actually been waiting on her.

Twenty minutes later, they were seated at the open dining room in the Lighthouse Bar and Grill. Somehow, Ginny managed to avoid adjoining condos. There were only three buildings that separated them, but it gave Ginny the space she needed. She loved her sister, but she could certainly get on her nerves. Their meals and socializing provided them with plenty of time together.

"So Mom, are you all settled?" Aspen peered up from her menu.

"For the most part, I am. I'll probably have to buy a few pieces of furniture, but your aunt and I can worry about that later." Susan removed her reading glasses and set them on the table. She gave her daughter a long look before frowning. "When was the last time you ate?"

Aspen rolled her eyes. "Mom, seriously, I'm thirty-three years old. You don't need to mother me."

"You mean smother." Ginny snorted loudly.

"Hmm." Aspen shot her aunt a cheeky smile. "Like you."

Ginny feigned shock then broke out in laughter. "Well, sister, how on earth is she going to survive without us?"

Aspen shook her head and buried her face in her menu, ignoring the laughter of the two older women. "I'm ignoring you right now." She waved her hand in a hurry along gesture and sighed loudly. "Perhaps you both can stop picking on me and decide what you want to eat. I'm starving, and I'm not getting any younger."

This brought on a new round of laughter, and it was several more minutes before they could get themselves settled down enough to even think about reading a menu. Susan slipped her glasses back on and eyed the menu. "Are you all ready for your show?"

"Yes." Aspen nodded and looked up from her menu briefly. "I'd like to get another couple of pieces finished, but if I don't I think I can stretch it out. It's Gallery 29 in the Chelsea art district. I had them email me the layout of the gallery, and it lends itself well to my exhibition. It's just a small, industrial space, but the entire front is glass and faces the street; so all three walls are visible when you walk by. Plus, it's on the Chelsea gallery walking tour in the middle of spring. I should get a ton of exposure."

Susan watched her daughter's face light up, but the sadness in her eyes hit home. It was the same forlorn look she had seen in them since Lex had left five years ago. Aspen didn't talk much about their time in the bunkhouse, and Susan hadn't pressed. "How long is the exhibition?"

"It's a bit over a month." Aspen offered quickly. "I know it's not a long time, but it's a start. I'm hoping to get a permanent show somewhere. I think I'll look a little closer to home. There are some neat galleries in Burlington."

"Are you going to be okay by yourself?" Susan asked quickly. She knew she shouldn't worry about her daughter so much, but moving so far away was making her maternal instincts more honed.

"My goodness, Susan. Leave the poor girl alone." Ginny patted Aspen's hand. "She's fine. Let her be and order your dinner." She smiled at the waitress who appeared at the table.

"Evening, ya'll." Her southern accent was very strong, and they knew right away she was not from Florida. "I'm Meghan and I'll be your server tonight. Can I start ya'll off with some drinks?"

"Give me something strong." Aspen said with a laugh. "Something that will make me forget I'm getting lectured by my mother."

Meghan laughed and pointed to a drink on the back of the menu. "Try this one." She winked at Aspen and shot her an understanding smile. "Couple of these and you will have to park the golf cart and walk back to the condo."

Aspen smiled gratefully and ordered an Overboard martini. "Either that or I'll be looking for the nearest ship to jump off of."

"Let me know if you need someone to pull you in." Meghan smiled, and her gaze lingered a moment longer before she turned her attention to the other women. "What can I get ya'll to drink?"

Susan and Ginny both ordered lemonades and Ginny added an order of fried clams and sautéed mussels.

"Sounds good." Meghan didn't bother writing the orders down before she hustled away and stopped to check on another table.

"Well now, that was interesting." Susan glanced sideways at Aspen. "Did you see that?"

"Did I see what?" Aspen's brow furrowed quizzically.

"She was totally checking you out." Aspen's mother smiled mischievously. "I think she's interested in you, honey. I think it's high time you start living again."

"Mom, I'm living." Aspen rolled her eyes in exasperation. "Besides, she's like twelve."

"Honey, she is not twelve." Susan huffed loudly. "That's not the point. The point is, you're holding on to the past, and you need to let go and start living in the now."

"I'm doing that." Aspen countered defensively. "I'm moving on."

Ginny smiled and swatted at her sister. "Leave the girl alone. She's doing fine."

"I'm leaving her alone." Susan glared at her sister. "And if I wanted to give her a hard time I could."

"I think she's had enough of that the past few years." Ginny squeezed her hand and smiled. "But it's looking up now, right, honey?"

"Right." Aspen smiled proudly. "One foot in front of the other."

"That's my girl. See, Susan, she's fine." Ginny shot her sister a snide look. It seemed they would always disagree and fight no matter how old they got. "Whatever happened with Lex, honey?"

Aspen frowned. "Nothing happened."

"I really thought that you would get back together." Ginny smiled apologetically. "Just the way she looked at you...I knew she still loved you."

Aspen sighed. "Sometimes, love isn't enough. Being back with Lex reminded me of that. I realized that I'm not the same person I was five years ago. Going through that damaged me, and if I'm ever going to be whole again, I need to do it my way. I can't rely on someone else to fix me."

"Oh, honey, you're not broken. You're heartbroken." Susan's heart went out to her daughter. Despite her tough exterior, she still hurt when her daughter hurt. "I'm proud of you for letting go."

"Thanks, Mom." Aspen's face broke into a smile when Meghan set a full drink in front of her. Maybe it wouldn't be so hard to move on. Meghan was cute and while Aspen wasn't interested in her, she could at least acknowledge that she was alive and not oblivious to attention. "Thank you."

Meghan winked. "You're welcome, darling'." She set waters and lemonades down for the other two women. "You're appetizers will be up soon. Ya'll ready to order?"

Everyone ordered the fried fish sandwich. When Meghan left, the sisters turned their attention back to Aspen. "Are you okay?"

"You know what? I am." Aspen ran her finger along the edges of her glass distractedly. "Letting go was hard, but necessary." Aspen wanted to believe that. She wanted to believe that she was actually ready to let go. Saying good-bye to Lex had taken everything she had and left her hollow and lost. But she had reached her low place, and the only place now was up. "Besides, it's better this way. We would never have worked. There was too much history between us."

"Everything is built on history, honey." Ginny sipped her lemonade and studied Aspen's face. "That's all any of us have. Days, months, years of history that we grew out of and that made us what we are. Tomorrow is just history that hasn't happened yet. Don't knock your history. It's what got you to this point. You say history like it is a bad thing. It's not. It's your story. You may have let go of Lex, but something tells me your story isn't done yet."

Aspen shook her head. "My history is what I am learning from. I made mistakes that I don't intend on repeating. I can't explain it other than to say that our stories are going in different directions now. I have to make a new history, one that I live for myself and not for anyone else."

Susan smiled at her daughter. However much she was like her aunt, Aspen was still her daughter. She paused and waited for Meghan to set two plates with mussels and clams on the table. "I know I give you a hard time about letting go, but I also know you are so much like your father in that you hold onto every aspect of your life. I don't know what that is like. But what I do know is that you're strong like me and when you set your mind to something, I know you will do it. Whether it's getting a permanent exhibit for your art or letting Lex go, you will succeed. Just don't forget to live while you're doing it."

"I won't." Aspen popped a fried clam into her mouth and moaned quietly. "That's good. Maybe I'll just move down here with you."

Ginny laughed and squeezed Aspen's arm. "No, honey, you are not hiding yourself down here with a bunch of old fogies. You're gonna get out there and live."

"Yes, Aunt Ginny, I know." Aspen smiled wickedly. "I'm going to get myself out there and start sleeping with every lesbian I meet."

"Aspen." Susan's stern tone couldn't even stop the laughter. She finally decided it would do her no good to preach to her daughter. Instead, she quieted and drank her lemonade, ignoring the raucous laughter that filled her ears.

She knew her daughter would be okay and as a mother, that was all that mattered.

Chapter 24

Aspen reached out and straightened one of her pictures. She stepped back and surveyed her handiwork. A smile settled on her face. The past couple of months had flown by in the blink of an eye. It seemed like just yesterday that she was setting everything up and not almost two months ago. Her exhibit had shown really well and there had been some interest from other gallery owners. She wasn't sure if that interest would turn into a show, but she was hopeful.

"Can you believe this is the last weekend?"

Aspen jumped then turned and smiled at the approaching woman. "No. Honestly, I think I blinked, and it was over."

Gabrielle Larson returned her smile and stopped beside Aspen, brushing her shoulder against Aspen's. "It looks really good in here. The pieces showed really well."

"Thank you." Aspen couldn't help feeling proud. An exhibition here in Chelsea was the big time. She finally made it. "I really appreciate what you've done for me."

"Don't thank me." Gabrielle chuckled softly and flipped her long blonde hair behind her shoulder. "You did it yourself. You have a really good eye. I've never seen anyone capture raw emotion like you do. You have an amazing talent. The feedback has been nothing but positive, and you've sold almost every piece."

Aspen felt the heat rise in her cheeks. "I guess I had better get back to the drawing board, so to speak."

"How about you let me buy you a drink to celebrate?" Gabrielle turned and studied Aspen closely. She had been mesmerized by Aspen's blue eyes from the moment she stepped foot in her gallery. "You deserve it."

Aspen hesitated. "I really appreciate the offer, but I'm not..."

Gabrielle put her hand on Aspen's arm and stopped her. "Don't say it. Let me guess, you aren't looking to date anyone. You just got out of a relationship, and you're going to focus on your career for a while. Am I close?"

Aspen blushed again. "Yes. But tonight, if I wasn't exhausted I would totally take you up on it...as a friend."

Gabrielle smiled shyly. "I could start with that. The rest can wait. Although, I have to warn you, I'm pretty persuasive."

"Why does that not surprise me?" Aspen chuckled softly. "Thank you, though. I really appreciate the offer."

"Maybe next time then." Gabrielle shrugged her shoulders. "She must have been something special to do such a number on you."

"It's a long story." Aspen stopped talking, and her eyes locked on one of the drawings. "*Someone Like You* sold? When?"

Gabrielle followed her gaze. "Umm, earlier today. The woman who bought it wanted to meet you though. I said she could pick it up tomorrow, since you would be around."

Aspen frowned. She priced that one much higher than the others. She didn't want to let it go. It was the last one that she had done of Lex, and she had an emotional connection to that sketch over any of the other ones.

"That's good, right?" Gabrielle inquired quickly, her interest piqued. "The picture...it's of her?"

Aspen nodded, her heart beating in her chest. If she had this much trouble letting go of a picture, how the hell did she think she was going to let go of the real thing? Three months had passed since she last saw Lex, and she still dreamed of her more nights than not. Aspen was all settled in her new home, but she still longed for the closeness of the bunkhouse with Lex nearby. "Lex. She's my ex. I did that sketch years ago, right after we met."

"She's beautiful." Gabrielle studied Lex's profile. "What is she thinking?"

Aspen chuckled softly. "I, uhh, probably shouldn't say."

"Oh." Gabrielle's eyebrows shot up. "I see. Well, no wonder you didn't want to sell it."

"It's okay." Aspen shook her head. "It's better that way."

"Sounds like there is a story there." Gabrielle pressed, interested in the woman who still held Aspen's heart. "An unfinished one, maybe?"

Aspen shook her head again. "No, it's done."

"Is it?" Gabrielle studied Aspen's face. "You sure about that?"

"No." Aspen sighed. "You know what, on second thought, I think I'll take that drink after all."

Twenty minutes later, they were tucked in a small booth near the back of The Park restaurant on Tenth. Gabrielle ordered them both a glass of Cabernet Sauvignon. She watched Aspen closely, studying her face. "Tell me more about Lex."

Aspen sipped her wine before she answered. "We met in college. She was the most beautiful woman I'd ever seen. I fell in love with her the first time I saw her. We started dating and eventually got married."

"What happened?" Gabrielle leaned forward and rested her hands on the table. "I am guessing she broke your heart."

"Hey." Aspen laughed. "Like I couldn't break hers?"

"I'm not saying that." Gabrielle smiled ruefully. "In my experience, when a face clouds over at the mere mention of an ex, it's pretty likely you were the dumpee."

"Ouch." Aspen shot Gabrielle a mock glare. "You go right for the gut, don't you?"

Gabrielle laughed out loud. "Honey, I'm a New Yorker. We're direct and to the point." She glanced at her watch and relaxed against the back of the booth. "I have time for a story…unless you have somewhere to be."

Aspen laughed sarcastically. "Yeah, I've got a full date book.""

"Well, you are an up-and-coming artist. The possibilities are endless." Gabrielle winked and sipped her wine, patiently tapping her fingers on the table.

"Really?" Aspen leveled Gabrielle with a piercing glance of her ice-blue eyes and chuckled in response to her gasp.

"Wow, do you have a license to carry those?" Gabrielle's breath had caught in her throat when Aspen pinned her with her gaze. She had seen those blue eyes for over a month now, but had not had them focused on her with such laser-like intensity until now. "How is it possible that anyone could say no to you?"

Aspen smiled shyly. "I didn't realize wine turned you into such a tease."

"That's the better change." Gabrielle looked chagrined. "It also has a habit of making me talk way too much…which is why I'm going to shut up now and let you entertain me."

"Thanks, I think." Aspen took several gulps of her wine, feeling the cool liquid slide down her body and settle in her stomach, stealing her nerves. "I met Lex a little over ten years ago in college. A mutual friend set us up on a blind date. It was love at first sight."

"I can tell." Gabrielle swirled the contents of her glass. "Everything you are thinking is written all over your face."

Aspen bowed her head, hiding the pink tinge on her cheeks. She finally looked up and met Gabrielle's amused expression. "Guilty. I'd be a horrible poker player."

"If that's the case, let me be playing against you." Gabrielle paused and smiled at a waiter who appeared wordlessly beside them. "Do you feel like a quick bite as well?"

Aspen heard her stomach grumble in response, and she smiled sheepishly. "I think that's a yes."

Gabrielle picked up a menu. "Do you mind?"

"Not at all." Aspen nodded, hiding a smirk behind her hand. Only Lex had ever ordered for her before, but it seemed that Gabrielle was the type to take charge as well, which was perfectly fine considering Aspen didn't know the Arts District well enough to have an opinion on food.

Gabrielle ordered an Artisanal Cheese Board to start followed by a wood oven pizza topped with soppressata, sun-dried tomatoes and goat cheese. Handing the menu back, she instructed the waiter to wait at least thirty minutes before bringing the main course, so they could enjoy their appetizers. She asked him to switch their Cab to a Zinfandel.

It was obvious that Gabrielle was in her element here, and it fascinated Aspen to watch the woman interact with skilled confidence. It surprised her when Gabrielle turned and focused her attention once again on her. Gabrielle's sudden burst of laughter startled her. "What?"

"I just wanted to make sure you were okay with all of that." Gabrielle smiled expectantly. "I can call the waiter back over and order something else, except..."

"Except that you ordered the best thing here." Aspen laughed easily. So far, her daily interaction with Gabrielle had been on a strictly business level and to see her out of the gallery afforded Aspen a new perspective. She was meticulous to a fault; one might almost say a perfectionist. But there was softness to her personality that smoothed out potential harshness of someone so fastidious. Her strawberry-blonde hair, which normally sat perched in a tight bun atop her head, had fallen loose and cascaded around her shoulders, framing her deep green eyes and high cheek bones, giving her the appearance of a young Maureen O'Hara. All in all, Gabrielle Larson was a very attractive woman, and Aspen tried to make her body react, especially given the fact that Gabrielle had given her plenty of clues that she was interested in her. None came. Shaking her head in frustration, Aspen smiled. "That sounds perfect. I can always do pizza."

Relief spread over Gabrielle's face. To say that she was taken with Aspen was a bit of an understatement. Normally, a take charge woman, she hadn't worked up the courage to ask her out until her attempt this evening, and only had been able to do so by disguising it as celebratory drink. Now, she was here with Aspen, and she was encouraging her to share the story of her ex, one she was obviously not entirely over. "Good. I tend to just plow ahead sometimes. Where were we? Ah, yes. Lex. You met in college. Blind date. Love at first sight. Continue."

Aspen marveled at how succinctly Gabrielle had said the words. No wasting time with unnecessary pronouns or the like. "We started dating immediately and when we graduated, we moved into our first apartment together. It was so tiny. A lot like the place I'm renting while I'm here in the city. We couldn't move without bumping into each other. Those first years were amazing. I couldn't have been more in love."

"What did she look like?" Gabrielle smiled at the waiter who had just returned with their appetizer and glasses of wine. She situated the board and began pointing out the different cheeses. "This is a smoky blue cheese. They smoke it overnight in hazelnut shells. It's amazing." She cut a small piece off and set it on a thin cracker, topping it with a thin pear slice. "Try this."

Aspen took the cracker and popped it in her mouth, savoring the pungent smokiness of the cheese as it blended with the sweetness of the pear. She moaned. "That is really good. Next."

Gabrielle smiled, obviously pleased that her choice had been well received. She sliced a small piece off the next chunk, placed it on a cracker and handed it to Aspen. "This is a gruyere from Wisconsin. It just melts in your mouth, doesn't it?"

Aspen could only nod. The subtle nutty flavor of the gruyere melted on her tongue. "That was delicious. Okay, this one worries me." She pointed at the last chunk that had an oddly purple tint.

Gabrielle chuckled softly. "This one is the something special. I'm just going to let you taste it and see if you can pick out the flavors." She sliced a thick piece and handed it to Aspen.

Aspen looked at it closely, seeing small bits of purple. She smelled it and detected a hint of something floral. Finally, she took a small bite and chewed it slowly. She smiled at the impatient look on Gabrielle's face. "Mmm, I taste flowers, maybe lavender."

"Yes." Gabrielle's clapped her hands together excitedly. "And?"

Aspen rolled the sweet cheese over her tongue, allowing it to dance over her taste buds. She cocked her head and closed her eyes in concentration. "There's an herb in there too." She chewed slowly, tasting every subtle layer of the delicious cheese. "Fennel!"

"That's it." Gabrielle's eyes lit up brightly. "You must be a foodie."

Aspen held her thumb and forefinger a hair's breadth apart and smiled conspiratorially. "Maybe a little."

"That makes me happy." Gabrielle confessed with a shy smile. "I guessed you might be."

"You were right." Aspen acknowledged the comment with a smile. "And this foodie is hungry, so start slicing."

Gabrielle laughed and cut into the gruyere, handing several slices to Aspen. "Now, you were telling me what a gorgeous creature Lex is."

Aspen blushed. "So I was. Honestly, she is one of the most beautiful women I've ever seen. Her parents are from Greece, so she has the typical dark coloring and strong features. The first time I saw her, she literally took my breath away. Her eyes are so soulful. I can get lost in them for hours and not even realize that time is passing. You think you can see everything on my face. You should see Lex. They just reach out and pull you in, long brown hair that falls around her face, sculpted cheek bones and full lips that you just want to kiss." Aspen shivered as she thought about Lex and how every time she looked in her eyes or even thought about her, it left her breathless. "Anyway, we were together for five years before she left."

Gabrielle's eyes narrowed thoughtfully. "She's the woman in the picture *Someone Like You*. Isn't she?" Her mind flashed to the woman who had visited earlier and bought the sketch. She had been wearing a baseball cap, and her hair was pulled into a ponytail. Even so, Gabrielle was struck by her beauty. She was almost certain that she was Aspen's Lex.

"What?" Aspen noticed how quiet Gabrielle was, and that she was no longer eating.

"Nothing, I was just thinking it's a beautiful piece. I can tell just from looking at it that she would be hard not to fall for. So what happened? Why did she leave?"

"Mmm…" Aspen shrugged. "We went through a rough patch, and she realized that she didn't want the same things anymore."

Gabrielle sensed that there was more to the story, but she didn't push. "Five years is a long time to hold onto someone."

Aspen laughed. "It would seem so."

"I guess when you love someone that much, you never really let go." Gabrielle slid the empty tray to the edge of the table. Somewhere between discussing lavender cheese and Aspen's break up, they devoured the entire tray of cheese. "Any chance she feels the same way?"

Aspen nodded. "Yes."

"So what's the problem? Why aren't you together?" Gabrielle pressed. She could tell from the emotions that flashed across Aspen's face as she talked about Lex that there was more to the story, but she could also see what any fool could see. That Aspen still loved her.

"It's not always that easy." Aspen admitted quietly. "Sometimes, love isn't enough."

"Oh, honey." Gabrielle reached across the table and squeezed her hand softly. "You still love each other. That's all that matters." She pulled her hand away quickly, making room for the waiter to set their pizza down between them. "One more glass then cut us off, or I will start telling my deepest, darkest secrets."

Aspen sat quietly, watching Gabrielle serve them both slices of hot pizza. She blew on hers and bit off a small bite, savoring the flavor of the spicy sausage, paired with the pungent goat cheese. All the while, her mind repeated Gabrielle's words. *That's all that matters.* For the first time in months, she began to wonder if she had made the right decision by saying good-bye a second time.

Chapter 25

Aspen zipped up her portfolio and let out a contented sigh. This was it; her big debut in New York had come and gone as quickly as the changing of the seasons. She glanced outside and saw the spring rain bouncing off the window and smiled. She was eager to get back to the ranch and see the girls. Jonathon Riley had cared for them while she was gone, and she knew they were fine, but she just had the urge to see her babies again.

"Is that everything?" Gabrielle stopped beside Aspen and smiled. "Need any help?"

Aspen shook her head. "That's everything, I think. I'm sure I'll get halfway home and realize I forgot something." She heaved the heavy portfolio onto a bench. "Oh, I almost forgot. I wrapped *Someone Like You* and put it in your office. I hope they enjoy it."

"What's next for you?" Gabrielle toyed with the silver chain around her neck. Last night, dinner had been amazing and the conversation never lagged. She and Aspen discovered many shared interests. She regretted taking so long to finally ask her out and regretted even more that Aspen's heart was taken, despite her protests that she and Lex were over. "Promise you will come back and do another show."

"If you are offering, I'm in." Aspen laughed softly, her eyes twinkling brightly. "The drive isn't bad. Hint, hint."

Gabrielle's smile widened. "You read my mind. I'd love to have you in the fall...I mean have you come down...ugh, I would love to have you exhibit in the fall." Realizing that her words would be misconstrued, Gabrielle smiled ruefully and shook her head. "That did not come out right."

Aspen smiled shyly. "It's okay. I think I know what you were trying to say, and I would be honored."

"Good, that's good." Gabrielle took a deep breath and smiled again. "So this is it. You're really leaving. Are you still going to try and get a permanent show back home? You could make it big here. You're willing to give that up?"

"Yeah." Aspen smiled reminiscently. "That's my home now. This past month was amazing, but it made me realize I'm not a city girl. I have no aspirations to be the next Braque or Renoir. I draw because it's inside me, and I have to let it out. If I can share a little piece of myself with a small part of the world, then that is enough for me."

"Something tells me that Aspen Lane is going to be a name we hear a lot of in the future. You may not have grandiose plans, but it may be out of your control. You have an amazing talent, don't forget that when you're holed up at the farm." Gabrielle's eyes danced mischievously. "I know it is because you just love mucking stalls, and God forbid, you give that up."

Aspen shook her head. "How did you know?"

"Honey, you may be able to take the girl out of the farm, but you can't take the farm out of the girl. Believe me, I've tried." Gabrielle looked down at the floor. "There's a reason I still spend my vacations back home. There are some things you just don't let go of…no matter how hard you try."

"True." Aspen agreed, but she had a funny feeling that Gabrielle wasn't just talking about the ranch. Aspen glanced at her watch. "Well, I guess I should be going. I've got a bit of a drive ahead of me, and the rain is going to make it even longer."

Gabrielle studied Aspen's face and smiled. "Thank you."

"I should be the one thanking you." Aspen rested her hand on Gabrielle's arm. "Thank you for letting me have this experience. It means more to me than I can tell you."

The two women stared at each other for several more seconds before Gabrielle pulled Aspen into her arms awkwardly. She held her close, probably longer than she should have, but the feeling of Aspen in her arms felt too good to let go of right away. Gabrielle finally broke the embrace and held Aspen at arms' length, holding her gaze. "If anything ever changes with you know, let me know. I'd love to take you back to the farm and show you my life."

Aspen bowed her head and smiled. "I'll remember that."

Gabrielle pulled away and adjusted her suit jacket. A movement outside caught her eye, and she stared out the window. "Umm, Aspen?"

"Yes?"

Gabrielle nodded towards the window, a cryptic smile touching the corners of her mouth. "I think someone is here to see you."

Aspen looked confused. She followed Gabrielle's gaze, and her jaw dropped. Standing outside the window, watching the exchange with a perplexed look was Lex. Aspen's breath caught in her throat the second her eyes met Lex's. She wasn't sure how long she stood there staring before Gabrielle nudged her forward. She walked on auto-pilot towards the front door. Aspen pulled the door open and stepped onto the stoop. "Lex."

"Hi." Lex shuffled apprehensively, unable to hold Aspen's piercing gaze. She bobbled her umbrella nervously and smiled apologetically when she splashed tiny droplets of water on Aspen. "I'm sorry."

Aspen shook her head dismissively. "What are you doing here, Lex?"

"I…" Lex stammered for several seconds and finally rubbed the back of her neck uncomfortably. She took several deep breaths, only meeting Aspen's eyes when she thought

244

she could speak without hesitation. "I need to say something. These past three months have been dismal without you. I realize what I took away from us when I walked out. I know what a hell you lived in because of me. I can't change that, but I would like a chance to make the next five years and every one after that better. Not a second chance, a first chance. I'm asking you to give me a first chance at making us happy. I'm not the same person I was five years ago, but my heart never stopped loving you."

Aspen stared at Lex in a stupor; after all this time to find her here and make a declaration of love made Lex either really optimistic or just a fool. "Lex, I thought we decided this already."

"No, we didn't. You did. You didn't give me an opportunity to say much before you walked away. Now it's my turn and damn it, you're going to listen before you run away." Lex dropped the umbrella and let the rain come down on her. Putting her arms out, she twirled around, letting the water drench her body. "You told me a long time ago that you wanted someone who would dance in the rain for you, do whatever it took to show you her love. That's what I'm doing now. This is me, dancing in the rain, asking you to love me. I'll do flips, whatever you want me to do to prove to you that I love you."

Aspen shook her head, blinking back tears. She felt the ache in her heart push into her throat and leave her breathless.

"Aspen, you own me. You control me. I belong to you." Lex stopped and let the rain drench her. She searched Aspen's face. "Every feeling I have is controlled by the look on your face."

Aspen's eyes took in every bit of Lex's face, the rain-soaked ringlets that fell across her brow, into her eyes, teasing her cheekbones, her soulful eyes, sad and lost, but hopeful in every glance, her full lips, with tiny droplets of water bouncing off of them. It was enough to make Aspen's heart ache with want. She swallowed hard, biting back her tears. Maybe Gabrielle was right, maybe, just maybe love was enough.

"I can't breathe without you. I can't sleep without you. I exist to be with you." Lex stepped under the awning, cupped Aspen's chin in her palm and brushed a tear off her cheek. "Can't you see? I love you. I'm in love with you. You're the love of my life."

Aspen's heart pulled her body closer to Lex without her realizing it, two magnetic forces meeting their perfect mate. The ache of wanting Lex pierced her chest painfully.

"I realized I will never want someone like you. I want you." Lex pulled Aspen close, the heat from her body taking away the chill. "My life is you. My future is you. Without you, I'm nothing. I love you. I belong to you. We're in this together." Lex felt her heart pound in her chest. All the emotions that she tried to keep down were tripping through her body, love and fear coexisting in discord." I want to face the world and everything in it with you by my side. One word from you and I'm yours. But if you don't want this, tell me no and I'll walk away forever."

Aspen finally let the tears fall. She wouldn't fight her love, couldn't even if she tried. She knew what she felt was bigger than she or Lex combined. Her heart was and always would be Lex's. This time, when she let Lex inside, she knew that there would be pain, but she knew that this time, they would face it together. The thought of living the rest of her life without Lex hurt more than anything that they would encounter. Aspen cupped Lex's cheeks in her hands. She leaned forward and captured Lex's lips against hers. She kissed away the fear and the hurt, leaving room for hope and love. Breaking the kiss, she smiled, truly smiled for the first time in years. "Yes."

Lex felt her body explode. It was all she needed to hear to make everything right. She leaned her forehead on Aspen's and hugged her hard. "Forever."

Aspen felt a calm overtake her body. She found her way back home. She grabbed Lex's hand and pulled her out into the rain, letting it soak them both. "And always."

Epilogue

Aspen hung the sketch on the wall and stepped back, surveying her handiwork. She felt Lex's strong arms slip around her waist, and she leaned backwards into her.

"It looks good."

"Mmm, yes it does." Aspen turned her head and kissed Lex's chin. "The subject was quite beautiful."

"Was?" Lex's eyes danced. "She isn't anymore?"

"Well…."

Lex growled and spun Aspen around to face her. She kissed her hard on the mouth then broke away, laughter in her eyes. "Care to rescind that, Mrs. Tataris?"

"I'm not sure." Aspen's blue eyes twinkled mischievously. "I might need some more persuading."

Lex smirked. "Is that so?" She leaned forward and met Aspen's lips, sliding over them slowly. She pulled Aspen's bottom lip into hers and ran her tongue over it slowly, the heat building between them. Lex's tongue brushed against Aspen's, electricity shooting through her body. Reluctantly, she broke the kiss before it was out of control. Their company would be arriving any minute, and Lex didn't think that Aspen's mother and aunt needed to find them in a compromising position and naked at that. "Did you know I was the one that bought it?"

"I had a sneaking suspicion. I'm glad. I wouldn't want your face in another woman's house."

Lex kissed Aspen's nose and smiled. "Then it's a damn good thing you didn't turn me away twice."

"Mmm, yes it was." Aspen returned Lex's playful smile. "Deep down, I knew you belonged to me, on paper and in person."

"Don't forget." Lex teased. "I would have to tie you up."

"That, my dear wife, sounds like a perfect proposition." Aspen waggled her eyebrows suggestively then left to answer the door.

Lex watched her walk away, jaw halfway to the floor. She smiled, knowing that she had a lifetime with Aspen to explore that proposition.

Not quite the end....

Author's Notes and Ramblings

Aside from writing, I have a few other things that I'm passionate about. I consider myself a bit of a foodie, which you will notice in my novels. My characters love to eat as much as I do! With that in mind, I'm taking a few moments to include Lex and Aspen's favorite recipes, as they love to share their secrets. Some of them are a bit outside your normal pizza and burgers, so a sense of adventure is necessary. I hope you enjoy!

Pear and Prosciutto Pizza

Ingredients
1 (.25 ounce) package pizza dough yeast
1 cup bread flour
1 teaspoon salt
2 teaspoon white sugar
2/3 C warm water (110 degrees)
6 cloves of garlic, peeled
1/2 tablespoon olive oil
8 slices prosciutto, cut into halves
1 ripe pear, peeled, cored and sliced
8 ounces shredded gruyere cheese
1 tablespoon cornmeal for dusting
1/2 tablespoon olive oil

Directions
Preheat oven to 375 degrees. If using a pizza pan, allow to preheat for twenty minutes to come to temperature. Spread garlic paste over crust and top with sliced pears and prosciutto. Sprinkle cheese over the top and brush edges with olive oil. Bake for 10-15 minutes or until golden brown.

Pizza Crust – In small bowl, combine dry ingredients and mix well. Add warm water and combine. Add flour if necessary to make a stiff dough. Turn dough onto floured surface and knead for two minutes. Roll out dough to form a 12" circle.
Garlic Paste – Place the garlic in a small square of aluminum foil. Drizzle ½ Tbs of olive oil over the garlic and seal foil. Roast garlic in the preheated oven until soft, about twenty minutes. Smash garlic with a fork.

Pasta Puttanesca

Ingredients
6 ounces dry pasta, cooked al dente
1 ounce olive oil
1 tablespoon minced garlic
4 anchovy fillets, chopped
32 ounce can of diced tomatoes
1/4 teaspoon red pepper flakes
2 tablespoon capers
3 tablespoons Kalamata olives, pitted
1 teaspoon fresh minced oregano
8 fresh basil leaves, torn into pieces
1 tablespoon minced fresh parsley leaves
Salt and freshly ground black pepper
Freshly grated Parmesan

Basic Directions – Aspen changes the order some
In a saute pan, heat the olive oil. Add the garlic and saute 1 minute. Add the anchovy fillets, tomatoes, and red pepper flakes. Bring to a boil and lower to a simmer for 15 minutes. Add the cooked pasta, capers, olives and oregano. Toss to mix and coat pasta with sauce. Turn off heat. Add the basil and parsley. Season to taste with salt and pepper.
Divide between two plates and grate fresh Parmesan cheese over the pasta. Serve immediately.

Lex's Pan Seared Filets with Shitake Mushroom Sauce

Ingredients
1 1/2 cups sliced shiitake mushroom caps
1 tablespoon all-purpose flour
1/3 cup merlot or other red wine; keep the rest for drinking.
1/3 cup minced shallots
1 tablespoon balsamic vinegar
1 cup beef broth
2 teaspoons Worcestershire sauce
1 teaspoon tomato paste
1/8 teaspoon dried rosemary
1 teaspoon Dijon mustard
2 6 ounce filet mignon
1 tablespoon black peppercorns, crushed
1/2 teaspoon kosher salt
1 tablespoon butter

Directions
Preheat oven to 350 degrees. Heat an oven safe skillet over medium-high heat. Sprinkle steaks with peppercorns and salt. Add steaks to pan and cook sear 3 minutes on each side. Add butter and cover. Cook to desired doneness in oven, 8-10 minutes for medium well. Allow steaks to rest before eating. To make the wine mushroom sauce, combine mushrooms and flour in a bowl and toss well. Combine wine, shallots, and vinegar in a medium skillet. Bring to a boil and cook until thick. Reduce heat to medium. Add broth, Worcestershire, tomato paste, and rosemary and cook 1 minute. Add mushroom mixture and cook 3 minutes, stirring constantly. Stir in mustard. Keep sauce warm, serve over steaks.

Parsley—Leek Vegetable Soup

Ingredients
4 leeks, white part only, finely sliced
2 cloves garlic, finely chopped
1 stick celery, finely chopped
1/2 onion, finely chopped
2 Potatoes, peeled and chopped
5 tablespoons butter
4 large handfuls parsley leaves
6 cups chicken stock
1/3 cup sour cream

Directions
Place leek, garlic, celery, onion and potatoes in a large saucepan. Add butter and gently sweat over a low heat until vegetables are tender. Add the parsley to the pan and mix well, cook for a further few minutes. Add enough chicken stock to cover the vegetables and season with salt and pepper. Simmer for 20 minutes or until potato is tender. Puree soup in batches and then return the saucepan - thin soup with extra chicken stock as needed. Serve with a dollop of sour cream. Serve with a dollop of sour cream and grilled cheese.

Ham and Taleggio Grilled Cheese on Ginny's Homemade Bread (sadly, Ginny won't share this recipe)

Ingredients
3 tablespoons butter
8 thin slices homemade bread
10 ounces taleggio cheese, rind removed, sliced
8 ounces thinly sliced ham
1 green apple, thinly sliced (optional- I do prefer mine with the apple)

Directions
Lay out 4 slices of bread. Top with half the cheese, then half the ham. Layer the apple slices and the remaining ham and cheese on top, then the remaining bread slices. Melt 1 tablespoon in a large skillet over medium-low heat. Add 2 sandwiches and cook, pressing gently with a spatula, until the bottom is golden and the cheese begins to melt, about 4 minutes. Slice and serve with soup.

Lemon Drop Shots

Ingredients
1 ounce lemon-flavored vodka, Citron
1 lemon wedge
1/4 teaspoon sugar

Directions
Pour vodka in shot glass. Rub lemon wedge over wrist and sprinkle with sugar. Lick sugar off and immediately chase with vodka. Stealing kisses is entirely optional and highly recommended.

Other titles by Syd Parker:

Immediate Possession - Regan Sloan has had her share of bad luck in her relationships. She isn't sure she is even willing to give it another shot. But all bets are off when she "runs into" Darcy Grey. Darcy leaves more than just an impression. She gets inside Regan like no other woman has. That should have been just fine with Regan…except Darcy isn't exactly single and she isn't exactly a lesbian. Can the two women get past the hurdles and accept their love is bigger than the hurdles they face?

Secrets of the Heart – When Chase Berkley learns that her best friend was killed, she decides to finally visit the B & B they co-owned. At the funeral she finds out that Avery was carrying a huge secret that she is left to deal with. Avery's attorney, Jude Stafford, doesn't plan on making her stay any easier. As a matter of fact, Chase quickly learns, her life is about to get turned upside down…again.

Love's Abiding Spirit – Soren Lockhart knows heartbreak. Unable to get past her wife leaving and taking their daughter, she runs away so she doesn't have to face the pain. She buys a rundown house and hires contractor Merritt Tanner to do the renovations, unaware that they are waking up a ghost who is intent on telling her love story and pushing Soren toward the love of her life.

Just Tonight – At forty-five, Adrienne Thomas thought she was done being a mom, but when her son and daughter-in-law die and she inherits her granddaughter, and her partner of fifteen years subsequently leaves, she feels like she is right back at the beginning. Putting the heartache behind, she moves back home to collect herself. Nothing she experienced before could have prepared her for Dylan Montgomery, a loner who makes Adrienne's blood boil. Can Adrienne figure out a way to be a mother again and win Dylan's heart?

Twist of Fate – Storm chaser Remy Tate doesn't mess around when it comes to storms or women. She knows what she wants and goes after it. A chance encounter with fellow chaser, Sarah Phillips, has lingered in her mind for years and when they run into each other again, she puts everything on the line to prove to Sarah that she is interested in more than just a one night stand.

The Killing Ground (A Gray Foxx Thriller) – A serial killer is working his way through Chicago, leaving behind gruesome victims. It's up to Detective Rebecca Foxx to find him and put him away. Much to her chagrin, the latest victim pulls in the FBI. Special Agent Jordan Gray is up to the task of finding the killer, but can she get past the walls that Rebecca Foxx puts up, both in the case and in their personal life?

Biography

Syd Parker was born in California and lives in Indiana with her partner of seven years. She loves golfing, biking and spoiling her ten nieces and nephews. She loves to travel and anywhere on the water feels like home. She spends her days toiling away at her day job until she figures out a way to drop the last fifteen strokes to make it on the LPGA tour, although she's totally mastered Tiger Woods Golf on the Wii.

Most days when she's not writing you will find her on the trails or riding her road bike and praying she doesn't end up in another ditch.

She loves to read a good love story and thoroughly enjoys writing them as well. "It isn't just about writing a story, it's about creating a world and having the reader climb into it, experiencing it in first person. That's my goal...that's why I write."

Check Syd out on Facebook and online at www.sydparkerbooks.com.

Made in the USA
Lexington, KY
18 July 2013